NO TIME
FOR WORK

NO TIME
FOR WORK

A HUMOROUS NOVEL

By George Ryan

****

Dedicated to

Arthur Reynolds

****

NO TIME FOR WORK

© Copyright George Ryan 1979

ISBN 0-9547771-0-7

Printed and bound in Ireland by
ColourBooks Ltd.

**Proof read, corrected and paged by Brian Oliver,
whose temperament was sorely tested by the author.**

*In this novel no unfavourable reference is intended
to any living being except George Ryan.
All the characters are fictitious, and there is
no such place as Ireland.*

FOREWORD

George Ryan is an extremely funny writer and in No Time For Work he has given us a richly comic novel in the humorous tradition of Myles na Gopaleen and Donal Foley.

Readers will smile at the efforts of him and his friend Cecil Chuckleworth to outwit headmasters and school inspectors. They will grin at their encounters with parents and parish priests. And they will roar with laughter at their escapades with landladies and publicans.

No Time For Work is a hilarious work of fiction which even the most dour reader will find highly entertaining.

Eugene McEldowney

NO TIME FOR WORK

by George Ryan

AN assistant teacher I am, who never sought assistance from, nor gave assistance to, any of those fourteen headmasters, seventeen parish priests, and twenty eight inspectors, whom with the minimum fuss, and the maximum speed, I've deftly managed to put through my hands to date.

Headmasters! God love them. They have their own troubles too, and I was often among them. However, I never insulted them by attempting to become one of them, nor was there the remotest possibility of such an absurdity occurring.

When my colleagues and I passed out of the training college we were all bursting with ambition. Theirs', without exception, was to become a headmaster. Mine was to remain a nobody. Effortlessly I have achieved my target, while many of them have sobbed their way to the grave impatiently waiting for their bosses to die.

As for the school-managers, I seldom exchanged a cross word with any of those reverend gentleman. Enthusiastically, wholeheartedly, humbly, I usually accepted whatever advice they gave me, and then went off, and did the opposite. In my own time too. I was never one to rush.

Inspectors! How I love to listen to the welcome stamp of their feet - when they are leaving my room. Nevertheless I can tell you that lately I must have become a very important, a very interesting, a very unusual teacher. They have started coming to see me in twos, at regular, and unexpected intervals. An uncharitable friend described them as 'dogs hunting in pairs,' whereas I regard them as doctors looking for a second opinion, but if they think they are going to cure me they are barking up the wrong tree.

#####

Long ago I discovered that teaching is an easy way of earning a living provided that one does not make the mistake of actually teaching. I come in every morning. No! That's an exaggeration. Every morning that I come in, I first of all usher my faithful dog, Lazarus, on to the emergency pillow, beside my armchair, which is situated at

1

the farthest possible distance from where the children are prone to congregate.

A characteristic of my dog which never fails to fascinate me is, that the moment he mounts the pillow he gives me a hint that he is interested in geometry by making three circles on it, before coming to a decision to lie down.

When I have seen to Lazarus's comfort to our mutual satisfaction, I proceed to the classroom door, and unlock it. Then I return to my armchair, and take the lid off my super-size flask of tea - coffee makes me too alert - and pour myself a generous mug of the cup that cheers, as a buffer against the blights of the five-hour day that lies ahead.

Meanwhile the children will have started drifting in, with their coats and caps, satchels and teddies, dolls and guns, games, comics, and jig-saw puzzles, which they enjoy while waiting to get their orders to go asleep.

Having deposited their coats, and caps in a tidy heap on the floor... (Excuse me for a moment for going off at a tangent. This regulation about every single pupil being allotted a specific numbered hook at the beginning of each school year, and being marshalled to and from cloakrooms four times a day, is an unjustifiable waste of time both for the pupils, and the teachers).

Having lodged their surplus clothing in its allocated locality, they open their bags, and form a queue at my desk, and my morning's work begins. Methodically I take out each child's lunch, unwrap it, and inspect it. I have a very sweet tooth and some of the mothers are great bakers. Rarely have I been known to take a child's whole lunch. If I did I always gave him a share of somebody else's.

After filling my biscuit-tin with my sustenance for the day I cater for Lazarus's needs, as he too depends on charity.

Another queue is formed in which only those with meat sandwiches are qualified to join. This time they themselves are permitted to unwrap whatever is left of their lunches. They open their sandwiches, and hold the meat to my nose. Lazarus refuses, unless very hungry indeed, to eat stale meat, especially corned beef. So I have to be choosy, or else I'd find myself saddled with the drudgery of handing back to the pupils half of what I've taken from them.

When I have seized enough to ensure that Lazarus would have no justification in knocking over garbage bins on our way home, I call a halt to the proceedings, consoling those from whom I've taken nothing with a guarantee that they will get first chance to offer their wares on the following day.

Then they all in chorus say their innocent little morning prayers rounded off with a solemn promise to God that they will give me no trouble today. That, the most important deed of the day done, they are permitted to sit down and launch into their favourite hobbies, the only condition being that they are not allowed to talk above a whisper. I have sensitive ears, and noise does get on my nerves.

Analysts of teaching systems, both here and abroad, and all those young men and women who aspire to be part of the noble pedagogic profession, will be grateful to be informed that after years of observation, I have noticed - whenever I have found the time to spare - that the weaker ones are happier playing with soldiers or dolls, the average ones go in a lot for Ludo, whereas the bright ones have a distinct preference for Snakes and Ladders, probably because going up and down requires a lot more concentration.

Seldom am I tempted to join them, even though I do like my game of Ludo. No! I keep to myself as much as possible when they are around. If you are too intimate with children they will lose their respect for you.

My normal procedure, the moment prayers are over is to instruct my prefect - chosen because he has the longest legs in the class - to take from my briefcase my three daily newspapers, each of which he opens at the death columns for my perusal.

Perhaps you have jumped to the conclusion that I am looking for an excuse to abandon ship, pretending I'm heading for a funeral. Not a bad guess, but it's wrong. I don't need an excuse to go home. If I feel like walking out of my place of work, I go, and that's that. If you don't believe me ask any headmaster who ever worked under me.

I peruse the names of the dead every day purely for conscientious reasons.

I am a man of many parts. I've been the erstwhile occupant of teaching posts high up in the mountains, and low down in the cities, and have been miles up country lanes where even a postman never came unless he was being chased by a bull.

Having been to so many places, having got to know so many people - before they got to know me - thus having borrowed so much money, I scrutinise the names of those who have snuffed it, to see if

3

I can lighten the load on my conscience, by deleting some of them from my list of creditors.

That chore done I give my prefect the pair of scissors - which I always carry to trim the threads on the frayed sleeves of my shirt. He cuts out the racing pages from all three papers, and then sticks them to the blackboard with chewing gum.

Next, if the previous day had been an exceptionally disastrous one, I call forward the three most pious-minded pupils in the class, and having ejected Lazarus temporarily from his place of rest, I go down on my knees on the emergency pillow, while the chosen children do likewise on the bare boards, and having formed a ring around me, holding hands, start intoning hymns, while I do a half-hour's meditation, in the process of which, I call on God to wreak his vengeance on the souls of the crooked jockeys, who deliberately threw themselves head first off their horses, crossing the final fence the previous day, and then I pray for the atonement of the sins of the racing correspondents, who, with malice aforethought, engendered by iniquitous bribes, succeeded in leading half the country astray, to the benefit of the coffers of the covetous leeches who are commonly known as bookies.

Sometimes, after having completed my spiritual half-hour, by the grace of the good God, the bitterness evaporates from my heart, and my faith is somewhat restored in the suspect tipsters, but usually I make out a list on the left-hand side of the blackboard, of all the horses which they have forecast will win, and put a note under them to the effect, that they are clear favourites to drop down with exhaustion, and not finish the race.

I'm a great believer in coincidence doubles ever since that day, 17 years ago, one of them came off. So, each morning I run my eyes down the various fields to see does the name of any horse tally in any way with that of another. I thought I was on to a good thing last week when I coupled 'Hasty Lady,' with 'Shy Gentleman,' but the latter refused at the first fence second time round.

Next I study the records of each runner, and on the right-hand side of the blackboard compile a list of all the horses which finished nowhere in their previous six outings. My reasoning being, that on the law of averages, sooner or later, one of those long shots must romp home a sensational winner at a fantastic price. So, taking no chances of not being in on the act, with that crazy optimism, for

4

which all true gamblers are noted, I back each of them on the nose, and throw in a few trebles just for good measure, having been overcome once more with the happy sensation that this is going to be my lucky day.

I feel in my bones that you are sniggering at me now, and saying to yourself that I must have lost a fortune on the horses. First of all I never had a fortune to lose. Secondly, apart from my monthly salary, and whatever I could scrounge, I never lost anything worth talking about.

Sending pupils out of school 'merely to go to the bookie's office,' is strictly forbidden by the rules of our department of education. I didn't find that I had to stay up all night to figure out a way to drive a coach, and four through such ridiculous red tape. I send a different pupil every day to one of the self-service supermarkets, to buy the nearest thing he can find to a rotten banana. On his way back he drops into the bookie's shop to place my bets.

As there would be neither rhyme nor reason in me investing my money in rotten bananas when the children bring them in by the dozen every day, as soon as my messenger returns, I send him posthaste to the same supermarket to demand my money back, and to make an official complaint to the manager about the poor quality of the fruit he stocks. Once when I was in a bad humour I didn't bother making a complaint. I just told the child to go back and ask him did he himself enjoy eating rotten bananas.

One day, a busybody of a headmaster, acting on a tip-off, burst in to my room in a rage, and demanded to know why I had racing pages stuck to the blackboard.

As cool as you like, I explained to him that I was training the pupils' memories by getting them to learn lists of racehorses off by heart, which, I added, would be every bit as useful as some of the geographical junk he was ramming down the throats of the unfortunate members of his own class.

Then I told him that this was my room, and my blackboard, and that I'd stick whatever I liked to it, and that if he didn't get out quickly, I'd have no compunction about pinning him to it as well, and that when I'd have the job finished it would take a hell of a good surgeon to stitch him together again.

From that morning until the day he prematurely retired he never put his foot across the saddle of my door. A colleague asked me to contribute towards a memento for him. I told my friend that I would willingly do so on two conditions: if they unanimously agreed to present him with a rope to hang himself; and that I would be allowed to make the presentation speech.

Many people maintain that the more diligently one is engrossed in one's work the more quickly the day will pass. There must be something radically wrong with those people. They feel so insecure that they use work as an escape from the responsibility of doing nothing.

And there is a responsibility attached to doing nothing. There is the responsibility of keeping oneself in a happy frame of mind. Doing nothing is a greater challenge, a greater test of one's character. I'll give no man a pat on the back for rushing here, rushing there, doing this, doing that, and thereby putting in his day. Anybody can do that. But put that man in front of 57 children, and him sitting there silent, and motionless, throughout the day, every day. How long will he be able to stick it without becoming fidgety, without allowing it to get on his nerves, let alone driving him mad! That's what I mean when I say that it's a test of a man's true mettle. Modestly I'll mention that I've been doing it successfully for years.

I will admit that I do indulge in a little physical training for health reasons. Occasionally I get up in front of the children and practise my golf swing. There are dangers involved in this exercise, as was brought to my attention when the head flew off my wedge and hit a child - who could never keep his mouth shut - between the teeth. Luckily they were merely his milk teeth. The mother didn't harbour any ill will towards me, but did ask me to aim at anyone bar her son for the future.

Eventually I realised that putting is the only facet of the game tailor-made for the classroom. I have a strip of carpet which I took on loan from the stairs of the local police-sergeant the night I brought him and his wife home drunk from the Christmas party. I put them to bed first. I even took off his boots for him, but I didn't take them with me. I tried them on for size. They were the wrong fit. That's why I took the carpet. He never suspected me. My theory is that with me living in a lodging-house he didn't think that I could have a motive for lifting a carpet. Don't people do queer things to improve their golf!

Anyway, whenever the urge comes on me I bolt the door, take

my carpet out from behind the big press, stretch it on the floor, put a bucket on its side at one end, and me at the other, and putt balls into it until I'm blue in the face. The children used to cheer when I scored a direct hit, but as they cheered louder when I missed I ordered them to stand up, and turn their backs to me.

More sedentary pastimes however are really my dish. Crosswords I find to be a most useful way of idling away the time. So, every morning after my elevenses, and the children's obligatory piddle in the toilet, they receive instructions to place their heads on their desks, and shut their eyes - with them all looking in one direction - and go to sleep. Snoring is banned as it disturbs my concentration while I'm having a go at the crosswords in each of the newspapers in turn. I don't always finish them, but I never allow myself to feel frustrated about it - as some people do. I didn't get where I am today by worrying over crosswords.

At the lunch break I keep them in for English reading. I met with some hostility from the more ignorant parents when I first did this. They withdrew their opposition when they saw the light of day. It dawned on them that all play, and no work makes Jack a dull boy.

The children themselves take a delight in learning their reading. My teaching methods are simply ingenious, and ingeniously simple, from a labour-saving point of view.

When I was at school as a pupil I never had the good fortune to have as a teacher, a man gifted with the ability to attract momentarily, let alone capture continuously, my attention. As a result school life for me would have been one long bore, had I not repeatedly resorted to transporting my mind to a world of my own. Nosey people sometimes ask me why I go around with a constant stare in my eyes. That affliction developed from my gazing into space when I was attending school.

The daily lesson on reading in particular was a yawn from start to finish. We were compelled to stay at the same page until every child in the class was able to spell, and explain every word on that page. That could take a fortnight in which time some of us might have read the whole book twice.

Nowadays there are available an abundance of graded readers, each one slightly more difficult than the preceding one. If teachers so wish, all the children in the class can be on different books, depending on their aptitude. The snag is: with them all on different books, how can they all be taught, how can they all be examined! I gave the matter some slight thought, and came up with this solution.

When the lunch hour bell rings the four best readers in the class - hereafter known as the 'subs' as they are my substitute teachers - take up their stations in front of the four rows of desks in which the other children start reading silently until they come to a word which they don't know, whereupon they put up their hands, and the subs solve their problems.

After ten minutes I examine the No 1 sub who will keep reading until he or she makes a mistake. I put a tick in front of the error to indicate the point from which that pupil will start the following day. The other subs are dealt with in the same way. Then they examine the whole class in like fashion.

On the blackboard I have a progress report. Beside each child's name is put the title of the book, and the number of the page he is on, with the leading reader numbered one on the list, and so on. They study that list in the same way as soccer fanatics study league tables. I have them indoctrinated to focus their interest chiefly on who is immediately in front, and behind them.

Do they strive or do they not to keep ahead of, or jump over both friends, and enemies! They have their parents driven to distraction teaching them their reading at home every night. Since I invented, and started working this method NO child has gone through my hands unable to read.

When the bell rings indicating the lunch break is over my children are given permission to tackle their grub, and read their comics at their leisure, while I take a nap.

Usually the last hour is spent at singing which is taught by them bringing in records of Irish ballads, Country and Western songs, and anything else they fancy. From listening to the records they pick up the words and airs quite quickly because children have much better imitative powers than parrots.

With the first shake of the dismissal bell I wave bye-bye to my charges. My dog is the only one I allow to beat me in the run for the door.

#####

When refined parents come to my classroom door to quiz me about how their offspring is progressing they sometimes obliquely enquire about how the likes of me was let loose out of a training college. Vulgar ones invariably go directly to the headmaster to ask him how the likes of me was let in to a training college. He gets great satisfaction out of confronting me, to quote verbatim their complaints about me - including the foul language used to describe me. My stock reply to him is that I'm glad to be of service to society, because when they are criticising me they are leaving somebody else alone.

My dear reader, in case you too are wondering how I gained one of the highly competitive admission places to the training college it will be my pleasure to satisfy your curiosity.

Places are won by obtaining exceptionally high marks in the leaving certificate. As I had never done a tap throughout my primary, and secondary school career, I hadn't a snowball's chance in hell of gaining a place, unless I resorted to unorthodox tactics, which I did, and in the process nearly wrecked my health.

With many authors readily available on all the subjects I was doing, I decided to enlist the aid of the best among them by smuggling their books along with me to the relevant exams. That happens to be illegal which I don't think is 100 per cent fair. A few marks should be given for knowing which page to look up.

Be that as it may, I was nervously conscious of the fact that I'd get the boot if I were caught, but I couldn't think of an alternative, so I had to take every precaution to keep whatever Nosey Parker of a supervisor I had to contend with, as far as possible away from me. Hence I went into training with the objective of developing a heavy cold, bordering on pneumonia, but not quite the real thing.

I worked up sweats, wore damp vests, and wet socks, and sat in a draught for a fortnight before the exams, as a result of which I was in fine fettle when they began. I could cough like a chain-smoker. I had a red, raw, running nose, and I could sneeze at will.

My heart lit up when I set eyes on the little shrivelled-up excuse of a thing who was our supervisor. Obviously he was a man who had reason to worry about his health. I approached him muffled up in my father's railway overcoat - it had spacious pockets - and told him that my twin brother, and my only sister had died from tuberculosis, that I was going into a sanatorium the moment the exams were over, and asked him in a croaking voice if he would have any objection to putting me at a desk well away from all draughts. I gave a sudden sneeze into his face to bring home my point.

As I had anticipated, he put me sitting at the end of the hall, and never came within forty feet of me during the eleven days of the exams, but as a safety play for the following day, I always showered him with three sneezes, when handing up my afternoon papers.

I developed some bronchial trouble towards the end of the exams, which cost me the summer in bed. I recovered fully thanks be to God. Anyway it was all in a good cause.

I used more or less the same tactics for the training college finals. The only incident worthy of mention was that on the afternoon of the last day I noticed that the supervisor was peering in my direction, more often than at others, which called for some kind of retaliation.

On my way out I swiped his spectacles which he had short-sightedly taken off to blow his nose. As they have shoddy frames which I wouldn't be seen dead wearing I had often intended to post them back to him, but I didn't get around to it yet. Perhaps I will next Valentine's Day, along with an indecent card just to set him wondering what kind of a nut would do that to him.

#####

Life in the training college was quite interesting and very profitable. In the study-hall I used to study the students who were studying. I was intrigued that they were able to concentrate intensely on musty old books when they should have been thinking about fresh eager women. Where was their sense of values! Where was it all going to get them! They were going to hold only the one job, but they could have dozens of women if they played their cards right! By the looks, and capers of some of them, they would gain more satisfaction from grappling with a geometric problem, than coming to grips with an unwilling young woman who has the habit of shouting:

'Stop!'

'Stop!'

'Don't.'

'Don't stop!'

There was one particular professor, a bald, fat, little man, who used to capture my imagination almost to the point of obsession. At this moment, as I relive those days of yore, I can see him as clearly as if it were yesterday, looking down at us from his rostrum, staggering through his lecture, shaking and stuttering with excitement when an idea would threaten to come into his head.

He'd throw in a minimum of three 'ehs' for every two sentences he managed to ejaculate. The 'ehs' could come at the beginning of a sentence, or even three or four of them consecutively in the middle of a nonsensical sentence, when he'd be at the top of his form.

I used to run a book with my friends on how many he'd utter in the 55 minutes we had him at bay. The lovable, lame duck must have been encouraged by the rapt attention we paid him, by the manner in which we used to hang on to every word he babbled from his quivering lips, and us merely waiting for the next 'eh.'

A trainee teacher used to spend three weeks before the Christmas, and Easter breaks doing practice teaching in the city schools under the watchful eye of the teacher whose class was being taken over. All but one of the teachers, under whose wing I was put, were generous, and considerate.

The guy about whom I have the unpleasant memory was a tall, round-bellied, cantankerous cur, whom I'm confident, never got on with anyone, especially himself.

I was barely inside his door on that Monday morning when he handed me a lump of chalk, and arrogantly snapped: 'Here you! Introduce them to long division!' Then he took his newspaper out of his coat pocket, sat down beside the fire, and began reading it.

When people treat me like a doormat I inwardly rage against them. I scheme against them, and I seek revenge. I know it's wrong, and I try to turn the other cheek but my nature won't let me.

I decided to defy the long division decree, and instead show him as much disrespect as he had shown me, by going up to the blackboard and plastering it from top to bottom with simple addition sums that an infant could do. I then turned to his class of ten-year-olds and ordered them to: 'Do those sums now, and make sure you don't make too many mistakes.'

Then I sat on the table in front of his majesty, and said: 'Hand me the sports pages of that rag you're reading.'

He looked at me with his mouth shut first. Then he opened it. Then he looked at the blackboard. Then he looked at the children giggling among themselves. Then he looked at me again. Then he stood up, and roared: 'Get out of my classroom before I kick you out!'

My curiosity didn't get the better of me. I didn't wait to see would he carry out his threat.

Money is never a problem to students. They could readily list numerous ways of getting rid of it. It's the lack of it that presents the difficulties, especially if one is a smoker.

On the day after I first arrived in the training college, I made out, during the maths class, my budget for the term. Having deducted the cost of one box of matches per week, I found - with some assistance from the chap next to me, who claimed to be a financial wizard - that I could afford two and three quarter cigarettes per day, up to Christmas. Then I got a brainwave: instead of buying matches I could bum lights, which would bring me to the very verge of three full cigarettes per day.

Happy at that thought, I was then hit with this sudden crazy urge to go out, and spend every last penny I possessed on one mad splurge of ice-cream, chocolate, and cakes, and then come back in, and bum cigarettes for the rest of the term.

Across the road from our resident college was a cheap cafe. Within five minutes I was there gorging myself.

As I was licking the fingers, and thumb of my right hand after finishing my fifth cream bun, a well-dressed, well-spoken young man came in, and sat down opposite me. He ordered a cup of coffee and a few cakes. When the waitress came to collect the money he produced a wallet bulging with notes.

'You are not a student,' said I.

'Oh I am. I just arrived across the way yesterday.'

'Is that money all your own, or are you minding it for somebody?'.

'It's my own alright,' said he, giving his wallet-pocket a proud pat.

'Where did you get it from?'

'I worked on the building sites in London all summer.'

'Tell me,' said I, 'do you play poker?'

'No. I never played card games in my life.'

'I'll teach you.'

'Is it hard to learn?'

'Dead easy.'

Within a week I had that fellow bumming cigarettes off me.

Inspired by that successful start to my college career I cultivated friendships with those who had had summer jobs as builders' labourers, ice-cream packers, or fruit pickers, and persuaded them to take up jackpot poker. It says a lot for my integrity that I rarely resorted to cheating when stripping them of their worldly goods, to enable me to live in agreeable, if not luxurious comfort, during my sojourn in the training college.

#####

Out of the training college into the world where job seekers without character references are as impotent as anglers without bait.

All leaving the college were supplied with a neatly typed reference. That's all you could say in favour of mine: That it was neat, and that it was typed; but the authorities didn't consider me neat, nor did they like my type. So my document read: 'George Ryan passed through this college between the years 19XY, and 19XZ.

I'd have been proud of that reference had every other student been refused one; but none were refused, and as far as I could ascertain, most of them had received glowing reports loaded down with adjectives normally used only when referring to someone stretched out in a coffin.

Seeking your understanding, I'll ask you to do me a favour now, and look at me from the point of view of the person with the power to dish out the jobs - the reverend school manager.

He advertises his vacancy. I apply for the position, enclosing my references. Unfortunately, five or six of those brown-nosed craw thumpers, who tied their shoelaces every day of the week, and wore clean shirts on Sunday, also apply, and also include their training college references.

Whose reference goes into the wastepaper basket first!

But wait! I've more to tell you. Along with a reference from the training college, there is also required, one from one's parish priest, whose duty it is to know the members of his parish.

I went along to my reverend gentleman but didn't get off to a good start. Urchins were playing football on the street in front of the parochial house. If there is one thing I can't resist it's a game of soccer, especially on a wet and windy day, with the challenge there for me to stay on my feet, wearing Wellington boots. So I joined in. Before I had even dirtied my rubbers I met the ball on the volley, slightly misjudging it. I followed its flight with great interest, as it went sailing straight for, and through the lovely, stained glass window of the parish priest's porch door, and knocked the pipe out of his mouth, and him sitting there in his armchair, reading 'Way to Inner Peace,' by Fulton Sheen.

The children vanished. Up the steps I went, and politely knocked on the door, even though I could see him through his shattered window, picking pieces of glass from his hair, while attempting to stamp out the smouldering tobacco on his snow-white, sheepskin rug.

The moment he opened the door I explained that I had miscalculated the timing of my kick, but emphasised that there were extenuating circumstances involved, which I hoped he would take into account, namely, that if the wind hadn't gusted unexpectedly he'd still have a window.

Ignoring my waffle, he asked sharply what I wanted. I told him. He claimed that he didn't know me well enough to give me a reference, whereas I knew that he knew me too well to give me one. However, I wasn't willing to take no for an answer as I wanted to get a job immediately, not because I was of an industrious bent, but rather the opposite. If I succeeded in getting a job quickly I'd be paid to do nothing for two months.

We qualified from the training college in the middle of June. Schools closed for the summer holidays in the first week of July. So, if a chap had the good fortune to be appointed to a position even one day before the holidays started, he could arse around for two months, and be paid for it - a loafer's dream. Then I could consider resigning on the evening of the day the school reopened, and find another post just before the next holiday period.

Therefore it was vital that I would persuade his reverence to relent, and grant me a character reference. So I launched into a long-winded sermon, the theme of which was, 'Love thy neighbour as thyself.' As I showed no signs of drying up, he could bear it no longer, and retreated to his office, to emerge shortly afterwards with a sealed envelope, which he stuck in my fist, and hooshed me out of his house.

Trembling with anticipation on his doorstep, I burst open the envelope at the wrong end to find: that he had free, gratis, and for nothing, supplied me with written evidence that I had been born; that I had been baptized; and that as far as he knew I wasn't living in sin with a woman, but that he wouldn't put it past me.

As there was nothing to be gained by my applying for teaching posts enclosing the two above-mentioned documents as proof of my suitability as a teacher, I applied without sending any references whatsoever, for seven positions in different parts of the country, via facsimiles of the following:

Reverend, and respected sir,

I wish to apply for the post as advertised. If you appoint me to the vacancy you'll regard it as the wisest decision of your life for the following reasons. You will discover that I am of a diligent, industrious, hard-working disposition. You will find that I will produce results, never before heard tell of, in your well-run parish.

You will be charmed to learn that I will be zealously interested in the spiritual welfare of the dear little children under my care, both before, and after, and during school hours.

If you want me to take charge of your church choir you will be thrilled to hear that I have a fine baritone voice, and I know every hymn in the book.

Herewith enclosed please find copies of my excellent references, from: (a), the training college; (b), my own dearly beloved parish priest, who showers me with praise every time he meets me. I also enclose a stamped addressed envelope as I expect you are too busy a man to be licking stamps.

Your obedient servant,
George Ryan

P.S. If I forgot to enclose my references please let me know, and I'll forward them to you without delay.

Not a single reply did I get.

Remarkably, the only time I had any trouble with references was in seeking my first teaching post. After that, the various managers were so relieved at the prospect of seeing the last of me, that they gave me first class references to expedite me on my way.

Usually I was given the option of leaving a parish or being sacked - not much of a choice. Once I did volunteer to leave, but withdrew my resignation within 24 hours because my financial circumstances suddenly changed for the better.

I was an assistant in a little town which I quite liked, the only snag being that the population was so small that it didn't take long for me to run out of people prepared to lend me money. So I decided to move on.

I went to the parish priest, an affable man, who enjoyed a few pints. When I told him the good news that I was leaving, in a moment of impetuosity he said he was sorry to be losing me, but recovered in the next breath, and handed me my train fare, which proved to be lucky money, when I used it at the dogs that night, and backed six winners in a row for the only time in my life.

Next morning I sent a pupil with a note to the parochial house informing his reverence that he would be relieved to hear I had changed my mind, and was staying on indefinitely, as I had lost the train fare at the dogs the previous night.

#####

To go back to that first summer with me as a qualified teacher, I failed to obtain a pre-holiday position, so I turned my thoughts to another possible source of revenue.

Apart from the fact that I had once kissed a farmer's daughter on the cheek, and that we had a small field behind our house, from which I used to pick weeds in the summer, to find that they had grown again by the following summer, I knew nothing about farming, but I saw no reason why that should deter me from reading the agricultural ads in the local paper: 'Wanted. Willing worker. Good milker. Ability to plough would be an advantage. Live in.'

The farm was only 17 miles away, so I took the loan of a neighbour's bicycle and headed for it. The man himself came to the door of the thatched cottage with his peaked cap pulled down near his nose, and his head thrown back so that he could make use of his eyes.

'You're looking for a farm labourer!'

'That's right.'

'I saw it in the paper.'

'Can you milk?'

'The last place I slaved in, there were 37 cows. A dairy farmer you know.'

'I know. Can you plough?'

'I've been following horses all my life.'

'Do you object to working seven days a week?'

'I don't, if I'm off the next seven.'

'Smart Alec! Have you any references?'

'Produce yours first!'

'Huh. Are you honest?'

'What do you mean? Are you trying to tell me I'm a chancer?'

'You have the look of one!'

'Right. That's it. Thanks for the information. Goodbye.'

'Come back! I'll take you on, on a week's trial.'

'You must be joking! Do you take me for a guinea pig?'

'I'm badly in need of help. You'll oblige me for a week?'

'I will. If you pay me in advance.'

'That's a ridiculous thing to ask a farmer.'

'No more ridiculous than me giving you my labour on tick.'

After a bout of bad-humoured haggling he parted with half of what he reckoned I was worth, which pleased me no end, because I knew I wasn't worth tuppence. Then he ushered me around to the yard at the rear of the house, where his sister, sporting a greasy bag-apron on her belly, and a bun of grey hair on the back of her head, was throwing oats to the hens, out of a bucket, the bottom of which was plugged with a wisp of straw.

'I'm after taking on this fellow on a week's trial. I paid him in advance.'

'You what!'

'You heard what I said.'

'Not only do you look like an eejit, but time and again you prove to me you are an eejit. Can he milk?'

'He says he can.'

'Can he plough?'

'So he tells me.'

'Show him up to the loft.'

I didn't know what she meant until himself did as he was bid, and conducted me into the horse's stable - which had a springy carpet of dry dung - and up a rickety ladder, held together with binder twine. In the corner was a truckle bed, on which lay two moth-eaten grey sheets made from flour-bags, and one slimy horse-rug, which served the dual purpose of quilt, and blanket.

Overhead hung, on a double string of binder twine, a drooping line of dusty empty sacks. By the bed was a sack scales. Keeping it company were five dust-laden iron weights of various denominations. On the scales sat a sconce, in which was stuck a stub of a candle, patiently waiting to throw the shadows of the sacks on the bare cement wall behind. In the far corner were the miserable remains of last year's harvest, in the form of fusty-smelling oats.

'This is your bedroom.'

'I presume it's also my living room.'

'Many's the one would be glad to have it.'

I didn't respond, instead looked out the cobweb-curtained window, in the bottom pane of which was thrust a threadbare, half-rotten sack, which had played the part of a goalkeeper, for God knows how many years, against the wind, the rain, and the frost. In the distance I could see children frolicking in a clover-covered field. My thoughts were not on children. I wondered how many men had looked out that window. What were their thoughts? Did they look forward to getting drunk on Saturday night? Did they look forward to having a real room, with real clothes on the bed, with real curtains on the window? Did they look forward to minding a woman, to giving all their love to a woman? Or did they merely look forward to getting out of this dump by the gates of death!

'Have you lost your tongue! I suppose you had your tea.'

'Your supposition is incorrect.'

'You speak very well for a farm labourer.'

'What's wrong with the way farm labourers speak?'

'I didn't say there was anything wrong with the way they speak.'

'Nor have you any right to. You don't pay us according to our fluency in the king's English.'

'You're a quare hawk to have around the place. I'm wondering are you the full shilling.'

'And I'm wondering are you going to give me a bite to eat. I wouldn't be surprised if you told me to have a feed of those stale oats there on the floor in the corner.'

'You could ate worse,' said he, as he turned to grapple his way down the would-be staircase, and then, having reached the carpet of dry dung, shouted up at me, 'Knock at the back door in ten minutes, and your grub will be ready for you.'

Twenty minutes later I gave the door a rap. There was handed out to me by the lady of the house, a tin mug containing a liquid which had a vague resemblance to watery tea, and a chipped enamel plate, on which reposed four thick slices of brown bread, each with a centimetre of butter scraped on.

'Thank you,' said I sarcastically. 'Are you saving your eggs for Easter?'

'None of your lip, or you'll get the sack.'

'Is it the sack that's stuck in the window of my disgraceful sleeping quarters?'

'By the look of you, you're well used to worse. He'll call you in the morning at seven o'clock to milk seven cows. So you can sleep tight.'

'I won't sleep tight alongside you, thanks be to the good God.'

The door was slammed in my face. I went and sat on an upturned wheelbarrow in the middle of the yard, and partook of my feast. Then I threw the crumbs to the hens, and retired to my dusty den.

As I had no intention of attempting to milk one cow let alone seven, before I fell asleep that night I concocted a crazy excuse which only a stupid man would swallow.

#####

'Get up! Hi you there! Get out of your bed, and come down, and milk them seven cows this minute.'

I threw on my clothes, and went down, and told him: 'I've a touch of the eczema on my hands. It's almost gone now. It'll be better in a week or so, but it's highly contagious. Has been known to turn fatal when taken in tea, and certainly would cause gangrene in the cows' udders.'

'You didn't tell me that when I was handing you your week's wages.'

'When you are selling an animal at a fair do you point out its flaws to the prospective buyer?'

'No sensible farmer would do that.'

'Well then, it's thanking me you should be, for being honest enough to admit it before it's too late, before your whole herd would be ruined.'

He paused for some time, apparently weighing up the validity of my confession, then took the winkers off a nail on the door of the stable, handed them to me, and ordered me to, 'Go up, and catch the horse in the far field. I'll milk them myself.'

Off I went through the dew-wet fields, wondering how one goes about catching a horse. Was he quiet, or one that kicked with both legs at the same time! If he was a kicker my neighbour would have his bike back quicker than I had intended, for which he'd be grateful as it would save him having to walk to work.

Anxiously I approached the horse. He looked at me, his two ears pointing towards me. Then he rudely turned away and started to walk. I followed him, easily at first, not wanting to panic him. I quickened my pace. He quickened his. I took longer steps. He took faster ones. I broke into a relaxed run. He broke into a relaxed trot. (This procedure took longer than it takes to tell. We had now completed three rounds of the field, and were nicely into the fourth). I galloped. He galloped. We galloped all two.

I retired temporarily to a seat on the ditch, while I smoked a cigarette to alleviate the pangs of hunger. Then I got to my feet, and tried to sneak up on him. He waited until I was within arm's length, then suddenly swung around, threw his heels playfully in the air, and went off with a snort. My morning's work done I headed back for my breakfast.

'Where's the horse?'

'He made strange.'

'I knew you were a chancer the moment I laid eyes on you.'

'Don't be showing yourself up to be a fool. If you knew I was a chancer why did you pay me a week's wages in advance?'

'I want none of your smart answers. Come with me now, and I'll show you how to catch a horse in jig time.'

'I will. As soon as I get my breakfast.'

'Give the back door a knock. She has it ready for ages.'

It may have been ready for ages but it didn't take her ages to ready - a few slices of bread, with no milk in the tea.

'Are the cows gone dry?'

'When you start milking you'll get milk in your tea.'

'I prefer it without milk.'

Breakfast eaten, back to the field with the boss, who, as soon as he went in the gate, held his cap out in front of him, and whistled. The horse came running, whinnying, to eat the oats that weren't in the cap, while he grabbed him, and threw the winkers over his head.

Pointing to the other end of the field, he said, 'Do you see that cement tank, and pump yonder! Over you go, and fill it with water for the cows. I'll have him harnessed, and ready for you in the yard when you come back.'

'Ready for what!' said I to myself. 'If it's to go to town for a bag of meal, I can manage that, and take all day about it. Anything else and I'm on thin ice.'

Tank filled. Me in yard. Horse in yard. Horse harnessed. The lord of the estate, a straw in his mouth, commands his serf to, 'Go up to the long field, and grub them turnips. You won't come out of it until you have the whole field done. Your dinner will be brought up to you. The grubber's lying inside the gate. And don't abuse the horse.'

As my horse, and I set off for the long field I felt a tingling thrill of anticipation, something like the excitement I experienced on my way to my first date - which incidentally turned out to be a flop. What was a grubber! What did he mean by grubbing the turnips? My crossword knowledge of words told me that grub doesn't only mean food, but also means to dig up. I wondered was it to dig up the turnips. What else could it be!

The minute I entered the field I understood what he meant. The turnips were there alright, but barely visible in a forest of weeds. He wanted me to get rid of those weeds, and I was willing to oblige.

For you readers who never saw a grubber I'll paint a picture of the one I steered. It was an implement with a long, narrow, rectangular, iron frame, with lots of wee legs, in the shape of miniature spades or shoehorns attached to it underneath. You don't push it. The horse pulls it. That's his contribution. There was a small wheel at the front, and two handles sticking up out of it at the back. With a rein in each hand, and your hands on the handles, off you go, up and down the field between the rows of turnips, and the shoehorns rooting away at the weeds.

After four or five experiments I managed to get the horse properly yoked to it. I let a shout at him, and gave a strong chuck on the reins. He must have had a tender mouth because he took off at a furious pace - considering what he was pulling - diagonally across the field. Turnips, weeds, stones, and clay went flying in all directions. I tried to stop him, but the more I shouted the faster he went, until he reached the far headland. Then he stopped suddenly, and started to tear away at the grass as if nothing had happened. 'The grass must be extra nice up here,' said I to myself.

I sat down, and had a smoke. He looked over at me several times as if waiting for my next move. My cigarette finished I managed to get the grubber and its haulage contractor facing more or less in the right direction. This time he kept in a dead straight line, but he got it into his head to walk on the turnips, and if he walked on the turnips, the grubber grubbed them. I was nervous of pulling hard on the reins to shift him off them, for fear he'd go into another gallop, as I had had enough galloping for the one day. So I let him have his way. There were plenty of turnips in the field, and one drill would never be missed.

Then I turned him around. This time he chose to go on a zigzag course, not rooting up more than 75% of the turnips. 'I'm learning,' said I to myself, and I persevered with the job I had been paid to do.

I had him down to about 25% spoilage when she arrived in the field with a basket in one hand, and a pint can in the other. She looked. She stepped forward, still looking. She dropped the basket. She dropped the can. And went running back to the house.

And I went running over to save my black tea. The lid was tight. I hardly lost a drop. Meanwhile the horse, dragging the grubber all over the place, had started off for the far headland, where the sweet grass grew. I didn't try to stop him. Why should I work during my dinner hour! Besides I'd get no thanks from either of the two tulips for letting my bacon, and cabbage go cold.

I was peeling my third spud with my nail when, through a gap in the hedge, I saw an interesting sight. He was coming running faster than was good for a man of his years, and her not far behind. He had neither coat nor cap on him, which indicated that he must have been having a lie-down, when herself shocked him out of his siesta by bringing him up to date on what was happening to his field of turnips.

He came in the gate, and without so much as a glance at me, strode up and down the field with his arms raised to his ears, taking stock. He looked, and looked, and still his horror grew. Then he headed in my direction. When he got within firing-range he started pelting me with medium-sized turnips. Between shots he was roaring, and crying to the skies, 'My grand field of turnips. My grand field of turnips.'

Dodging most of the missiles I shouted back:

'It was a field of weeds when I came into it.'

'Give me my money back, and get off my land.'

'You hired me on a week's trial. This is only the first day.'

'You got money out of me under false pretences. You told me you were able to milk. You told me you were able to plough. Come on! Out with my money or I'll sue you for both it, and the damage you did to my crop.'

'I didn't do any damage to your crop. It was your own horse that did the damage. I didn't say I was able to milk. I didn't say I was able to plough. You twisted what I said round to what you wanted to believe. Sue me! I'll look forward to it. I'll enjoy the publicity, because I was never up in front of a judge before, and I'll get my name in the paper for the first time in my life, but my name will only be in small print. You're the one who will steal the show. You're the one who will get the banner headlines: 'Mug of a farmer hires farm labourer not able to milk or plough, and pays him a whole week's wages in advance.'

A mad glint came in to his eyes, and he rushed for me, trying to grab me by the throat, but I was too quick for him. I turned, and ran for the gate. She tried to trip me. I sidestepped her with delicate ease.

When I had put a comfortable distance between me, and them I slowed down to a walk. Approaching the bike I looked back to find that they had made commendable progress, and were now only twenty yards behind. I waved bye-bye to them, jumped on the bike, and headed for home.

From that day to this I have never heard a word about them with the exception of this ad which appeared in the local paper on the Saturday after they had chased me off their farm: 'Wanted. Genuine farm labourer. The successful applicant will not have any skin diseases, and will not be paid any wages in advance. Each candidate will undergo a proficiency test in - (a) milking my seven cows; (b) grubbing his own field of turnips.'

#####

Towards the end of the summer holidays the ads looking for teachers were being published again in the columns of the daily papers, pricking my conscience into remembering that a teacher of my ability owed it to my country to use my talents for the betterment of the nation's children.

Prior to the long break my letters to the seven reverend managers failed to earn a rejection, never mind a summons for an interview. So, in late August I got down to the business of trying to sell myself again, hoping to be more successful this time, by going off on a new tack:

Reverend, and respected sir,

I wish to apply for the post as advertised. Unfortunately I can't forward my references to you, as the last reverend manager to whom I sent them, put them in the fire.

Nor can I send you a stamped, addressed envelope on the chance that you'd favour me with a reply, because I can't afford such an extravagance, as I have an aged, feeble mother, who can't even mope her way from her bed to her favourite spot beside the kitchen fire without the aid of two makeshift, broken crutches, and I can't resist buying her little delicacies with every penny that comes my way.

If you appoint me to the post I will bring her along with me, as I know the mountain air will do her a power of good, even though she is not expected to last until Christmas.

Hopefully your obedient servant,
George Ryan.
P.S. I'll say a prayer that God will direct you in your decision.

I received a lovely letter back from the saintly Father Smith telling me the job was mine. He mentioned that nobody else had applied for the post, but had there been 40 he still would have chosen me, because his mother living with him, was in the same boat as mine - not expected to see the year out.

He suggested that the two old ladies should get together for a chat now, and again in the parochial house as soon as my mother settled into her new surroundings. To crown it all he promised to have her measured for a new pair of crutches within an hour of her arrival.

When the letter arrived she was out in the field behind our house, digging potatoes for the dinner. I ran down to tell her that at last I had got a job for which I was trained. She threw herself on her knees on the stones, and clay, and thanked the good Lord for answering her prayers, and then asked me to promise her that I'd always be a good boy, which I duly did.

On the day before the school was due to reopen Father Smith met me off the train. He was surprised that my mother was nowhere to be seen. I told him the poor thing had suffered a fall, and had to be carted off to the hospital with two broken hips, but that otherwise she was alright. Noticing how distraught I was, he wanted to know if there was anything he could do to help.

'Well Father, I'm reluctant to ask you. It wouldn't be fair on you.'

'What's on your mind, George? I'll be glad to help you any way I can.'

'That being so Father, I was wondering if I put in an appearance in school tomorrow to officially start the job, would you mind if I then went home for some weeks to visit Mammy twice a day. Being her only son, it would mean a lot to her. I'd be back for sure on the last day of the month to sign the salary form.'

'That's the right thing to do. Your first duty is to your mother.'

As we walked out of the station towards his car he asked, 'Have you no luggage with you, George?'

'The clothes I have on me are my luggage. I always travel light.'

'And what do you do for a shave or even a change of socks?'

'I've a razor in one pocket and a spare pair of socks in another. What more does a man want. Weren't we all born naked!'

'I don't follow your logic, George!'

'Don't get me wrong, Father. As soon as I get a few pounds together I'll buy myself a nice, big leather case. If I have it for nothing else, I'll have it for show.'

No further words were exchanged until we reached the parochial house, where he brought me into his sitting room, and introduced me to his mother, a beautiful white-haired lady, without a trace of a wrinkle on her face, even though she was on the brink of her 89th year.

She laughed heartily when I told her I never saw her looking better. We got on famously together. Her lively, blue eyes danced again with the fire of youth when I got her going about her young days, about the men she had put through her hands, about the captain of the sailing ship whom she had been due to marry the week after he had been lost at sea, and then about the pulsating romance she had had for 44 years with the passionate, wonderful man who had been

25

her husband.

My heart went out to her when she went in to a fit of coughing, which racked her frail body from head to toe. Her son stood up with anxious eyes, and fingers extended. When she stopped coughing he said, almost in a whisper, 'Are you alright, Mammy?'

'Yes Christy, I'm alright, but I am looking forward to rejoining my wonderful husband.'

I envied her her simple faith in the life hereafter.

After a wholesome meal I mentioned to him that it would be no harm if we went through the formality of us signing 'The Agreement Form,' which tied him down to giving me three months notice, or three months wages, if he ever imagined he had a reason to get rid of me.

That done, he drove me to my digs, and introduced me to my landlady. She seemed to be taken aback when I told her I was stay-ing only the one night. However, when I explained to her about my mother she was all sympathy, and understanding. She told me that too many young men forget too quickly about their mothers, as soon as they start earning money, and that she had great admiration for sons who were good to their parents.

I let a sad little smile play on my lips, and told her that I wasn't giving myself any credit for what I was doing.

Next morning I breezed into my first headmaster, Mr Samuel McVeigh, about an hour late - just to test his temperament. Subsequently I discovered that he was a man eaten away with ambi-tion. Was he proud or was he not that he was the first native of the place to attain the rank of schoolmaster! Was he proud or was he not that he had won 'The Murphy and Mulligan Award,' presented annu-ally only to schools with exceptionally high standards in everything, from the flowerpots on the windowsills to the splits in the children's hair in the classrooms! However, for the moment I had to take him at his face value.

Wearing a superior smirk on his ugly dial, he held out a fish-cold hand for me to shake, while he cracked a sardonic joke about me coming in late on the first morning I arrived.

'I wonder will he be cracking jokes,' said I to myself,' when I tell him in a few hours time that I'm doing the disappearing trick for a month.'

With him strutting down the corridor to my room, and me

ambling after him, he remarked over his shoulder, that there wasn't another minute to be lost.

While introducing me to my 52 pupils - divided in to three classes of the age-group eight to ten - he confidently predicted that I was going to work myself to a standstill. His forecast was right to a limited degree, as always, on my first day in a school, I do work like a Trojan, and when I set to it, I can do as much in a day as an average man in a fortnight, or a lazy one in a month.

How do I do it! To me children's minds are like plasticine. I can mould them any way I choose. I motivate them in various ways. I arouse their curiosity. I use their keen sense of rivalry. I animate them to the pitch where their enthusiasm is bubbling all over the classroom.

You mightn't believe me, but I am able to do that!

The catch is that I have only enough petrol in my tank to do it for one day. After that I'm like a wet rag - a mental wreck - and I need a long holiday. And I take a long holiday; either in the classroom or out of it, but generally one finds that it is easier to keep up appearances by appearing at one's place of work.

I am aware, when I walk in to a class for the first time, that every child in the room is watching me, sizing me up, looking for weaknesses, and deciding how far they can go with me. I am also aware that when they go home Mammy and Daddy will quiz them about what kind of a person their new teacher is. And it has not been unknown for reverend managers to put harmless questions to innocent children about what they learned from their new master.

Perhaps you don't agree with me, but I think that the right time to sell them the dummy is the first day. After that it's often a month before most of them suss me out. By then I've myself worked in to a fit of enthusiasm for another day's teaching.

Maybe you believe that I'd find it more exciting, if, when taking up a new job, I didn't do a tap from the word go. I've considered that line of inaction, but dismissed it as being imprudent, for the very reason that if I tried it, as sure as you are reading this book, before long there would be parents bursting in my door, saying that Sally forgot her scarf, or Charley forgot his cap, and then apologising 'for interrupting the work,' while I'm slouched half asleep in my chair. Then there would be fireside chat, followed by letters to the department of education, followed by inspectors breathing down my neck before I'd have my derriere warmed in the place.

So, having offered you a reasonable excuse for doing a day's work, I'll get on with the autobiography by sketching a snippet of my technique in my fight for survival.

I believe in finding out by subtle probing, what type of a character I'm immediately going to be compared with, namely, my predecessor. If he or she was popular with the parents, one has to be diplomatic about how one sets about undermining their professional reputation, which bitter lesson I learned in my early days, when I was stationed for a brief period in a country school at the back of beyond.

I had taken over from an old lady teacher, who though due to retire at 65, had got, through the good offices of the parish priest, a three-year extension. That woman didn't know how to form a letter let alone write legibly on the blackboard. If you saw the figures her pupils made! Their attempts at an '8' were like an 'S' gone haywire. Hardly any of them were able to spell 'cat' never mind read.

How did she get away with it for 48 years! The answer is simple. She spent her days telling them lovely stories with lovely morals attached; telling them how lucky they were to have such lovely mammies, who bought them such lovely clothes; and teaching them how to knit lovely socks for the lovely inspectors.

She peeled their oranges. She wiped their noses, and other places, and generally acted as a first-class babysitter. I was run out of that parish because I said she was a disgrace to the teaching profession.

To return to my debut in McVeigh's school, after I had questioned them to find out what stages the three classes had reached in the programmes of the various subjects, it was obvious that they were excellent in all except mathematics, in which they were of an incredibly low standard. Apparently their previous teacher had no interest in arithmetic, so I zoned in on that, taking the three classes as one.

'Hands up those who like arithmetic problems!' Only three hands were raised out of 52.

'There's something radically wrong here. Don't you know, don't your parents know, that the most important subject of all is mathematics! How will you get a job when you leave school if you can't add, subtract, multiply, divide, and solve simple problems!

'You boys there! You'll be costing your parents a fortune feeding you for the rest of your lives, when you come home starving every evening, after spending your day holding up street corners, unless I do something about it. As for the girls among you, don't ever think of getting married because you won't be able to add up the cost of a shopping list, and you'll be diddled left right, and centre, by the shopkeepers. However, if you work hard for me I'll save you. I'll put you on the right road.'

I took the loan of a maths book from the child nearest to me, and read a problem in it to myself: 'Kathleen bought 20 sweets. She gave 6 to John, ate 7, and gave one to the baby in the pram. How many were left?' I converted it into a story, which I wrote on the blackboard.

'Mickey Full Trickey went in to a cake shop, and bought 20 fleas. He came out, and sat on his hunkers on the side of the road. He put all the fleas standing in a straight line on his long nose, which reached down to his belly-button.

'6 of them jumped into a milk bottle, and swam to the bottom. 7 of them climbed up into his hair and went to sleep. One of them fell into his shoe, and gave him a fierce kick on the ankle. The rest played a game of "Hide and Go Seek," on the tip of his nose. How many were playing?'

They were all agog to find out. I taught them how, and gave them more similar problems. When we came in after the lunch break they were yelling up at me, 'Please sir, can we have another game of Mickey Full Trickey.' They didn't realise that I had conned them in to loving maths problems. That day I did likewise in every subject.

As the hour for quitting approached I took out my watch, and started the countdown. If McVeigh had the right to moan to me about my lateness in the morning, I was entitled to complain to him about his unpunctuality in the evening. Much to my disappointment he rang the bell on the dot.

Having sent the children home, I went to his room, and casually asked him to supply me with the name, and address of the inspector for our area as I wished to notify him, as stipulated by the rules, that if he intended swooping down on me in the next month, he had better think again, because he'd have a hard job finding me.

McVeigh refused to believe that he wasn't going to see me again for a month. I told him that I didn't ask him to believe me, that I didn't care whether or not he believed me, that his beliefs were personal matters in which I was not remotely interested.

With his eyes blazing, and his pimpled nose in my face, he demanded from me a reason for taking a month off after a day's work. I told him that I didn't come all the way to this pokey little place to supply him with reasons for what I did or didn't do, for where I went or didn't go, and that he, as chief bottle-washer of this tuppence-halfpenny, three-teacher, village academy, would be better employed minding his own business, and figuring out what he'd do with my pupils for the four weeks he'd have them all to himself, along with his own, rather than prying into my private affairs.

I left him to ponder over that suggestion, and went off, and caught the train satisfied that I had done a good day's work insofar as I now had a foolproof excuse for not informing the inspector of my absence from school, as the headmaster had ignored my request to give me his address.

#####

Starting the long journey I had every intention of taking it easy at home for the month until I began thinking about the unsought advice our next door neighbour, Mr Ginty, had shoved down my throat a few years previously when he heard that I had been called to the training college.

Ginty, a retired teacher, uninvited, visited our house and urged me not to take up teaching: that it was the last job under the sun for anyone with worldly aspirations; that you'd hear about auctioneers dying leaving thousands; that you'd hear about butchers dying leaving thousands; that you'd hear about vets dying leaving thousands; that you'd hear about everybody dying leaving thousands; but that you'd never hear about teachers dying leaving thousands; that it was the poor man's profession; and that if I were depending for my existence on a teacher's salary I'd be struggling all my life.

With remarkable civility I listened to the old bore's exhortation, and then told him that I would get no satisfaction whatsoever out of dying leaving thousands, that my ambition was to die owing thousands.

As the train rumbled along I wondered was there any way that I could prove Ginty wrong about there being no money in teaching. I opened my daily paper, and looked up the teaching ads: 'Wanted immediately, substitute for one month in school adjacent to city. Phone: 280155.'

Considering that I had four weeks at my disposal what was to prevent a man with my itchy feet holding down two jobs, especially as Mr Samuel McVeigh, my headmaster, in his wisdom, had warned me that there wasn't a moment to be lost.

When I reached the city at which I had to change trains I rushed to a telephone booth, and rang the number. No! The job wasn't gone. Yes, it would be alright if I started the day after tomorrow.

#####

Much always wanted more, so the moment I clinched the deal to have two wage packets due to me at the end of the month, my thoughts turned to the more attractive possibility of having a third coming in.

For that to come to pass I'd have to put a substitute in my place in McVeigh's school. However, I could not put a sub in without a doctor's certificate stating that I was too ill to work. I would also be supposed to pay that sub out of my own pocket, but then on production of a receipt proving same, I could recoup the outlay. Of course I'd also be paid my month's salary.

It would gain me nothing to pay the person who took my place, but I had in mind a way to obtain a receipt without doing anything dishonourable. My mother is a qualified teacher, who had been headmistress in a seven-teacher school until she got married. Then the notorious 'Marriage Ban,' which at that time was in operation, forced her to resign, as the wiseacres of the department of education considered that those who might have children were not the right people to be teaching children.

She was not a wealthy widow. I, the only son, had four sisters older than me. Two were married. The other two kept the home going - barely I'll concede, but my mother always said that the happiest people were those struggling, and succeeding in making ends meet. She maintained that they had a challenging purpose in life, whereas most of those rotten with money led aimless unhappy lives.

If I talked her in to subbing for me, as I knew I could, I would

31

be downright inconsiderate if I forced hard cash on her, thus diminishing the pleasure she would derive from obliging me. Besides, I would only create problems for her. She wasn't used to having surplus money, and would be lying awake at night worrying about what she should do with it.

Getting a cert demanded more initiative as I was not on intimate terms with any crooked doctor. I decided to stay overnight in the flat of my cousin, Charlie, a medical student, who armed me with a little knowledge, which I didn't find to be a dangerous thing when I went seeking my ill conceived credentials early the next morning.

After knocking on the surgery door I bent down in a compassion-inducing crouch, with my chin almost at the same height as my knees, and my left hand on my hip to prevent myself from keeling over altogether.

The doctor himself answered the door, and to my gratifying astonishment was also very stooped. I bent over a little more just to go one better than him.

'A lot of use in me coming to you when you can't cure yourself,' said I, with our two heads looking at each other about two feet off the ground.

'What happened to you?'

'I was balancing on one leg this morning, pulling a stocking on the other, when my back locked, and I've been in excruciating agony ever since. Do you think I can claim compo against the hosiery manufacturers? There was a fault in the sock. It was too tight for my ankle. Only for that it wouldn't have happened!'

He looked at me with interest. Said nothing. I knew that he was thinking: 'It's not a doctor this fellow needs. It's a psychiatrist.'

'I suppose you can't help me. I've an awful pain running down my right leg towards the outside.'

That cousin-inspired symptom swung him into sympathy with me.

'Sorry,' said he, 'sit down there.'

'No I won't. If I sit down I mightn't be able to get to my feet again. I've got to go to my work.'

'You're not going to work like that!'

'Yes I am. Aren't you working, and you're every bit as bad as me if not worse.'

'What do you work at?'

'I'm an overseer in a pig slaughterhouse. Can't you give me a tablet or something to kill the pain?'

'I think you should have your back X-rayed.'

'Aw no. You wouldn't know what they'd discover if they X-rayed me. My brother went in for an X-ray on his knee, and his doctor got a note three days later confirming that he was pregnant.'

'All I can advise you to do so, is to rest for a fortnight. I'll give you a certificate.'

'Can you make it for a month? I don't want to have to pay you twice.'

With suspicious amusement in his eyes he looked at me.

'Funny,' said he, 'I didn't think you were going to pay me at all.'

'I will as soon as my back is better.'

Not interested in making a fuss over a bit of paper he handed me the desired cert.

A few yards down the street I straightened up, and went for the station. As I turned the corner I glanced back. He was still at his door looking in my direction. 'I've made his day for him,' thought I. 'He'll be delighted with himself for curing me so quickly.'

#####

'Mammy I'm home. Are you there Mammy?'

'What on earth happened? You're not sacked after one day, are you?'

'No mammy, I got on great. A grand school. You'd love it.'

'Well then, why are you home? You started on Monday, and this is only Tuesday. There must be something wrong. You not up to your antics of dodging work already are you? The same as when you were going to school yourself, you stayed at home every second day.'

'Mammy have you forgotten that I passed my exams with flying colours!'

'I often wonder how you did. Sometimes I feel that it took more than my prayers to do it. They must have got your name mixed up with somebody else's, or there was some skulduggery somewhere. Sure you never spent five minutes studying in your life.'

'Ah Mammy you have it all wrong. I know you're disappointed that I'm home, and you have every right to be, after you being so proud to see me off last Sunday morning, to take up my first job. But Mammy we never know what's in store for us. I had a bit of an accident. I'm surprised you didn't notice how straight I'm standing. I injured my back, but as long as I don't try to bend I'm alright. I was with the doctor. Here's the certificate. Sacroiliac strain.'

'My poor boy! How on earth did it happen?'

'I was bending down to tie this wee girl's shoelace, so that she wouldn't trip out in the yard at lunchtime yesterday, when I felt something cracking in my back, and a fierce pain shot down my right leg. I didn't tell a soul about it but carried on bravely until school was over.'

'Ah George you were very foolish. Why didn't you get the headmaster to send for the doctor?'

'Mammy, I wanted to avoid the expense of a doctor. If you give those crooks half a chance they'll order you to bed, and visit you twice a day. So I decided it would be cheaper to go up to the city, and see cousin, Charlie. He put me lying on the floor of his flat hoping I'd be better by morning. I didn't sleep a wink all night. Every time I moved a muscle I was in agony, and I kept him awake with the moaning.'

'Why did you not ring Mrs Murphy last night to let me know about it?'

'What good would that do Mammy! It wouldn't cure me, and it would upset you, and you have enough worries of your own without me adding to them. Anyway, at seven o'clock this morning Charlie decided that there was nothing for it but to call in a doctor. A nice young man I'll admit. He pressed something in my back. There was a sound like a click, and lo and behold: the pain vanished; but I'm afraid of my life it'll happen again. That's why I'm holding myself so straight. The doctor gave me strict instructions to rest for a month. I don't know what to do Mammy. I was thinking of going against his advice, and returning to work tomorrow. I can't have you going down there, teaching those kids. It just wouldn't be fair.'

'Would they accept me as a substitute?'

'Of course they would. Aren't you a fully qualified teacher! But Mammy, I think it's asking too much of you.'

'If I wouldn't do a turn for my only son who would I do it for!'

'Alright Mammy. You've talked me into it. I'll go over to Mrs Murphy and ring Father Smith.'

Mrs Murphy wasn't at home. She had neglected to secure her kitchen window, so I scrambled in, and made my call.

'Could I speak to Father Smith. Aw it's yourself, Father! I didn't recognise your voice. The line's not too good.'

'How is your mother, George?'

'It's a sad story. The cratur has slipped down the hill an awful lot in the past two days. She didn't know me at first when I went in to visit her last night. She thought I was her brother, who's dead this forty years, but she's not quite as bad this morning.'

'I'll drive up to see her myself tomorrow.'

'You're very good, Father, but you'd put the fear of God in her, if she saw a strange face in the black clothes coming at her. She'd know for sure she was on her last legs. The parish priest drops in to her every evening. He's an old friend of the family. So spiritually she's being well looked after.'

'Alright so George. Where there's life there's hope, and God is very good.'

'Your very good too, Father. I feel I don't deserve the kindness you're showing me.'

'What can we do in this life but try to help everyone as best we can.'

'That's what I always think, and my mother always says that God helps those who help themselves. By the way Father, my eldest sister, Anne, was giving out stink to me for coming home, and leaving you stranded short of a teacher. She says that I must have no conscience, and that she'll go down herself, and teach them for a few weeks.'

'Is she not worried about her mother?'

'I'm ashamed to say it, Father. She has no feelings whatsoever for Mammy. They couldn't be together for three minutes but they'd be at each others' throats. They've had some terrible rows. Only last week she threw a pot of boiling macaroni at her own mother, because Mammy advised her not to be always plastering herself with make-up. I wasn't going to tell you, Father, but that's how Mammy fell, and broke her two hips.'

'I wouldn't have the likes of her in my school.'

'You don't understand. My mother believes that the cause of Anne being the way she is, is that she, herself, fell off a bicycle when she was pregnant with Anne, as a result she was born two months premature, and has never been right since.'

'Isn't there a danger that she'd be violent with the pupils in the school?'

'Not at all, Father. She dotes on children. It's only with her own family that she's aggressive. And she's an awful lot older than me. An awful lot older. She didn't get married until she was well past the gander, so she could have no children herself. Worse still, six months ago her husband ran off to England with the vicar's wife, and hasn't sent her home a penny since. She's too proud to go back teaching in her own area, and won't look for a job elsewhere. It could be the makings of her, if you allow me to put her in as a sub, until the end of the month. It would be an angelic act of charity, Father.'

'Alright so. When will she be down?'

'She'll be on the last train this evening.'

'I'll meet her at the station, and if anything happens to your mother let me know at once. I'll break the news gently to her, because if I know human nature she'll suffer dreadful remorse of conscience.'

'Right, Father. Goodbye, and God bless.'

Going out the door I nearly knocked down featherweight, Mrs Murphy, and her coming in at the same time, with a bottle of milk in one hand, and a loaf of bread in the other.

'George! You gave me the fright of my life! What on earth are you doing in my home?'

'Mrs Murphy you're a shockin' careless woman. You went off, and left your door wide open. Any tramp could have come in, and taken anything he wanted.'

'I could almost swear that I pulled it after me.'

'Well there you are. You must have had your mind on something else. When I saw it open I took the liberty of making a local phone call in your absence. Here's the money for it.'

'Don't bother, George. It's only a couple of coppers.'

'No, Mrs Murphy. I insist. One must pay one's lawful debts, and give everyone his own.'

'We won't argue over it, George. By the way, I thought you were down the country teaching school.'

'I am but we've two days off. The parish priest, and his mother were killed tragically. A car accident. He had a sup too much taken, the poor man, and ran into an ass and cart in a thick fog. The ass

36

escaped without a scratch. Did you not read about it in the papers?'

'I don't have time to read the papers.'

'You're as well off Mrs Murphy. Half of what's in them is lies. I better be off now. I promised my mother I'd dig the potatoes for the dinner.

#####

'Mammy, you have the job alright. You'll have to dye your hair.'

'Why should I dye my hair! I'm not going in for a beauty competition. Am I!'

'Well then, will you give it a blue rinse?'

'What are you talking about, George? Tell me what blue rinses have got to do with teaching children!'

'Very little Mammy, if the whole truth were told. So I'll come clean, and tell you the whole truth. The parish priest is a screwball who lives in a fantasy world. He is convinced that you're in hospital with two broken hips. When I told him that you'd teach in my place for a month he said he'd fit you out with a new pair of crutches. To save him going to the expense of buying the crutches I suggested that I'd get my sister, Anne, to sub for me instead. He jumped at that idea. So you'll have to pretend you're my sister.

'Incidentally, the landlady is twice as mad as him. They're in cahoots together. They've put out a rumour that you're dying. Just to humour her, fob her off with the first thing that comes into your head.'

'I'll do no such a thing, George. You're treating me as if I were an idiot. I don't believe a word you've said. I'll soon find out the truth when I go down there. I'll be able to judge the landlady, and the parish priest for myself.'

'Alright Mammy. I couldn't cod you. We're too much alike.'

'I've never been so insulted in all my life.'

'You're only joking me, Mammy. Aren't you?'

'You know well I am, but you're much more like your father than me. God rest his soul. He was forever playing outrageous practical jokes without giving a damn about the consequences. However, he wasn't as bad a liar as you.'

'I think you're being a bit harsh on me, Mammy. For a highly intelligent woman like you, I'm surprised you don't realise that just as some people have big feet, and others have small feet, some people are afraid to tell lies, and others are afraid to tell the truth, and I fall in to the latter bracket. However, I'll pluck up my courage now, and make a clean breast of it.

'It's only a yarn about the parish priest, and the landlady being mad. You couldn't meet two nicer people in a long day's travel. When I was applying for the job I believed I'd have a better chance if I played on the priest's sympathy by telling him that my mother wasn't well. The one mistake I did make, was in saying that I was going to bring you with me, if I got the job. I had to tell a dose of lies after that to cover up, but Mammy, if you go through with this I'll give you my word of honour that I'll never tell another lie in my life.'

'What about your back? Is that a yarn too, to play on my sympathy?'

'Ah, Mammy! You know that's genuine. Didn't you read the doctor's certificate!'

'I always heard it said that if you wanted to cod a doctor all you had to say was that you had a pain in your back, and he couldn't prove otherwise.'

'Mammy, I'll bring you straight up to cousin Charlie, and you can ask him yourself if I kept him awake all last night, moaning with the agony.'

'You know well that I wouldn't take a trip to the city just to prove that my own son is a liar. Anyway, you and Charlie were always as thick as thieves.'

'You won't believe me, Mammy! I'll tell you what I'll do. I'll bend down now to see will it happen again. Maybe then you'll believe me when you're running for the ambulance.'

'Alright son, you win. What have I got to do?'

I filled her in on the details. She didn't know whether to laugh or cry so she did a bit of both. The idea that she'd have to pretend she was her own daughter, while she herself was supposed to be in hospital, at first horrified her, and then on second thoughts appealed to her sense of devilment. I was telling her that being in such a situation was not all that strange because I had heard of a chap about whom a song had been written. When matters were investigated it was conclusively proven that he was his own grandfather. As I was finishing that titbit the two sisters arrived for their lunch, and to some degree thwarted my plans.

'I thought you had a job down the country, George! Did they cop on to you already? Why are you here?' asked Nellie through her sarcastic teeth.

'I tripped over a straw and a hen kicked me, as a result of which I lost my memory, and came in to this house by mistake. Who are you anyway? Or should I know your name!'

'Don't mind him, Nellie. He injured his back, and I'm doing sub for him for a month. You'll have to fend for yourselves girls, and look after George as well.'

'That's great news, Mammy. You've hardly stirred out of this house since Daddy died. The change will do you good,' said Susan.

'Mammy, I forgot to tell you. Charlie has asked me to do him a favour. He has a lot of expensive medical equipment in the flat - skeletons, and such like. The fellow next door to him was cleaned out at the weekend, and Charlie asked me to stay with him for the month, to keep an eye on the place during the day. I couldn't refuse him, especially as he was so good to me last night, getting up every hour to hand me cups of tea.'

'That's grand so. The girls won't have to look after you.'

'Mammy, what are you going to do with the money you make for the month?' asked nosey Nellie.

'I wasn't going to take anything off George. Let him do what he likes with it.'

'Mammy, I feel embarrassed walking up the middle aisle of the church every Sunday morning, with you in your shabby coat, and tatty hat,' said sensitive Susan.

'We'll go on a shopping spree at the end of the month, and dress you out from head to toe,' said full-of-suggestions Nellie.

'What do you say, George?'

'Mammy, that was what I had planned for you myself. I was going to keep it as a surprise. They're after going and spoiling it.'

'I always knew you had a soft spot for your poor old mother,' said Mammy.

'The only one he has a soft spot for is himself,' sniped Nellie.

'Come on girls, you'll have to eat up your dinner or you'll be late for work.'

#####

Mammy did give her hair a blue rinse, and dolled herself up as best she could. We went to the city together. She then transferred to

39

the other train, and I returned to Charlie's flat.

He was having his cheese sandwich tea when I arrived. I filled him in on my sisters' shopping spree plan for my mother, which meant that I wasn't going to gain a penny from her month's work. He nearly choked with good humour.

'Poetic justice, George!'

'I suppose you'll be just as delighted if I'm not paid for the job I'm starting in the morning!'

'Ah come off it, George. If you're not able to laugh at yourself, you shouldn't laugh at anybody else. Anyway, won't you be sharing everything you earn with me, and we'll have a great time together.'

'I suppose so.'

Next morning I arrived at the school armed with two Edgar Wallace crime thrillers as I'm a speed reader, and saw no sense in working up a sweat when the man for whom I was subbing would get the credit for it.

The headmaster was a fine strapping countryman. Though in his late thirties, he was still the star of the local football, and consequently was idolised by the children. He told me that mine was the senior class, and asked me what my favourite subject was. 'English composition,' I replied, and assured him that they would be much improved therein when I was finished with them. Which they certainly were at the end of the month, as I piled on compositions till welts were coming up on the two fingers in which they held their pens.

Unlike a bats in the belfry acquaintance of mine, who used to give his ten-year-old pupils subjects such as, 'Uneasy lies the head that wears the crown,' on which to write essays, I chose topics in which I knew they'd be interested.

I'd take time-out from Edgar Wallace to allow them the thrill of reading aloud their compositions, each of which was discussed by the class. Suggestions were made about how mistakes could have been avoided, and how stories could have been improved. They quite enjoyed the experience.

I gave them loads of homework, and made sure that I put a tick on each child's exercise the next morning to prove that I saw it. That doesn't mean that I looked at it. It's amazing the number of parents who judge a school, who judge a teacher, on the amount of homework given.

The headmaster never came near my classroom from the day I arrived until the day I left. I respected him for his faith in me.

Every Friday I collected my wages. Charlie was most obliging in helping me to spend it, but I didn't mind in the least. The acquisition of money always generates in me a burning desire to get rid of it before I think of something sensible to do with it. Besides, I saw in Charlie a perpetual provider of doctor's certificates as required, from the morning he would qualify.

Nearly every night we went dancing. I found it exciting looking across the floor, admiring all the beautiful girls, and wondering would I get off my mark. More often than not I failed to score because of my callow approach, but I always bounced back on the resilient wings of immature youth, and the month flew.

Towards the end of the second week there, the following letter arrived at Charlie's flat for me:

Dear son,

How is your back? Coming down on the train after leaving you, I was thinking about your granduncle, Ted, who also claimed he had a weak back. His wife never gave him a day's peace, only at him morning, noon, and night, about how quickly the pain disappeared the moment he got between the sheets

When she died suddenly he didn't act the hypocrite, and feign grief. More power to him, on the day of her month's mind he married a young girl whom he had put an eye on at the funeral. At the wedding breakfast he told me privately that he couldn't believe his luck that two such happy ceremonies occurred in the same church within a few weeks of each other. Ted was a hard man, but he was always good for a laugh. Lord have mercy on his soul.

The parish priest met me at the station. When out of pure friendliness, I asked him how his mother was he released a grunt, and drove me straight to the lodging house.

The landlady is a nice, softhearted woman, and quite a good cook too, in an economical sort of a way. She couldn't hide her astonishment when I told her you were my brother. I confided in her that our mother had you when she was 56. She said that a woman never knows when she is safe. She's that age herself.

She made great enquiries about how I was doing in hospital

with my two broken hips. I was finding it difficult to keep a straight face. To cover up, I forced myself to burst out crying. She started crying in harmony with me, and then insisted that we'd both get down on our knees to say the rosary that I'd make a swift recovery.

Write soon and let me know what Charlie, and yourself have been up to.

Lots of love,
From your only mother.

Mammy,

I received your welcome letter the week before last. I had every intention of replying to you sooner. Unfortunately I wasn't in form for writing because I suffered a relapse. It happened so simply Mammy that it sounds ridiculous.

I was doing nothing in particular one morning, only looking at Charlie's skeleton, and wondering what kind of a man it was who used to wear the flesh on it. I was trying to figure out by the look of him whether he was more likely to be a wife-beater or a saint, when I accidentally knocked off his head, which rolled in under the bed.

I crawled in after it, chasing it, when I felt at first a twinge, and then a shot of agony right through my whole system. I made a brave attempt to manoeuvre out from where I was but the more I edged out the worse it got.

I can only conclude that I lapsed in to unconsciousness for some time, because I couldn't believe that six hours had gone by when Charlie returned, and me still stuck in under the bed. I was rushed to hospital. Was there for eight days, but thank God I've made a complete recovery. The surgeon assured me that if I don't stoop suddenly, and avoid lifting weights, it need never happen again.

I'm not saying that just to ease your mind. So there is no need for you to worry about me, Mammy, but I'm sick worrying about the hospital bill. What a shock I got when it was handed to me. You could have knocked me down with a feather. I don't know how I'll pay it. Could you see your way to postponing that shopping spree for the present? Anyway Mammy, Susan has no taste whatsoever. I've admired that coat on you for years.

I'll see you on Friday. I'll be down before the school clos-
es, to sign the salary form.

With all my love,
Your only son,
George.

On Thursday night my mother walked in to Charlie's flat.

'Mammy! What's wrong? You weren't due to finish till tomorrow. Are you sick?'

'No, but McVeigh is. (Hello Charlie). When I dismissed my
classes today I went to the staff room to collect my coat. Yer man
was at the table with his head down correcting copies. The ignorant
jinnet didn't even acknowledge my presence, but went on with what
he was doing. Going out the door I passed the harmless remark that
my brother was resuming on Monday but was coming back tomorrow to sign the salary form.

'Huh,' said he with a sneer, 'I was hoping that that young pup
wouldn't darken the door of this school again.'

'You know George that I'm not of a violent nature. I never raised
my hand to you or any of your four sisters in my life. Isn't that true?'

'Of course it is, Mammy. You were always too quiet. I don't
know how you put up with the way those girls used to go on, fighting about who owned which pair of knickers every Sunday morning.
You had the patience of Job.'

'It was all in a day's work, George. Anyway, I wasn't going to
let yer man away with calling my only son a pup. I drew out and hit
him a clatter across the face that set his two plates of false teeth
going round the room like flying saucers. Then I gave him a dig
under the chin, and followed up with a right to the eye. I was about
to finish him off with one to the stomach, when who walked in the
door but the parish priest himself. He grabbed me from behind, and
pinioned me by the arms.

'Having always had such a great respect for the clergy, I was so
mortified at him catching me red-handed giving yer man the works,
that I calmed down instantaneously, and apologised for losing my
temper, but McVeigh was on for suing me for assault, and battery.

'Father Smith wouldn't hear of it: that it would bring disgrace to
the school, to the teachers, and to the parish, and that the papers
would be full of it. He then ordered me to leave the parish, and not

to put my foot inside it again.'

'He told McVeigh that he'd buy him a new set of false teeth, the best on the market, both top and bottom. Yer man accepted the offer, but his last words to me were: that he'd have you sacked at the first available opportunity. So George, I think it's better if you leave that school altogether.'

'Mammy! For God's sake will you be sensible. Just because you have a tiff with the headmaster doesn't mean that I should start looking for another job. I'll go down there tomorrow as if nothing happened. You'll have a nice cup of tea now, and Charlie and myself will see you to the train.'

'You're one cool customer, George! Just like your father, God rest his soul, you always have your eye on the main chance, and to hell with trivialities, such as boxing matches between 40 year-old men, and 60 year-old women. How is your back by the way? It went clean out of my head until this minute.'

'Not a bother on me.'

'And what about you Charlie? How are your studies going?'

'To be honest auntie, I didn't do much recently, but I intend settling down to work as soon as this fellow goes tomorrow.'

Mammy had a cup of tea, and a rasher sandwich, and signed a receipt, for what she would have been entitled to, as a substitute. She missed out on one day's pay I know, but I had no regrets when I measured it up against the job she hammered on McVeigh. I was relieved, delighted that she got out of that place without giving the game away that she was my mother. We saw her to the train, and went off dancing.

Next day, at the lunch-break, having collected my wages, I took off for McVeigh's academy, and landed there just before closing time, believing that the man himself would be absent due to multiple pains in the head, caused by a misadventure with an elderly lady.

Not alone was he there in all his gummy pomposity, bedecked with a royal blue eye, but so also was the reverend manager, and the inspector, in the corridor, chatting with him.

'Ah hello! I just dropped in to sign the salary form before you send it off.'

'We were just discussing how we'd send you off,' said the vindictive McVeigh.

'What do you mean?' I've done no wrong.'

44

'Why didn't you notify me of your absence?' asked the tetchy inspector.

'Because Mr McVeigh declined to give me your address.'

'Is that true?' asked the inspector, turning to McVeigh.

'I don't remember,' answered slippery Sam.

'Maybe if I balanced up your face with another black eye you'd remember,' said I.

'Cut out that talk,' said the inspector.

'Wait now,' said I, 'I want to know what you mean, McVeigh, by sending me off. First of all you haven't the power to hire or fire me. Secondly, even if you had, I have not neglected my duties in any way. While I was in this school I worked hard. When I was out of it I produced a doctor's certificate justifying my absence. I sent it along with my sister to you, McVeigh.'

'Your sister!' said McVeigh in a tone dripping with sarcasm.

'George, I want to speak to you alone. Come in to the staff room,' said Father Smith.

He ushered me in, and shut the door.

'I brought you in here because I didn't want to humiliate you in front of those two men. I am deeply disappointed in you. Mr McVeigh rang your own parish priest last night, and discovered that your mother was never in hospital in her life, let alone being there at present with two broken hips; that in fact she was down here for the past month doing your work.

'You have flung at me a tissue of lies. You have played on my sympathy. You have played on my charity. I don't mind that too much because I'm well used to it. It's one of the hazards of our profession, but what I do object to, strongly, is the unjust treatment that both you, and your mother meted out to our respected headmaster, Mr McVeigh.

'You were only one day in the place, when - as I heard for the first time last night - without any provocation, you insulted him, and made little of this school, of which both he and I, and all my parishioners are so proud. Then to add injury to insult, your mother beat him up yesterday evening.

'I don't know what kind of a family you Ryans are, but I do know that there was peace in this parish before you came, and there'll be peace in this parish when you go. And I'm asking you to go now!'

'You are asking me to resign!'

'Yes I am.'

'There's nothing further from my mind. I found it hard enough to get a job without giving it up voluntarily. I'm sane enough to know I'm a bit mad, but not that mad.'

'George! The simple fact is that there's not room in the one school for both you, and Mr McVeigh. I've my mind made up on that.'

'A minute ago you were asking me to go. Are you now telling me to go?'

'You will never again stand in front of a class in this parish, as long as I'm in it.'

'Well then I'll sit down all the time. I'm not a bit fussy.'

'This is a serious matter, and you are being flippant about it.'

'It's more serious for me than it is for you.'

'As you sow, so shall you reap! Consider yourself sacked this minute. And please go quietly. I do regret that we are parting like this.'

'So do I, but I have my rights, and I won't go quietly unless I get them.'

'What do you mean?'

'I worked very hard while I was in this school. You can't deny that. Ask any of the children! And I want a reference to that effect.'

'Well, I'll give you a reference stating that you worked diligently for one day.'

'Ah no Father! You can leave out the one day bit. That wouldn't impress anybody.'

'Alright so. The Good Lord said that we should always be charitable, and out of charity, I'll give you a decent reference.'

'I'm not here on my knees begging for charity. If I don't get my rights I'll contact my union this evening, and I'll be walking up, and down outside this school next Monday morning, with a placard in my hand: 'Strike on here.' The papers will be full of it on Tuesday.'

'You wouldn't do that, would you!'

'Try me, and you'll find out.'

'What exactly do you want?'

'Firstly I want my reference. Secondly, I've an agreement form in my wallet, which states that when sacking me you are bound by law to give me three months' notice, or three months salary in lieu of notice. As you have decided not to give me a day's notice, I'm willing to accept three months salary.'

'Sit down George, and we'll have a smoke to calm our nerves.'

'There's nothing wrong with my nerves. Sit down yourself while you're writing the cheque.'

'Have a cigarette, George.'

'Thanks.'

We talked, and smoked until his cigarettes ran out. Then I let him off with two, and a half months' salary, and a reference which would warrant my being appointed as minister for education.

#####

I cleared out of that parish on the next train. For the following twelve years I wandered up and down the country, in and out of jobs, not knowing exactly what I was looking for, but worse still not knowing where to look for it, yet instinctively believing that some woman held the key to the door of the happiness I was pursuing. I did short lines, and long lines, single lines, and double-cross lines, and even one triple line which came to a sudden end when the three young ladies with whom I was involved happened to meet in the powder room of a dance hall, compared notes, and discovered that all three had the one, and the same lover boy. On the spot they decided to return to the ballroom, confront me, and give me the bum's rush, which would have been most humiliating had there been a decent streak in my nature.

One exceptionally serious female with whom I had become friendly, if not intimate, psychoanalysed me without charging a fee, and came up with the judgment that I gave little in a relationship, and looked for too much. I told her she was right, but the reason she was right was because she was the wrong woman for me. She reared up and told me that the right woman for me didn't exist on this earth. She was wrong on that score. I found the right woman. The problem was that I was the wrong man. I might tell you the story about that later if I manage to overcome my shyness.

As I was saying earlier I allowed my wanderlust gene steer me all over Ireland for twelve years. I then settled down in a thirteen-teacher school in Edenstown, where I got off to a bad start by ruffling the feathers of the headmaster, Mr Swan, within a few weeks of my arrival.

On the last working day of each month the salary form is signed by all the staff and then posted to the department of education. Otherwise we don't get paid. While in their possession the document is carefully minded by most headmasters, and treated as sacred by those of a niggardly nature, to which ilk Mr Swan belonged.

I decided that I'd cause the form to go missing for a while in order to get a taste of the reaction that would ensue.

I managed to obtain it during the midday break while the male members of the staff were walking in a line in the yard, with me in the privileged position of being on the headmaster's left. With one hand I pointed out to him a ruffian bullying a little orphan, and with the other I whipped it out of his overcoat pocket.

Ten minutes after we had returned to our classrooms, a courteous girl came to my door, and knocked timidly on it. Having been admitted, she sought permission to make an announcement: 'Mr Swan wants to know if anyone found a yellow piece of paper in a long brown envelope in the yard at lunch time.' No one had. She did likewise in the rest of the rooms throughout the school.

Twenty minutes later a big boy with a shrill voice bulldozed in the door, and squawked out a statement to the same effect with no effect.

Lastly came the despairing headmaster himself, who did a thorough investigation. After urging them to put on their thinking caps, he quizzed every single pupil separately, as to whether or not they had seen the precious piece of paper.

One imaginative chap thought he had got a glimpse of it being blown over the wall. Mr Swan, accompanied by a dozen senior pupils, who didn't wear glasses, climbed over the wall, and found: that it wasn't over the wall.

About a quarter of an hour before quitting time I chose my courier, Dickey, who is one of those giftless individuals, who should, but never does, excite our envy. He was then, and will be, as long as he lives, as happy as the day is short. He hasn't the brains to worry about anything.

He came to my notice on my first afternoon in Edenstown when I was doing a geography lesson. I put to him the question: 'What do you fish for in the river Shannon?'

'Fish,' he replied.

For that night, I told them to: 'Trace a map of Ireland, and put in all the counties, cities, large towns, rivers, and mountains.'

When he proffered his homework for my inspection the following morning, I was surprised to see that he had traced an outline map of Scotland, and squeezed in all the counties, cities, large towns, rivers, and mountains of Ireland.

I called Dickey up to my desk and said in a conspiratorial whisper: 'I want you to do a little message for me.'

'Okay sir,' answered he, and his face flushed with pride, excitement, and anticipation.

After much repetition, I succeeded in teaching him to say off by heart, these few words: 'Mr Swan, I was out in the sit-down toilet, going to wipe my arse with this bit of paper, when I remembered that it might be the thing you were looking for.'

I then gave him the salary form, and clear-cut instructions which any halfwit could follow. Out past the headmaster's door to the toilet he goes. Back in. Knocks on the door. Straight up to Mr Swan. Hands him the form, and trots out his party piece, having hung me with the cunning introduction, 'Mr Ryan told me to say...'

Mr Swan rushed to my room in a rage, and spat a torrent of abuse at me. Most of the interesting points he made have slipped my memory, but I do recall him mentioning that it doesn't come within the bounds of a teacher's duties to inculcate lies, and vulgarities in the minds of young children. The man was right to a degree, but I don't see why, if it's proper to call a nose a nose, it's improper to call an arse an arse.

The rest of the staff, with one exception, were both relieved and peeved to find that the form was found. Relieved that there was not going to be a hitch about them getting their pay, and peeved with the cheeky newcomer who had given them an anxious few hours fearing that there would. Yes, I have learned that you can get away with playing pranks on people provided that you don't cause them any inconvenience.

The one exception was a man by the name of Cecil Chuckleworth. A man destined to be my friend for life. Barrel-chested, bow-legged, hatchet-faced, cross-eyed as he was, he had a wicked sense of humour. He pretended to be disappointed in me for not holding on to the form overnight, 'just to give Mr Swan something to think about if he found it difficult to get to sleep that night.'

Your good taste prevents me from revealing what he suggested

Dickey should have been directed to smear on it, before handing it up to the headmaster.

From that evening Cecil and myself got on famously. Our class-rooms were next door to each other, with a wooden partition between, and a large window therein. Underneath the window was a hole about the size of a pullet's egg, through which one could view - without being seen - what was going on in the other room. I passed many pleasant hours watching him in operation. He was endowed with a raucous voice which penetrated the partition as if it were made of paper.

Generally the most interesting time to have him under observation was when he came in on a Monday morning after a hard week-end's drinking. However there was one memorable Friday he arrived in a semi-drunken state, straight from the pub, after an all-night session.

He gave the kids a composition, put his two elbows on the desk, followed through with his head, and tried to catch up on his sleep, but they had him persecuted, coming up asking him questions, and telling him tales.

'Sir! Spell shnite.'

'What did you say?'

'Spell shnite, sir.'

'Say the sentence.'

'Las shnite I went to the pictures with me granny.'

'Sir! Dermot O'Sullivan is walking round the room.'

'What do you want him to do! Fly round it.'

'Sir! My copy's full.'

'Do you think I've a stationer's shop under my desk!'

'Sir! I've a pain!'

'Don't be always boasting.'

'Sir! Mary O'Driscoll said dirty words.'

'What did she say?'

'You'd bate me sir if I said them.'

'I'll bate you twice as much if you don't.'

(There followed a whisper in to Mr Chuckleworth's ear).

'How dare you repeat such language! Go down you brazen brat.'

'Sir! Noeleen Cullen called me a creature.'

'God keep my hands off that girl.'

'Sir! Frank Martin is fighting with Joe Burke.'

'Who's winning?'

'Sir! Peter Guinness is eating his lunch.'

'More than I feel like doing.'

'Sir! Liam Hearty punched me in the stomach!'

'You're a tough man! He couldn't hurt you.'

Boy goes down. Holds out his stomach, and says: 'Go on, Liam. Hit me again. I bet you won't hurt me!'.

'Sir! Barry Nolan has a rubber band and is firing paper.'

'You gather up the paper when he's finished.'

'Sir! Noeleen Cullen pinched me!'

'Where?'

'I don't want to say, sir.'

'Go down, and pinch her back in the same place.'

'Sir! What time is it?'

'Time you shut your mouth.'

At this stage Cecil decided that it was too much of a strain to give different replies to every remark, and question, so he opted to give a stock reply to them all.

'Sir! Martin Crilly says he has a dreadful toothache.'

'Tell him to go to the toilet.'

'Sir! Noeleen Cullen is calling me names.'

'Tell her to go to the toilet.'

'Sir! Paddy Power is shooting peas.'

'Tell him to shoot them in the toilet.'

'Sir! Maggie Byrne's mammy is at the door.'

'Tell her to go to the toilet.'

'Sir! I'm dying to go to the toilet!'

'Sit down and shut up.'

Cecil fell asleep then, and started to snore. I kept an eye on his class, along with my own, for the rest of the day.

#####

I was only a few months in Edenstown when Cecil got me in to his digs. There was nothing wrong with the place in which I had been except that the landlady, a tall, slim widow, with a pleasant face, was more interested in flirting with me than feeding me. Perhaps I myself should shoulder some of the blame for the fare she provided.

On my first evening there she asked me what food I liked best.

Projecting the tough guy image, I told her that I didn't give a hoot what she put in front of me, as long as it didn't walk away before I finished eating it. Taking full advantage of my schoolboy exaggeration she wasted no time cooking my meals.

I entered regularly in my diary: 'Lemonade, and biscuits again for breakfast. 'Tea-dinner,' again for dinner.' When I used to come back from school in the evening she'd have ready for me what she described as a 'Tea-dinner,' which was neither a tea nor a dinner, but a salad which one might get as a starter in a run-down cafe. I had been her first experiment in the boarding-house business. When I told her I was leaving she asked why. As I didn't want to upset her I told her it would take all day to tell her.

The joint to which I moved would not excite an architect's interest except to make him wonder what madman designed it. Having entered by the front door one meets a nine-feet wide, forty-feet long corridor. What a waste of floor space! In the right-hand wall can be seen a pygmy window which sheds a lot of darkness during the daylight. On the left are two doors into two huge rooms, off which are doors into two more large rooms. The back ones are the dining room and the kitchen, and the front ones the sitting room, and the 'dead' room in which there is not a stick of furniture. It earned its nickname, according to the locals, because the previous owner hid her dead spinster sister there for a few days, before going public that she was stiff, so that she could draw her full week's pension.

Immediately inside the hall door is a stairs which leads to a spacious landing. The biggest room upstairs is the bathroom, in the centre of which is an enormous bath with an unofficial hole in its bottom, which, if not stuffed with a towel, will flood the place when one is taking a bath.

In the far corner is the thunder bowl, which, according to tradition, did have a wooden seat, until the night a former guest of the establishment wrenched it off, and wore it as a collar at a dinner-dance, in case people wouldn't notice that he could afford to attend the function.

There are eight bedrooms, none of which is big enough to swing a dog with a short tail, which reminds me to tell you that the landlady, Miss June Casey, always wears her grey hair long, and straight.

In her early fifties when I first went under her roof, she is a plump, plain-faced, wee woman, in whose life religion plays a dominant part. She never misses seven o'clock Mass in the morning, nor evening devotions whenever they're on. What's more, she has charity in her heart. Not once in my time there, did I hear her say a bad word about anybody.

She keeps the cheapest digs in town because there's not a greedy inch to her body, but like most of the landladies at whose mercy I've been, she's a mediocre, unimaginative cook. Against that, she's such a sincere, simple person, that she has always had a warm relationship with her boarders, and consequently a homely atmosphere permeates 'St Jude's.'

The evening I lugged my baggage - a case full of books interspersed with a few dirty shirts and socks - across Miss Casey's threshold, I wondered when I'd be lugging it out again.

Cecil and I shared the front bedroom over the corridor. When you came in our door, my narrow bed was on your right, Cecil's on your left. A chest of drawers under the window over the hall door, a slim fireplace below my bed, a slim wardrobe below Cecil's, completes your picture of the room where I so often tried to convince myself that 'better days are coming.'

#####

This minute, as I lie on my bed, I'm thinking about you, my dear reader, and wondering what kind of form you're in. I hope you're not lost in a fog of loneliness as I am. If you don't mind me asking you a personal question, do you take a drink? You don't. You're right too. You're far better off without it. Sorry. You do! I misheard you. That bloody radio is getting on my nerves! Wait till I turn it off.

Well, I'm delighted to hear that you do enjoy a drink. How would we live without it! I'll tell you what: we'll go out now, and have a session together. Too early! You must be joking. It's nearly four o'clock, and we'll be thrown out of the pub at twenty to twelve. We'll barely have time to wet our whistles. You don't believe in drinking like that! Everything in moderation you say. You're right. I won't argue with you.

Will you listen for fecks sake! I already conceded you were right, so don't start preaching temperance at me, please.

No! I won't go out on my own. Why! I can't. I've no money. I was depending on you to supply the drink, and I'd supply the chat. You feel sorry for me! Then lend me the price of a bottle of brandy, and I'll give it back to you first thing in the morning.

You're really giving it to me! Thanks. In all my life I never met anyone as generous as you. No I don't need the money for ginger ale. I don't use the stuff; but you can throw in the price of a packet of cigarettes since you have the loose change.

Do I spend all my money on drink! Not quite. I give a fair share of it to the bookies.

When did I first hit the bottle! Listen. I haven't time to tell you now. That money you gave me has set off a chemical reaction, and I'm after getting a fierce drought in the base of my throat. I better go before you think up some reason for asking it back. All the best.

#####

A pain in the stomach was the direct cause of me starting to preserve my body by saturating it in alcohol.

That first winter in Edenstown, I used to go to 'Barney's', a spit-and-sawdust pub, with Cecil, and the other lads from the digs, most nights of the week. I was the odd man out, inasmuch as I drank mixers, while they drank drink. They accepted my right to be a teetotaller - as I had, due to parental influences, always intended to be - and never tried to make me feel that I was a half-caste among a bunch of thoroughbreds, but some of them would tell me now and again in their cups, that I didn't know what I was missing. Cecil, though not of a mercenary nature, always took the opposite line and assured me that I was a wise man not to touch the stuff, that I'd never have a bob if I started. That to me was a joke because I never had a bob anyway.

Be that as it may, I continued to ride the virgin of sobriety until one night coming on towards the spring, through bad luck, I fell off. I was with them as usual in 'Barney's', joining in the repartee, and general chat about how to solve the problems of the soul, and the state, when suddenly I got an excruciating pain in my stomach. I excused myself from the company and spent a dreadful age in the gents, dry-retching, and violently vomiting.

After a while Cecil and another chap came out to see was I alright. The blood had drained from my face, and I was next door to going into a faint. The other man, (I won't give his name because he often expressed his regret about it afterwards.), urged me to take a brandy, and port, that it was the only thing to cure me, and back to the bar he went, and got it.

Meanwhile, Cecil advised me not to take it, that with my temperament I wouldn't know when to stop once I started, and that the pain would be gone in ten minutes. However, I was in such distress that I'd try anything to rid me of the feeling that my stomach was about to explode. And so, I took my first drink in the jakes of 'Barney's' pub in Edenstown, at the age of 32.

That first one didn't cure me, but the second made me feel much better, and I asked for a third. Thus I started down the alcoholic's avenue, on the road to the stutters, on the road to the shakes, on the road which leads nowhere but to mental hell on this earth.

Just as innumerable men, and women would like to go back to that moment at the altar, when they said, 'I do,' when they should have said 'I don't,' I would like to go back to the moment in that jakes when I said, 'I would,' when I should have said, 'I won't,' but, in the most important decisions in life we don't get second chances. Yet we do allow ourselves to be influenced by short-term factors, when we should be standing back a mile, to consider the long-term results.

Closing time came, and we returned to 'St Jude's.'

During those few, for me, momentous hours, with alcohol down my hatch for the first time, it didn't register with me that my mood was any different than ever previously, but next morning, when looking back on the night before - as drinkers often do - I realised that the three brandies had effected in me a feeling of good humour, a feeling of good fellowship, a feeling of exhilaration, which I had never hitherto experienced. Naturally, I liked the feeling, and went out, and bought it again, and again.

#####

Early in April, Cecil suggested that we should join the golf club. The idea appealed to me for a few reasons, the chief being that we had in the digs a golf bore by the name of Willie McGrath, who was under the impression that he could hold all his fellow boarders, except me, spellbound, by recounting shot for shot, every shot he played, even though he played a lot of shots, not alone in every round, but also to every hole.

The golf apart, he was a likable guy, so the others - more tolerant than me - used to listen politely to him, and then give out hell about him behind his back. If he could corner nobody else he'd fall back on yours truly for his ego trip. When he'd suspect that I wasn't giving him the attention which he deemed to be his due, he'd have the nerve to make a spot check by asking me: 'Where was I?'

I wouldn't have a clue whether he was at the 6th or the 16th, so I'd give him a reply such as: 'You were just after watching your ninth putt to the 18th horseshoeing round the hole, and staying out, whereupon you threw your bag of clubs in the lake, and crawled back to the clubhouse with your head down, justifiably disgusted with yourself.' To such mild insults he reacted with an amused expression on his face, and then continued his saga, from where he had halted to make his spot check.

Cecil and I agreed that it would be more attractive for us to bore Willie than to be his victims. Besides I had been keen on pitch and putt in the days of my youth, and Cecil had been a caddy, a first-class one at that - I have his own word for it.

Taking up the game was not all plain sailing. One difficulty was that one needs clubs if one is to play golf, and one needs money if one is to buy one's clubs. And one needs one bicycle if two want to get to the golf course which is three miles out of town.

As neither of us had a tosser we decided to hold a jumble sale in aid of charity. You probably have no experience of jumble sales, so I'll tell you how we went about it, in case you yourself want to take up golf.

The first essential was a venue for the stall. We had no intention of paying rent for the venue. We wanted to make money, not give it away. So we approached Miss Casey, with Cecil acting as spokesman: 'We happened to bump into dear old Father O'Shea, the parish priest, today, on our way home from school. After exchanging civilities about the weather, he looked us both straight in the eye, and asked us did we realise that little was being done by the laity, for the needy of this parish. On the spur of the moment we volunteered to do our bit, by running a jumble sale, to make a few bob for those less well off than ourselves. Father O'Shea immediately referred to your spare room which is never used, and suggested that we should approach you, to find out if you could see your way to allowing us have it as a venue for the jumble sale.'

Miss Casey was more than flattered that Father O'Shea thought of her, and said that she'd be delighted to oblige. She even offered to help us run it. We said that we'd consider the offer.

So that we'd have full control over the commodities collected, we decided that we'd allow only the pupils of Cecil's class, and my own, to go abroad soliciting items for the sale.

Each of us gave our pupils a sermon on the advantages to be gained by helping others, and clear instructions as to what they were to look for. We warned them that we were not going to allow our jumble sale to be turned into a dumping ground for cast-offs suitable only for scarecrows, but that we would accept golf jackets, waterproof trousers, and golf shoes if they weren't leaking; and also any kind of a golf club provided that it had a head on it. If they found that they had the urge to take a club or two out of Daddy's or Mammy's bag, to do so discreetly, when their parents were in the garden or the pub. We gave them an assurance that we wouldn't let them down, that we'd deny all knowledge of receiving same.

Lastly we said that we knew of two respectable men who had fallen on hard times, and were badly in need of a bicycle. If there happened to be an old one lying around at home, why not bring it along, and we'd see that it was put to good use.

The children's initiative surpassed our wildest expectations. We had set four o'clock on the Thursday afternoon as the time for receipt of the donations. By 5.30 p.m. we had Miss Casey's spare room chock-a-block with golfing equipment, from brand new irons to out-of-date wooden-shafted mashies.

What's more, there was brought to us a bicycle in good running order, except that the front wheel was missing. One of the tough backstreet boys said that he knew how to fix it. Off he went. Ten minutes later he returned with a shining wheel taken from a bicycle which had been chained to the church gate, while the owner was inside saying his prayers, and thanking God that he had a new bicycle.

One mistake we made was that we forgot to ask for golf bags. Cecil insisted that thick twine would serve the purpose just as well, and would look more impressive than a shabby old bag.

We spent that night sorting out the clubs, and golf attire. We found that we had a full mongrel set each, and loads left over. Therefore there was no necessity to sell anything. We shifted what we needed up under our beds, and then told Miss Casey that we appreciated her kind offer to run the jumble sale, and gave her the go-ahead to take over from there.

Next morning she was busy, not with people coming to buy her wares, but looking for their own back. Some of them called Miss Casey a receiver of stolen goods, to which she retorted that she'd have the law on them for defamation of character.

The fuss about Miss Casey's jumble sale fizzled out after a few weeks, by which time our applications for membership of Edenstown Golf Club had been accepted by a narrow majority.

We rode out, with me in the saddle, and Cecil on the crossbar, holding on to the 28 clubs, which were inclined to catch in the front wheel now and again, and upend us on the road. A squabble would follow about who should be in the saddle, and who should be on the crossbar keeping the 28 clubs safely under his oxter. As Cecil had never previously ridden a bicycle I always come out on top in that particular bickering match.

On our arrival at the clubhouse we strode in to the men's bar, with a bundle of clubs under each arm, and approached a colonel-like, old gentleman who was twirling his brown-stained, handlebar moustache, while taking stock of us two newcomers. We asked him would he be so kind as to give each of us the loan of a fairly new golf ball.

After taking two puffs out of his crooked-shanked pipe, and looking us up and down as if he considered us intruders on his private property, he said to Cecil: 'That's very like my jacket you're wearing.'

'A case of mistaken identity,' said Cecil. 'I found it on a rubbish dump, when I was on a skiing holiday in the Swiss Alps, but seeing that you've taken a fancy to it, I'll swap it with you for six new golf balls.'

The man must have been uneasy about Cecil's hatchet-faced, cross-eyed, glowering countenance, or else very fond of the jacket, because he walked up to the counter, purchased a half-dozen Dunlop 65s, and parted with them to my friend.

Cecil took off the jacket, and went to pull it down, back to front over the head of his benefactor, and him with his pipe in his mouth.

'What are you at?' asked Handlebar Moustache querulously.

'I'm only trying to be helpful. I want to see does it fit you,' answered Cecil.

'Don't treat me as if I were a baby. Give me that jacket!'.

He tried it on. A perfect fit. Then he put his hand in one of its pockets, and brought forth a tobacco pouch.

'That's mine!' he declared.

'Don't worry,' said Cecil. 'I won't charge you any extra. You can have it as a luck penny.'

He then asked us were we members. To which we replied by asking him was his own membership paid up. We also advised him to shave off his dirty moustache as it was lowering the tone of the place.

While I've often been berated for my lack of taste, condemned for not being clothes conscious, indeed accused of being 'positively scruffy,' I must admit in all humility, that I could never boast of being as badly dressed as was Cecil, when we wended our joyful way to the first tee, having put Handlebar Moustache in his box.

Divested of his zipped-to-the-chin jacket, there was on show, a wrinkled, egg-stained, greyish shirt, which had been pure white, after Miss Casey had washed, and ironed it, before he had put it on, seven weeks previously. The shirt, of the old-fashioned kind, had a detachable collar, which he did detach, to help reassemble the braces of his trousers, when they came apart, the second time we fell off the bike. He would have used his tie instead, only he doesn't wear a tie, because there is a department of education rule: that one must wear a tie.

Some of the thongs of his braces were giving the thumbs up sign, because there was only one button in all the places where there should have been two.

The right knee of his corduroy trousers was hanging down, providing double protection for his shin, and exposing the scrape he got the third time we fell.

His red golf shoe and his blue hiker's boot gave a colourful touch to his large feet.

'Good evening,' said Cecil to the dozen or so players waiting around to take their turns in hitting off.

Everybody looked at us. Then everybody looked through us. Then everybody looked everywhere except at us.

'Do you mind if we go next?' asked Cecil. 'We want to be back in town before dark, because we left our bicycle lamp at home on the mantelpiece, and I hear the police are a terror if they catch you with no light on your bicycle. Or maybe one of you would lend us a lamp?'

Apparently nobody was carrying a spare bicycle lamp as Cecil's request was greeted by a stony silence until somebody asked everybody: 'Are they members?'

'Couldn't be,' said a quality voice.

'Substantiate your assertion,' said I with my temper rising.

'Is it fight you're looking for?' asked Cecil.

'Let them off,' said an authoritative voice.

Cecil mounted the tee. Placed the ball with confident deliberation. Took up a classic stance, Then, after a slow drawl of a backswing, lashed the ball arrow-straight, 270 yards up the fairway.

'Good shot,' said I.

'If I had to catch it right,' bragged Cecil, 'I would have made the green.' Which was about 20 yards further on.

It was now my turn to show my skill. Nonchalantly I tossed the ball on to the tee. Selected my ten iron. Asked Cecil to keep a watchful eye on the rest of my clubs. Addressed the ball where it had landed. Hit a splendid pitch 90 feet high, and 50 yards forward. The ball gave three hops, then spun back two feet in the centre of the narrow path which bisected the waist-high rough that stretched out a cruel 100 yards from the tee.

'Cleverly placed,' remarked Cecil, which words of encouragement were greeted by an ironic cheer from the amused onlookers.

Cecil turned on them, challenged them: 'I'll bet any of you a fiver that the next shot will land on the green!'

'You're on!' said a gentleman with a big cigar, and a bigger mouth.

'Gather up your clubs,' said Cecil to me.

As we walked to my ball I asked him: 'You're not going to pay that fellow, are you?'

'I haven't the slightest intention,' answered he.

'This is crazy,' said I. 'I never used a wood in my life. How the hell do you expect me to hit the ball that distance! Barring I pick it up in my fist and walk a couple of hundred yards, and throw it on the green I wouldn't reach it.'

Having come to my ball I took up my stance, and was about to strike it, when he gruffly ordered me out of the way, produced his brassie, and planked my ball in the heart of the green.

'Now,' said he, 'I'll put on my debt collector's hat, and seek a financial settlement with Big Mouth.'

Back he went to the tee, and addressed the latter gentleman, with his hand out.

'A fool, and his money are easily parted. Pay up, and look happy.'

'What do you mean?' said Big Mouth, with both puzzlement, and stupidity written across his face.

'I mean that I want my softly earned fiver.'

'It was your partner not you that was supposed to hit that ball on to the green.'

'You were not paying attention to the bet, my dear man. The bet was that the next shot would land on the green. I did not specify, nor did you specify who was to play it!'

Then Cecil turned to the rest of them: 'Am I right?'

'That's true. You're right,' they all agreed.

'He did you, Fred. He codded you. Fork out your fiver!' added one of them.

Fred wasn't pleased with the gallery going against him, but was too proud to haggle over the fiver, and handed it to Cecil after telling him that he was the first gangster he had met that day.

'I'm not as much of a gangster as you're a mug,' replied Cecil. 'By the way,' he added, having given his nose a superficial wipe with the fiver, 'I'd like to thank you all for letting us off in front of you.'

'It was only because we wanted to see the back of you,' was Fred's parting shot.

And so I had my first round of golf. I'd put it on a par with a tantalising woman who wants to be on top all the time. I found it an exasperating, thrilling experience. No way could I feel that I was the master, but every instinct in my body told me that I must come back for more.

Starting off I had expected, with my high standard of pitching and putting, to have no trouble in breaking the century, and had looked forward eagerly to doing so. However, I wasn't allowed to live too long in that fool's paradise. I came back down to earth when I chalked up a 13 at the long second. My final total was a miserable 157.

In retrospect I realise that my approach to the game was crazy. I had reckoned that if Cecil could hit the ball 270 yards, I should be able to get a respectable 190 off the tee, and so I insisted - against Cecil's advice - in using the driver for every long tee shot, and the brassie for every long fairway shot. Much of the time, through my enthusiastic, whirlwind lashes, I managed to miss the ball completely, or else watched it scuttering along the ground 30 or 40 yards to come to rest in a divot mark.

You'll be surprised to hear, if you're a golf fan yourself, that Cecil took all of 88 shots. His long game was dazzlingly good, and his short game dastardly bad. He had no fine touch, no confidence in himself around the greens. He was the epitome of a jitters jabber. Sometimes his jabs worked, but when they didn't, his next quick-fire poke would give you the impression, that he was convinced that the hole was about to be stolen from the green.

On returning to the clubhouse we sought out the treasurer, and asked him for lockers. As there were none available at the time, we had to import, and export our clubs by two-wheeled transport every day, for our first couple of months as members.

That first night we had two pints apiece in the men's bar, and then headed back for our local, with Willie the bore, as our quarry.

Mocking is catching! We were stopped for having no light on our bicycle! On a dark stretch of the road who shouted 'Halt,' at us, and then followed up with a barrage of blue language, when we nearly ran him down, but Garda Arthur Morgan, one of the lads in the digs. However, when he recognised Cecil as one of the culprits he burst out laughing, and apologetically explained that there were no cases listed for hearing at the next court, and the sergeant had sent him out to, 'For God's sake issue a few summonses,' or else the public would be saying that the police were doing nothing.

He also mentioned that certain pubs, including 'Barney's,' were going to be raided that night, and unless we wanted to pay a fine for being 'found on after hours,' we should get out on the dot of closing time.

When we arrived in 'Barney's,' there was Willie, on his own, until one of us sat each side of him, on the high stools, up against the counter. We set a fierce pace at the drinking, away beyond his capacity, and didn't allow him get a word in edgeways. We went over our shots again, and again. Every so often we'd ask him: 'Where was I?' If he didn't know we'd abuse him. We'd ask him where his sense of justice was; that we always listened to him when he was reliving his rounds; but here were we, after our very first game, and there was he showing no interest whatsoever.

In fairness to the man, he did try to please us. He did try to listen, but with both of us talking simultaneously he found it difficult to digest the fanciful facts, and fictional figures flying into his ears.

The moment the legal hour for leaving licensed premises came we told Willie that for once we were going to have an early night, but that after us buying him all that drink it would be wanton waste if he left it behind. He tried to persuade us to help him out by drinking some of it. We said we were full to the gills, and back we went to the sitting room of 'St Jude's,' where Cecil produced two naggin bottles of whiskey, which he had obtained in the lounge on one of his visits to the toilet.

We discussed Willie's character, and agreed that he was a decent bloke, apart from being an unbearable bore. We decided that we'd skip school on the morning of the court to give him moral support when he'd be in the dock.

We wondered how long it would be before he, a bank official, would be transferred, as in those days bank managers took a dim view of members of their staff being named in local newspapers for being caught drinking after hours.

Some hours later Willie came in soaking wet to the navel. Being the gentlemen we are, we sympathised with him, and asked him what the dickens had happened to have him in such a state.

Soon after we had left, on the front door of 'Barney's' there was heard a loud knock, followed by a shout, 'Police on duty.'

Willie lost the head, ran upstairs, opened a back window, and slid down a drainpipe, into a barrel half full of water, which brought him to his sober senses. He decided to stay there until the coast was clear.

We congratulated him on the wisdom of his flight; told him how glad we were that he had escaped the clutches of the law; and urged him to take off his wet clothes at once, and go to bed.

Having no further reason to stay up, we also retired, disgusted that we had been deprived of the opportunity of discussing with Willie, the possibility of him getting off under the first offender's act.

That night, despite having put away a skinful of liquor, I couldn't get to sleep for ages as my mind hyperactively replayed every wasted shot in my round of golf. Eventually I convinced myself that if I could get the long game mastered, it would be only a matter of time until I'd win the British Open. I'm not fibbing. I really believed that!

Next evening, straight after school, we rushed out to the golf course for another round. We did the same, rain or hail, right through to the summer holidays. I devoured articles, and books on the game. Almost every night in bed I got a new theory on how to improve my swing, and went out full of hope the following day, to put it in to practice, the sum total of which was that I tied myself up in knots, and didn't succeed in breaking through the 100-barrier until placing came into operation at the beginning of that winter.

Meanwhile, we had received handicaps: Cecil off ten and me off 18. We didn't threaten to win a raffle, never mind a competition that first year, but looking back now it was a wonderful, healthy form of escape from the realities of life.

#####

After I had been carrying weighty Cecil for a couple of months on the bar of the bicycle to and from the golf club, the enjoyment of the daily, six-mile, round trip had diminished so much, that it had become a penance, which turned into a resentment. I reminded myself that I was not born to be a donkey. Furthermore, it didn't help matters, that while on our earlier trips he had always expressed his gratitude on our arrival at the club, he gradually reached the stage where he took the favour for granted, and indeed on occasions complained that I was pedalling too slowly, that it was going to take us all day to get to the course.

Because I'm as fond of him as if he were my brother, I kept the resentment buried for a while, but one night in the local I heard myself saying: 'Cecil, I'm fed up to the teeth of carrying you every day to the club. We'll have to do something about it.'

'I'm an independent man,' said he sharply, 'I'll walk out.'

'There's no need for you to get up on your high horse. I'm not asking you to walk out.'

'You mean that you want me to run out alongside you on the bike, and shove you the rest of the way when you get tired.'

'You needn't be so sarcastic, Cecil. You're taking me up wrongly. What I have in mind is that we should buy a car.'

'A great idea,' said he. 'Why didn't I think of that myself! But wait! Where would the likes of us, that's living from hand to mouth, get the money for a car!'

'There's always means of making money, Cecil.'

'It's easier to find ways of spending it. I hope you haven't in mind that we'll run another jumble sale. I wouldn't go through that again. Anyway, Miss Casey wouldn't let us have the dead room again, after the hassle she had.'

'Well, that shoots down that idea of mine before I even mention it. You come up with a better one so!'

'Let's face it,' said he. 'We'll have to start economising.'

'We won't give up the horses nor the drink. We might as well be dead as do that,' said I.

'True! What about us both going off the cigarettes?'

'I'll tell you what,' said I. 'You go off them first, and we'll see will you stick it. If you do, I'll think about it then.'

'You want me to be the guinea pig, while you act the sow, puffing smoke in my face!'

'That's an ugly way to put it Cecil. To be honest with you, I don't believe I'd have the willpower to go off cigarettes.'

'Alright so. I'll go off them myself... Another brain wave is after striking me. What about us buying a load of copies, and pencils in the wholesalers, and selling them to the children?'

'We won't make much money on that,' said I. 'There's only a month to go till the summer holidays.'

'It depends on how you go about it.'

Between our two classes we had almost a hundred children, so we bought 2,000 copies, and 400 pencils to do them for the month.

They wrote nonstop from they came in the door each morning until they went home that evening. Anyone who complained to me about a pain in his fingers or elbow was told that he'd have a pain somewhere else if he didn't keep writing.

Cecil was a star turn at shifting the copies. He used to go around his class tearing them up in a rage if he found the least alleged mistake. He went to town on the dot on the 'i'. After a week everyone was putting every dot on every 'i'. He then claimed that they weren't putting the dot in the right place - exactly over the 'i'. Who was to judge! He was the boss.

I showed more enterprise in the pencil line. I had a sharp

penknife. I reserved for myself the right to pare their pencils, and became an expert at putting on long, slender points, which broke at the least pressure.

We lodged our takings in the post office each evening. Cecil also put in the cost of 30 cigarettes a day, for which I admired him greatly, until after about ten days he started preaching to me about the dirty habit of smoking.

We nearly had a genuine row one night after we had gone to our beds. The light was off, and I was as usual chain-smoking, thinking about my golf, and hoping that the feeling of tiredness would come on me.

I will admit that the wee room was full of smoke. It had also been full of smoke when Cecil himself indulged in the habit, but then he never noticed it.

He passes some remark about me polluting the atmosphere, hops out of bed, stamps over, and bangs the window open. As you know I'm a man for peace at all costs, so I wait till he's settled in bed, then I stamp over and bang it closed. He waits till I'm back in bed, then opens it again.

This went on for quite a while, with each of us determined that we were going to give the window the last bang.

Then Cecil did the dirt on me. After I had got back in to bed for the umpteenth time, he gets out. Turns on the light. Roots under my bed. Pulls out my right shoe. Puts it through the top pane. Replaces it under the bed. Takes out my left shoe, and puts it through the bottom pane.

'Now,' said he, 'have it your own way. The clasp is on the window, so it's the way you want it. Closed.'

After breaking up at noon on the day the summer holidays started, we withdrew our savings, and went car-shopping to a second-hand dealer, who asked us how much we were prepared to spend. We told him.

'Come back when you have twice as much, and I'll sell you something that will go down a hill.'

'We'll be back this evening,' said we - both of us having been hit with the same brainstorm.

All our assets were placed on the nose of a sure thing, running at even money in the 2.30. Would you believe it? I bet you wouldn't! The horse lost - beaten by a short head.

'There's nothing for it,' declared Cecil, 'but to get a job in England for the holidays.'

'Agreed,' said I. 'I'll go home to see my mother first. I'll meet you on the nine o'clock boat in Dun Laoghaire on Monday night.'

#####

As always, my mother was delighted to see me, but bitterly disappointed to learn that I was off again on the Monday.

The two sisters, Susan and Nellie, who had remained single until their mid-thirties, had got married a year previously on the same day, and were both living with Mammy - along with their husbands: Susan and Oweney, Nellie and Henry. Mention of the latter 'gentleman' has set me reflecting on in-laws.

The butt of the comedian's ridicule is often the mother-in-law, and rarely the brother-in-law, possibly because the vast majority of comedians are male. As my experience of mothers in-laws is nil, and my experience of one particular brother-in-law is too much for me to take, I'll derive some satisfaction from redressing the balance slightly.

Long before Susan and Nellie got married they had made a pact that they'd stay with Mammy in our old homestead as long as she lived. So the husbands-to-be could like it or lump it. They had no say in where they were going to live if they wanted to hitch up with the sisters.

Oweney, a factory hand, didn't give a damn. It suited him fine. Whereas, Henry, a businessman, considered it a step down the social ladder to be sharing a house with an ordinary working man.

Whenever I visited home, the presence of the pretentious prick, Henry, in my company depressed me. Never mind talking to him, the sight of him was enough to make me feel sick. He always looked as if he was after stepping out of a washing machine, with his baby face soaked in aftershave lotion in a vain attempt to give himself a masculine touch. He never failed to have his blonde hair brushed, with every wave perfectly in place. Yet he was forever fingering, and patting it for fear it wasn't. His suits were always the best, and he used to change his shirt every day at lunchtime. Imagine putting on two different shirts in the one day! I never saw him in bed but I'd swear he wore pyjamas.

He never drank, smoked or gambled, and frowned upon those who did. He used to have the mistaken idea that he was making a great impression on me by telling me how well the hardware business he had inherited from his uncle was going. However he stopped that line of boasting when he realised that every time he did so I borrowed money from him.

I'd forgive him everything but for the despicable manner in which he used to try to score over Oweney, showing off his would-be superiority. It was obvious from Susan's body language that she'd be hurt at the manner in which her husband was being belittled, but was too considerate of her sister's feelings to make it an issue. So she sung dumb when she should have been kicking up stink.

What upset his wife didn't bother Oweney in the least. He only laughed when 'educated' Henry passed snide remarks about his etiquette at the dining table, and corrected his grammar ad nauseam, when they were chatting around the fire at night.

Oweney, a tall good-looking chap, had been a part-time professional footballer in his day. He was gifted with a bass voice which everyone was anxious to hear booming through the bar of my home town local, at the singsongs on a Saturday night, where we invariably went, whenever I did go home. I was amazed at the amount of free beer that used to be sent to our table by Oweney's generous friends, in appreciation of the pleasure he provided with his winning personality, and his favourite songs. There were always a few scroungers in his vicinity knowing that he'd get more drink than he'd need. I'll tell you this much: they bought their own when I was around.

Having done my limited best to make my mother happy, I headed back for the city on Monday afternoon, after listening to her well-meaning lecture on the danger of me losing my morals on my first visit to England. And as she had so often done, from I started going out with girls, she made me promise once more, that I'd never touch any of them below the belt or above the knee.

#####

As I had a few hours to spare in the city, I wandered in to a pub to pass the time away with a glass in my hand. I wasn't ten minutes there when I got a surprise slap on the back, and a 'How are you Ryan!' I turned around to see who I was going to consider suing for technical assault, and there beside me was a teacher. A teacher who worked!

Cecil, and myself had agreed that for our own peace of mind we'd never associate with, we'd never have any dealings with teachers who actually teach. Because those teachers who teach, talk about their teaching, and the last thing on earth that we wanted to hear was talk about work.

'What'll you have?' I asked.

'I'll just have a pint of beer.'

This chap, Rodney Dillon, was a six-footer with a pair of shoulders on him the size of a take-away blackboard. He had been going on for the priesthood - the Cistercian Order - and was within six months of being ordained when it dawned on him that it wasn't he, but his mother, who had the vocation. He pulled out, and went home, hoping to receive sympathy, and understanding, but instead was shocked to learn that neither of his parents wanted him in or about the house, as in their view, he had brought disgrace to the family - 'a spoiled priest.'

At 28 years of age he had managed to qualify as a teacher. His first appointment was to Edenstown about a year before my arrival there. He was a loner, but a congenial chap, even though he was a compulsive worker.

'I didn't expect to see you here, Rodney,'

'You know I'm not welcome at home. I've taken a bedsit around the corner for the holidays. What are you doing here anyway? I thought you'd spend the whole summer playing golf.'

'I'd love to, but I've other things on my mind. Cecil and myself are going to London tonight to get the money for a car.'

'A new one?

'Good God no. We're not prepared to work that hard.'

'Would you object if I went with you?'

'Well now... I'd have to ask Cecil about that.'

'Is there something wrong with me? Tell me honestly. Am I a kind of odd?'

'There's not a blasted thing in the world wrong with you, except that you love discussing your work, and neither Cecil nor myself want that subject brought up in our company. Talk about drink. Talk about horses. Talk about women, like any healthy man would do, but give what goes on in your class a miss, because we don't give a fiddler's feck what happens there.'

'Are you sure that that's all that's wrong with me?'

'Of course I'm sure! Are you trying to make out that I haven't the courage to speak my mind?'

'Not at all. If I promised that I'd never mention teaching from when we'd go, till we'd come back, would you let me join you?'

'Would you be able to stick to your word?'

'Certainly I would. No trouble to me.'

'Right so, Rodney. It's a deal. We'll be delighted to have you with us. And it's your turn to buy.'

'Sorry! I forgot. The same again, I suppose?'

'No. I'll have a drop of brandy to settle my stomach. By the way, this bedsit! Will you have to forfeit your deposit on it?'

'To hell with the deposit. To be quite honest, I wasn't looking forward to spending a couple of months here on my own in the city.'

Three hours later Rodney, and myself were on the boat, he with a big yellow case, and me with no luggage whatsoever.

'Where on earth is Cecil? Is he going to miss this boat! Ah, will you look at him! Coming up the gangway. Footless! He must have been at it for the last three days. Rodney, no more than yourself Cecil won't be let in at home. They don't approve of his drinking, and he has had some fierce clashes with his father who is a rabid teetotaller.

'Cecil, you old blackguard! It's great to see you. Rodney's coming with us.'

'What!.'

'Rodney's coming with us. He promised me that he won't mention a word about work.'

'That's alright so. As long as he keeps his word.'

'You've no luggage, Cecil! I was depending on you for a change of socks.'

'Can't you get them off Rodney! He'll have everything we need. Isn't that true Rodney?'

'I'll gladly share whatever I have with you both.'

We landed in Holyhead some time after twelve, and boarded the 'all through the night' train for Euston Station, and sat down opposite three attractive Irish girls, nurses, returning to work in London.

Within ten minutes Cecil had intimated to the company at large that he was not in a talkative mood by throwing back his head, opening his mouth, and starting to snore.

Within twenty minutes handsome Rodney had persuaded one of the girls to sit on his knee, and was kissing her passionately while caressing her neck.

That left me on my own with the other two young ladies. I went over, and sat between them. We passed the time in harmless chitchat until coming near our destination I asked them could they keep a secret. When they both earnestly assured me that they could, I told them that Cecil was a doctor who had been stripped of his title for interfering with his patients, irrespective of their sex. Not only were men, women and children in danger when the urge came on him, but he was also partial to hens.

Yes, they had heard about doctors like him, except for the hen angle.

I wondered what could be done to cure him.

They were of the opinion that he was a hopeless case, who should be locked up, and the key thrown away.

Coming in to Euston, Cecil woke up, refreshed after his sound sleep.

'Maybe the girls would put us up for a few days until we get settled in to a job,' suggested he.

The nurses climbed to high doh, and backed each other up with a string of vociferous excuses as to why they could not allow members of the opposite sex inside the door of their flat.

We helped them with their luggage to a taxi, and after a hearty breakfast in an early morning cafe, started looking for work, preferably where we'd all three be together.

We rode buses. We investigated subways. We trudged streets. We tried hospitals, hotels, seasonal canning factories, and building sites, but the only hint of a job we got was when we took it in turns carrying Rodney's big yellow suitcase, which got heavier as the day went on.

Coming up to six o'clock we walked in to a pub and ordered three pints of beer.

'You're Irish, aren't you,' remarked the landlord.

We agreed that we were not ashamed to admit that we were Irish, but what difference did that make!

'It makes this difference: I've had too much trouble with the likes of you fighting, and brawling in this bar. It's a rule of the house now, that we don't serve Irishmen.'

We told him that he had never seen us fighting or brawling, but that he would if he didn't give us three pints quickly.

He looked at us for some time, showing no signs of emotion.

Cecil had a wicked glint in both of his eyes. I had my shoulders hunched, my two hands on my hips, and what I hoped was an intimidating look on my face. Big Rodney was standing there cool as a sphinx, except that he was making short spits as if he were steaming up for action.

Then the publican addressed us in a firm, yet conciliatory tone: 'Don't make the mistake of thinking that I'm afraid of you, but, as a gesture of goodwill, I'll give you a pint apiece on the house. Then I want you to take your custom elsewhere.'

Whatever about the other two, I was never averse to getting drink for nothing, so I told him he was a gentleman, and asked him to supply us with a list of the other pubs in the area where the Irish were barred, so that we could hit them all up in the one night.

The tension was broken and he smiled, but Cecil wasn't satisfied with his pint. When he had it three-quarters drunk, he went over to the window, and held it up to the light.

'Look,' said he. And after a dramatic pause - 'It's flat!'

I went over, and held mine up to the window. Yes! It was flat too! We looked at the landlord, with our lips tight, our heads shaking in disapproval, and our index fingers pointing at our glasses. Then everybody else who was drinking beer held their glasses up to the light, and started muttering, and shaking their heads.

Cecil went to the counter, accused the boss of selling bad beer, and demanded his money back.

The counter was thumped, and we were given ten seconds to get off the premises, or he'd call the police. Cecil wanted to know was that all the thanks he was getting for trying to protect the public. However, Rodney stepped in, called us a pair of lousers, and persuaded us to leave, but not before we had finished our drinks.

Outside, Cecil said that he had never tasted a nicer pint in his life, but he wanted to see the expression on the landlord's face when he'd ask for his money back.

'There's a bus,' said I.

'Come on, we'll get on it,' said Cecil.

'Where will it take us?' asked Rodney.

'What difference does it make,' said Cecil. 'We're going nowhere.'

'Ah now listen lads,' said Rodney. 'You'll have to stop this messing. Do you realise that we have nowhere to sleep. We'll have to look for a nice quiet bed and breakfast place.'

'It's far too early to worry about that,' said Cecil. 'Instead we'll look for a nice quiet pub, and settle down to a few jars.'

Three pints later Rodney was still wondering where we'd sleep. Six pints later Rodney wasn't too worried about where we'd sleep. Nine pints later Rodney said that he was going to look for a woman to sleep with. Eleven pints later Rodney himself was fast asleep.

'What has he in that bloody case!' asked Cecil.

'There's only the one way of finding out,' said I.

'Will you look!' exclaimed Cecil. 'A new pair of shoes, an overcoat, two suits, a pair of pyjamas, four shirts, five pairs of socks, a razor, three brushes, a tube of toothpaste, and a tin of boot polish. The man's a millionaire, and we didn't know it.'

'I'm not going to lug that lap of luxury bag around London tomorrow,' said I.

'Neither am I,' said my mate.

'Hi chief!' said Cecil then, beckoning to an oily-looking customer, who had us under observation while we were inspecting Rodney's wardrobe.

He approached us, and addressed Cecil; 'Yes guvnor.'

'We're dealers in second-hand clothes. Do you want a bargain? A fiver for the lot, case and all.'

'I'll give you a pound.'

'Done,' said Cecil.

'They must be stolen,' said he as he humped the yellow case out the door.

Cecil carefully folded the pound note, and gently slipped it into Rodney's breast pocket.

'Now,' said he, 'my conscience is clear.'

'It's Rodney's turn to buy,' said I.

'Right,' said Cecil. 'We'll do the decent thing. We won't waken him.' And he fished the pound back out of his pocket.

Two pints later the landlord called time. Cecil gave Rodney a disrespectful push; 'Stand up you lazy, drunken bousy! We carried your case all day, and I suppose you expect us to carry you now.'

We found it beyond us to bring him to his senses. He did come to momentarily, and mumbled something about his mother not loving him. Then went back into a deep sleep. We dragged him out on the street, and poured him on to a windowsill, near a bus stop, and stayed one each side of him, in case the poor chap would fall, and bang his head against the ground on his first night in London.

Cecil asked a passer-by which bus would bring us to the city centre. Half an hour later we were in the middle of the capital.

Cecil stopped a different passer-by, and asked him for directions to the nearest police station.

Rodney's legs were still functioning as if they were made of rubber, but with a long arm slung around each of our necks, and a good grip apiece on his wrists, we managed to manoeuvre him down one street and up another, and in the station door, whereupon he took an ill-timed, abnormal fit of the staggers, which we both failed to get under control. As a result all three of us collapsed in a heap on the floor, in front of a sergeant and three constables.

'Don't think for one minute that we're drunk,' said Cecil, looking up at the sergeant. 'We just dropped in to report the theft of a suitcase.'

'Where did you lose it,' asked the sergeant casually, as if it were an everyday occurrence for him to be conducting a conversation with two dishevelled drunks awake on the station floor, and another asleep between them.

'We didn't lose it,' corrected Cecil. 'It was taken from us.'

'What is your name, and address?'

'I am Mr Cecil Chuckleworth of no fixed abode. I wish to make a statement while the outrageous larceny of my colleague's case is clear in my head!'

'Let's have it.'

Cecil got to his feet, brushed himself down, ambled over to the counter, behind which the sergeant, and the constables were standing, and made his statement, the gist of which was that our innocent friend, Rodney Dillon, had lugged his big yellow case in to a pub, where he intended to partake of some light refreshments, but then remembered that it was his birthday, and decided to celebrate the occasion with a few bottles of beer, as a result of which he became cockeyed drunk, and fell in to a deep sleep, alongside his case, while we sat guard over him, and continued to sip our drinks.

Unfortunately we both received a call from nature simultaneously, and went to the toilet, wherein no undue delay was made. On our return, Rodney was still there, but the case had vanished, causing Cecil to wipe a tear from his eye, because he knew that his dear friend would eventually realise that he had been separated from all his worldly goods apart from the suit on his back.

Every customer in the bar was questioned. Nobody saw anything. Neither he nor I knew the name of the pub or the street it was on, and Rodney wouldn't have a clue either.

Cecil then asked the sergeant what were the chances of the case and it's contents being tracked down, and returned to their lawful owner.

'None,' answered the sergeant.

'I thought so,' said Cecil.

Next he asked the sergeant to please do us a small favour, namely: to lock the three of us up for the night; after two of us would have been allowed out for a reasonable time, to purchase fish, and chips.

The sergeant looked at Cecil. Made no comment.

He then told the sergeant that he need have no fears about us throwing fish bones on the floor, as he, Cecil, would accept full responsibility for them, and if supplied with a brush, and shovel, would have the cell as clean as a whistle before we left in the morning.

He paused for reaction from the sergeant. There was none, so he continued by assuring the sergeant that he didn't expect him and his underlings to carry Rodney in to the cell; that we had carted his case around all day, and himself around all night; and that we might as well finish the job by chucking him in to the cell ourselves.

The sergeant continued eyeing Cecil but still considered nothing he had heard so far worthy of a comment.

Chuckleworth then wanted to know if it was because we had committed no crime that the sergeant was dithering about obliging us. If so, he was wrong. Rodney was drunk, and incapable, and we had no visible means of support.

The sergeant stared at Mr Chuckleworth.

Mr Chuckleworth eyeballed the sergeant.

'Have you been struck dumb?' enquired Mr Chuckleworth.

'Do you think I'm running a hotel?' snapped the sergeant.

'You'd have to answer to the customers if you were!' retorted Mr Chuckleworth.

'Take that body out of here instantly!' ordered he.

'Will you arrest us if we don't?' asked Cecil.

'Throw those two out, and lock up the heap on the floor,' shouted the sergeant to the three constables.

'That's not fair,' claimed Cecil. 'We're the ones who brought him here, and he's the one who's getting the reward.'

'You needn't use force,' said I. 'We know when we're beaten.'

#####

Cecil and I sat on the edge of the footpath outside the police station, and discussed our next move while I smoked a cigarette. We took stock of the street where the jailbird was lodged, so that we'd have no difficulty retracing our steps there in the morning. Then went and had a good feed in a cafe, after which we made our way to the Embankment, and had no trouble in falling asleep, as we had had an exhausting day, and it was a nice warm July night.

Next morning we awoke to find a tramp lying a few feet away from us with his throat cut.

'Let's get away from here quickly,' said Cecil. 'No wise man ever yet found a dead man.'

Rodney was enjoying a breakfast of bacon, and eggs when we went back to the station. A different sergeant was on duty. Nothing would do him but that we'd have the same, which hospitality we gladly accepted.

Our friend was panic-stricken when he awoke in the confined space of the cell. As he had no recall about the latter stages of the previous night he wondered what crime he had committed. He was relieved to hear that he hadn't beaten up anybody, and that there were no charges being preferred against him.

On asking about us he was told that we'd surely be along shortly. Until we came no reference had been made to his case, and he hadn't missed it, which meant that we had to break the news to him. Not being materialistic, he wasn't overly upset about its loss. His only whinge was that he'd be working his holidays for nothing to replace his possessions, which we both agreed was hard luck.

Cecil was on for giving a half-day searching for the pub from where the case had disappeared. As Rodney hadn't made a fuss about it, I'd get no satisfaction out of bringing him on a wild goose chase, so I pointed out the futility of the exercise, and we set off looking for work instead.

We weren't gone far when we met a building site gaping us in the face. We stopped and watched men, wearing nothing but a tan, plus trousers, and footwear, working away; paying no heed to anybody. Some were handling trowels, and others rushing to and fro carrying cement blocks. We saw a fellow doing nothing so we knew he was the boss. Over we went, and asked him would he like to give a start to three of the best builder's labourers Ireland had ever produced.

He admitted that he was short-handed, and said that he'd start us in the morning on a week's trial. We asked what kind of money we were going to get. To our pleasant surprise we learned that it was much better than what we were being paid as teachers at home. The snag was that we'd be working much longer hours, and by the sweat of our brows, to which neither Cecil nor myself were used, nor intended to get used.

Accommodation was now the only item on the agenda to be dealt with. We asked our employer would he have any suggestions in that line. He put us on to an Italian gent, in a run-down tenement area, ten minutes walk away.

Yes, he had an unoccupied, first-floor 'flat.' The terms were weekly in advance. He was right too. Nobody would be inclined, at the rear end of their last week in the place, to go running to him with money for a 'flat' which contained four single stained mattresses, securely nailed to a bare wooden floor, a water tap, and a gas ring. Nothing else. Not even a chair for Cecil to use when cutting his toenails.

He told us that he had given up supplying bedclothes, cooking utensils, chairs, and tables; that it didn't pay him. He'd hardly have them in the door when his patrons would have them out the window, and into a pawnshop.

Neither Cecil nor I gave a damn about bedclothes. What were they for on a summer's night but to kick out on the floor when one would be too hot in the bed. Besides, what could be handier than not having to dress oneself when getting up in the morning. Rodney, however, when we went shopping, bought himself, among other items, a pair of sheets, and pyjamas. We all contributed to the cost of a kettle, a large frying pan, and some delph, and cutlery.

Cecil was adamant that we should buy only the one spoon, knife, and fork between us; that anything more was an unjustifiable waste of good, beer money; and that we could easily agree on a relay system, whereby we could pass them around according as we needed them, without any great inconvenience to anybody. Rodney's objection on hygienic grounds was dismissed as the waffle of a hypochondriac. However, when I pointed out to Cecil that they would make a nice present for Miss Casey, when we returned to Edenstown, he readily agreed to the purchase of a quarter dozen of each.

Mr Dillon was appointed bursar, responsible for buying all foodstuffs.

We brought back to the flat a daily paper in which there was a cryptic crossword. As was customary with us two, Cecil had first go, and solved it in his head in twelve minutes. I was pleased to be one answer over halfway, filling it in, after 17 minutes, when Rodney declared that dinner was about to be served.

Our friend could not be described as a capable cook, nevertheless I praised to the sky the fare he planked in front of us - sitting on the bare wooden floor - as I did not relish the thought of coming home after a day's work, to start another day's work, standing over a gas ring getting a meal ready.

'You must think that you're silver-tongued, and that I'm stupid, George,' said Rodney. 'I know well what you're at. We'll take it in turns, week by week, doing the cooking. I don't mind doing the first stint.'

I proposed that Cecil would do the second week. He, always on the alert for fear anyone would pull a smart one on him, insisted that the fairest way to decide the issue was to toss for it, with which I agreed, while I felt around for, and found, in my hip pocket, the two-headed halfpenny I had confiscated from one of my backstreet pupils.

'Heads,' said I.

'Tails,' said the loser.

The meal over, Rodney was browsing through the paper when he let a shout of joy.

'What's this about, or do you always shout like that when you're reading a newspaper?' asked Cecil.

'Thank God we got the paper,' said ecstatic Rodney, 'or I would not have known that my favourite operatic soprano is the special guest tonight in a concert of classical music. You'll have to come lads!'

Neither Cecil nor I had the enviable ear to enable us to appreciate good music. I had been given an insulting 17 per cent in singing at the oral tests for the training college. Cecil was tone deaf.

'Will there be a bar in the place?' asked my practical pal.

'Yes,' said Rodney, 'it will be open before the concert starts, and at the interval.'

'We'll have to bring in our own drink so,' said Cecil.

Ten minutes before the 'off' we sat down in the front row, with Cecil beside a woman dressed like a dog's dinner, in an ignorant display of expensive clothes. She had rings everywhere except in her nose, and had a blatantly, phoney lah-de-dah accent. Cecil, ever a gentleman, offered her a swig from our bottle of whiskey.

'No thaunk you,' said she. 'It was a really gentlemanly gesture on your part to offer it to me. Actually, I only drink fine wines, and liqueurs. What kind of music do you prefer?'

'Loud music, Mam. Loud music is my dish.'

'It's mine also. Do you come here for the opera season?'

'No Mam. I'm just here for the summer season, working as a builder's labourer.'

'Oh dear! Imagine! A builder's labourer!'

And she turned off at an angle away from my friend.

'You wouldn't lend me a pound,' said he to her.

'How dare you ask me for money! A common beggar at a concert of classical music!'

'I didn't ask you for money! I said that you wouldn't lend me a pound. It's true isn't it, that you wouldn't lend me a pound! Or is your intelligence quotient so low that you can't recognise a simple statement of fact? In plain language, Mam, I'm asking you, are you stupid! You look it anyway.'

'Well I never! The cheek of you! Usher! Usher! This man has insulted me!'

Cecil was given the ultimatum to apologise or leave. He stood up, and walked out without uttering another word. Wherever he was going, I was going, especially as he had the bottle of whiskey. Full credit to Rodney! He was willing to leave too, but I wouldn't allow him to sacrifice his night of pleasure. I told him that Cecil and I would wait for him in the pub across the street, where we had the few, before we came in.

'You worked that well,' said I, after we had got our money back, and were leaving the hall.

'True,' said he,' Rodney was delighted that we had shown the spirit of good fellowship to go with him. Now he's where he wants to be, and we're going where we want to be. Could anything be more satisfactory than that!'

Rodney was thrilled with the concert. We also were in a mellow mood, as we wended our way back to the flat, conscious that we had ahead of us the pleasant task of finishing off the best part of a bottle of whiskey, which there would have been no sense in drinking in the public house, when other alcohol was available.

Only for Rodney we wouldn't have woken up in time the next morning as we had no alarm clock. He, however, with his monastic training, was an early riser. After giving us our bacon, and eggs, he had us down on the site a full two minutes before we were due to start at eight o'clock.

'Glad to see that you're good timekeepers,' said the foreman.

'He has a favourable impression of us already,' remarked Cecil to me under his breath.

'We're very particular about everything, especially punctuality,' said I to him. 'In fact, we came here this morning on an empty stomach so that we wouldn't be late for work. I hope you have no objection to us slipping off for a bit of breakfast, now that we have arrived?'

The boss, a fair-minded Yorkshire man, raised his eyebrows on hearing the request. He said that he'd let us do it this once. However, we were not to make a habit of it.

Rodney didn't let us down. He just remarked that he didn't feel like eating anything that morning. So off Cecil and I went for a cup of coffee, pleased that we had postponed for the moment, the evil hour when we'd have to actually make a physical show of working.

We came back at about nine o'clock to see Mr Dillon going hammer, and tongs, armed with a shovel, mixing cement, along with two other brawny chaps.

The latter two men were put doing something else. We were ordered to assist Rodney at the cement-mixing. Neither Cecil nor I had ever taken a shovel in our hands in our lives, except to throw coal on a fire, and we did that only if there was nobody else around to perform the operation.

We languidly scooped spoonfuls on to our shovels as we turned over the sand, and cement, while Rodney continued to go at it like a galley slave. We got away with it for some time as the boss was occupied elsewhere. At least that was what we thought. Apparently he had been spying on us from a distance. Then like a bolt from the blue he descended upon Cecil, and myself, and asked us did we suffer from some physical disability. As we had no desire to be kicked off the site on our first day, for the rest of the morning, we made an effort to prove to him that we were willing workers.

At the lunch break we walked to a self-service cafe where one could eat on the ground floor, or in the basement. We went downstairs, joined the queue, moved along the line, putting whatever we chose on our trays, received a chit showing the cost of what we took, then sat down, and ate. On the way out, at the top of the stairs, there was a girl at a high desk collecting the chits, and the money.

'That system's far from foolproof. They need to be taught a lesson,' remarked Cecil on our way back to work.

On a number of occasions subsequently, he and I joined the queue twice - firstly for our main course, and secondly for a cup of tea, and a bun. We handed up only the tea, and bun chits on our way out. They must have twigged us, because at a later date when we visited the place, the system had been changed. They had realised that it was more profitable to collect the money at the end of the grub line, rather than bestow chits on their patrons.

On our first afternoon at the site our only noteworthy task was unloading scaffolding from a lorry, which we did without knocking anybody down, though the boss-man had a few narrow escapes when he stepped too close to Cecil.

The next morning, Friday, himself set off with five of us in his van, to another site, to dig foundations for a house twelve miles out of town. Four of us were sitting in the back, on bags of straw, swapping bawdy stories, and laughing, when Cecil decided to put a brake on our progress through the traffic, as he deemed the boss to be driving recklessly, passing out everything in sight, in his anxiety to get to the job.

He got a match from me, and unselfishly set fire to his own sack of straw.

'Don't panic lads, it's too soon to tell him yet,' said he.

We kept our cool until the fire was beyond the stage where our respected foreman would attempt to piss it out. Then Cecil shouted: 'Stop the van quick or we'll all be roasted to death!'

The doubting Thomas of a driver, instead of taking my mate at his word, looked around to see what was wrong, which proved to be a disastrous decision, as the fellow in front of us stopped suddenly, to avoid running into a jaywalking pedestrian. Worse was to follow, as we also got a bang from behind, and a chain reaction set in for about 200 yards back.

As we were scrambling from the back of the van, choking from the smoke; and the flames from the straw licking us, the boss shouted: 'Save the shovels anyway.'

'If we do we'll hit you with them for trying to kill us,' retorted Cecil.

Ambulances, fire brigades, and police cars arrived on the scene within minutes, to find that the only serious victim was the van - burned to a shell. Undaunted, the foreman ordered us to go on by bus to the site, and wait there for him. He must have met some problems because he didn't arrive until the lunch break - in a hired van, with four new shovels, and a pickaxe.

Cecil and I spent that afternoon poking at the ground, and looking at the boss-man when he wasn't looking at us.

By the following Tuesday evening the foundations were in, and on Wednesday morning - the last day of our week's trial - we were back on the original site, carrying blocks to the block-layers.

Anxious though we were to hold on to our jobs, we found it painful to hold on to the blocks. The first few were easy enough, but quite quickly the friction from the cement began skinning our soft hands. In an attempt to alleviate the pain, we started carrying one block between the two of us, which brought laughs from our fellow-workers, but a scowl from the boss.

However, he held his tongue until we approached him that evening to find out if he was going to keep us on.

He told us that Rodney was the best worker he ever had, that he was worth three men on a site, but that we, by streets, were the worst

82

he had ever seen, and that he was retaining him, but letting us go.

Rodney proved to be a staunch friend. He told him that if we were going, he too was going, unless he gave us a week's notice to give us a chance to get another job. He demurred at first, but then yielded to Rodney's mild form of blackmail.

Being on our notice we found it difficult to work conscientiously. One always needs to have some kind of a carrot dangling in front of one's nose if one is to do any job under the sun. The way we read our situation was, whether we slaved or sat on our hands, at the end of the week we'd get our week's wages, and the boot. So it says something for our respective characters that we opted against doing absolutely nothing.

Apart from making tea every half-hour, we shifted blocks - one at a time in a rusty wheelbarrow, with one of us to each handle. On the next afternoon - Friday - we complained to the boss that the squeaking of the wheel was getting on our nerves, and as he was bone idle, we asked him to make himself useful by getting a sup of oil to doctor the squeak.

His temper got the better of him. He called us a pair of tramps, threw our week's wages at us, and ordered us to flee from the site, which we did, but not before checking our money to make sure he hadn't underpaid us.

We went back to the flat then, Mr Chuckleworth having told Rodney that fried steak would be on the menu for our evening meal. Incidentally, Cecil, to our delight, was a first-rate cook. Where he got it from I don't know. I suppose, just as some people have green fingers, others can intuitively work wonders with a pan.

Our meal over, Rodney spruced himself up, and out we went; Cecil, and myself with light hearts, as anyone should, who is fond of a drink, seeing that we were heading for a pub. Whereas Rodney was somewhat ill at ease as we strolled along the street. He said that he had something on his mind which he wanted to air. He hoped that we wouldn't take offence. Then he went silent.

'Don't beat about the bush, Rodney,' said Cecil. 'Get it off your chest!'

He reminded us that this was his first night out in our company since he had been in clink. Typical of what we had heard from too many sensible social drinkers, he said that he enjoyed a few jars immensely; but that he couldn't understand why we swilled it down like dipsomaniacs; that our way of drinking was pure gluttony. To end his homily, he made us promise that we wouldn't force drink on him; instead, allow him to drink at his own pace.

We didn't argue with him, but agreed among ourselves later, that because he wasn't able to hold as much as us, he was making a virtue out of necessity.

He and I sat down in a cosy corner, while Cecil went up and bought pints of Guinness for himself, and myself, and a glass for our temperate friend. That was the ratio by which we imbibed our way through the night. Rodney was at a financial disadvantage. What could we do about it, unless we put him drinking on his own, which would not have been sociable!

We were relaxing there for about two hours when our privacy was invaded. A bedraggled bum approached us. Stood over us. He had a nerve. He didn't beg for a cigarette. He didn't plead for the price of a cup of coffee. He didn't request the price of a bed to lie on. Instead, he cheekily informed us that we looked like three charitable men, and then bluntly asked us to furnish him with a large ball of malt.

We looked at him with interest; not uttering a word. Until Cecil, wishing to lead him to believe that we didn't speak English, said the 'Hail Mary,' to him in Gaelic. He listened with a poker face, and then addressed Cecil in fluent Gaelic: 'That was very good. Very good indeed! Do you know the 'Our Father,' as well?'

Rodney thought it was uproariously funny that the tables were turned on Cecil for a change, and up he went and bought our bum, whose name turned out to be Paddy, a large Scotch, which was lowered with indecent haste. We threw two more into him, for which he was thankful without being servile.

He had been, like ourselves, a teacher - in a Gaelic-speaking district of Ireland - who had lost his job through drink, and was now in the gutter, a resident of Rowton House. When Cecil mentioned to him that we were out of work, he gave us the name of a prestigious, centrally-situated hotel where he had once been employed as a dish-washer, and advised us to try our luck there.

Leaving him that night, each of us gave him a pound.

'There but for the grace of God go we,' said Cecil to me.

#####

On the following Monday morning, with Rodney long gone to the sweatshop, Cecil and I awoke with woeful hangovers. Despite that, we urged each other to get up, and go out, and look for jobs; then convinced each other that we shouldn't. And we didn't, but instead, lay in bed till lunch time. After a light meal, and a heavy investment on a sure thing, running at 3.30, we set off for Madame Tussaud's, to view the celebrated and notorious characters in the world-famous, waxworks museum.

We were astounded at how lifelike they were. One would swear that they were alive only they were so still. We did get a special kick out of seeing our own native Irishman, Eamonn Andrews, there among the best of them.

As we were about to go back down the stairs, Cecil spied a youngish, brown-haired woman coming up on her own. Like a flash he was over standing against the wall alongside a few of the figures, his hands hanging naturally by his side, his mouth closed, his eyes looking in to the distance, not a blink, not a wink, not a movement out of him.

She made her way along, casually glancing at the waxworks as if she were merely in the place to kill time, but stopped and stared when she came to Cecil. She stepped closer, no doubt admiring the art of the genius, who had created such a lifelike, ugly-looking being.

She turned to me, and said, 'Excuse me, would you be so good as to tell me who that is supposed to be?'

'An infamous bag snatcher,' answered I.

With that Cecil grabbed her handbag, and bolted down the stairs.

She screamed at the shock; then started to whimper. I assured her that it was only a joke.

'Some joke,' said she, after she blew her nose, and looked around to see if there was anyone in uniform to whom she could report the incident.

'No need to worry. He's a friend of mine. He's only having you on. He'll be back up in a second.'

'Are you sure?'

'I'm positive. Look! Here he is now, coming up the stairs. Not the least hint of a smile on his face.'

'I caught the robber,' said he, as he gave her the handbag.

She laughed heartily, whether with relief or amusement, I'm not sure.

'You're a villain,' said she.

'There are worse villains than me in this place,' answered he.

Then, after a few polite exchanges with her about the sights of London, he suggested to me that we had better be moving on, as he wanted to have Rodney's meal ready for him when he'd arrive home. We wished her luck, and went on our way, stopping only to find out how our horse had fared. The news was good, and bad. He came in first. It was a pity about the jockey falling off.

#####

Tuesday morning, bright and fresh, we rose from our beds at twelve noon. Funds were low but spirits were high. Here were we, a fortnight in London, having managed to obtain two weeks wages without rushing ourselves off our feet. If we kept that up for another six weeks, we would be able to buy a car when we'd return to Ireland, because both of our untouched salaries for the two months, would be lying there waiting for us at 'St Jude's.'

After our midday breakfast, we decided to go out job hunting, even though it was spilling rain, and us with neither caps nor overcoats. We saw nothing wrong with first trying the hotel which our bum acquaintance had recommended.

It was a snazzy-looking establishment for two scruffy, soaking wet, individuals to enter by the front door, but in we went as if we owned the place, and straight over to the long counter of a reception desk.

'Can I do anything for you?' asked a beautiful, blonde, young woman, wearing a low-cut blouse.

'You could do a lot for us,' answered I, 'but all we're concerned with at the moment is to find out how you're off for dishwashers!'

'Oh, you'd have to see Miss Mannix about that.'

'Get her for us so, and we'll look at her.'

'Miss Mannix! Will Miss Mannix please come to reception.'

'Tell her we're in the bar. We're going to have a drink in case she turns us down.'

There was a function of some kind on. The lounge was crowded with monkey suits, and fancy dresses. As we had no intention of waiting half the day to be served, we shouldered a channel to the front, with people holding their drinks away from us, as if they feared we were going to snatch them out of their hands.

'Two pints of Guinness please!'

'We don't serve pints here. We only serve bottles.'

'That being the case, give us four bottles quick, before we die of the thirst.'

Up came the drink, and over came the call on the Tannoy: 'Will the two gentlemen who are to see Miss Mannix please come to reception.'

'That must be us,' said Cecil, and out we rushed.

'Hi! You there! Come back! You didn't pay for your drinks!'

'Put it down to expenses,' shouted Cecil. 'We're here on business.'

Who was waiting at the reception desk! We couldn't believe our eyes at the astonishing coincidence. Miss Mannix was the woman whose handbag Cecil had snatched the previous day.

Her mouth dropped, agape in surprise. Then she smiled - one of the loveliest, most sincere smiles that it has ever been my joy to see forming on a pair of lips. However, the most attractive feature of her face was her eyes, her laughing, alluring, brown eyes.

She was not a pretty woman in the accepted sense of the word. Somewhat Roman-nosed, and pinched-faced, she was large-chested, and small-breasted, heavy in the hips, and thick in the legs.

Yet to me she proved to be a beautiful woman, because, after getting to know her, her unattractive physical features faded to insignificance, and one bathed oneself in the warmth of her personality.

It's sad to think that so many men can't see beyond a face, and a figure. Why is there always a rush for the 'best-looking' girls at a dance! Why do the 'best-looking' women so often receive the most attention at parties! It is a gross injustice. There is beauty in every woman, if only we had the eyes to see.

I'm not insinuating that I have the eyes to see beauty in them all. I wish to God I had. Some of the ones I met still give me a pain if I think of them. That's because, fool that I was, I let them hurt me.

Excuse me for going down a sideroad. Where was I? Yes. Miss Mannix.

Julia, that was her first name, was obviously delighted, indeed amused to see us - toting a bottle of stout in each hand, and us seeking employment.

'I understand you're looking for jobs as dishwashers. Have you any previous experience in that line?' asked she with a twinkle in her eye.

'Apart from licking our plates clean, none,' said Cecil, 'but we have occasionally watched other people, standing over sinks, doing the job. There doesn't seem to be much to it. I expect we'd get the hang of it after a few practice runs.'

'What about references?'

'What about them is right!' said I.

'I'm obliged to ask for them,' apologised she.

'You've done your duty so,' said Cecil, ' now forget about them, unless you want to give me the back of an envelope, and a pencil, and I'll supply you with the sexiest references you ever read in your life.'

She laughed and told us that she thought we were two hard tickets.

'Then buy us,' said Cecil.

'I'll start you at once. Come on down to the kitchen!'

'Give us a few minutes to sink this stout, and we'll be with you,' said Cecil.

The kitchen was a huge square room, which would remind one of the junction at Oxford Circus, people rushing in all directions, intense looks on their faces, one marked difference being, that instead of the aroma of carbon monoxide, one inhaled the fumes of boiling vegetables, and sizzling meats.

It was interesting to discover that there was a hierarchy of snobocracy in operation at our new business headquarters: on top was the chef de cuisine; beneath him the sous chefs; followed by a mixed grill of other chefs; below them, our Miss Mannix, the pantry woman; next, the kitchen porters along with those responsible for silver, plate, and glass; then, swimming underwater were we the dishwashers.

Dishwashing is a much more pleasurable way of putting in your day than cement-block carrying. For instance, if you let them fall they don't damage your toes, and then, to break the monotony, you can spend ages meticulously picking each piece up off the floor, while admiring the legs of the waitresses as they go about their duties.

It was early on the morning of our second day as dishwashers that I cooked my first and last meal at the flat. A well-done fry for breakfast did the trick. Mr Chuckleworth, and Mr Dillon were proffered for their nourishment: rock-hard eggs, fried to a cinder sausages, and black rashers to be washed down with coffee as thick as treacle.

As they were aware that I would stick to my set standards each time I stood in front of the gas ring, they thereafter let me have my way, and did the cooking week-about.

From the start Julia and Cecil hit it off like a bomb. Never before, in my company, had he evinced any interest whatsoever in women. With her it was different. We weren't a week in our new career, when to my surprise, he bought himself a toothbrush and paste for his yellow-black teeth. Within a fortnight he had invested in an expensive shirt, and tie - a man who, to the best of my knowledge, had never worn a tie in his life.

Then, in our third week as dishwashers, he asked her would she like to come out for a few jars with us. She didn't play hard to get. Warmly, gratefully she accepted the invitation.

Where previously Cecil didn't give a damn what kind of a low-down dive of a pub he went into, with her we had to go to a respectable hotel lounge. He had the cheek to ask me to clean myself up, and shave. If he hadn't asked me I might have done it, but no way was he going to order me around just because he was falling in love. For spite I didn't even comb my hair.

I will admit that even though I was usually playing the part of the gooseberry, we did have great times, great laughs together, that summer.

Julia was the most light-hearted woman I ever met. There was no such thing with her as talking seriously about any subject. Yet, at the same time, her eyes gave the game away that she was reciprocating Cecil's affections.

Out of pure mischief, one night I suggested to him that he should invite her to our place for a meal. I had assumed that he'd react by considering it an insult, or at least treat it as a farcical proposal to bring the lady of his life to a tenement flat, which consisted of four mattresses nailed to a bare wooden floor, and not even a chair for her to sit on.

My assumption was a mile out. He loved the idea. I realised later that he wanted to show off his cooking expertise to her. Which I suppose is only natural. If you're in love with a woman you want to impress her every way you can.

Meanwhile, Rodney had become involved with a tall, stunningly attractive, air hostess, Angela Stephens. We gave the poor fellow an awful time advising him to have nothing to do with her, as an exquisite creature like her would bring nothing but heartache to a possessive, passionate man like him; that like the sailors, air hostesses had a lover in every port; and that he'd never have a moment's peace, eaten away with jealousy, wondering what she'd be up to, when she'd be out of the country.

Not having the savvy to realise that we were teasing him for cheap entertainment, and that there's no satisfaction in hanging a man if he doesn't object, he used to rise to the bait, and lose his temper. Then we'd console him by saying that she'd probably drop him soon, and that that would cure everything. Anyway, he invited her to the party.

I brought along a madcap waitress, Liza Gregory - a buxom girl who lived for the moment, and to hell with tomorrow. She drank like a fish, and hence was regularly sloshed, but it wasn't that which appealed to me most. One night, us both leaving the hotel by a side door, I noticed that she was laden down with two heavy bags.

'What have you there?'

'The week's groceries for myself, and my mother.'

'Have you no conscience?' asked I, in feigned shock.

'Isn't it coming off a broad back!'

'Aye indeed,' said I, 'and the pay is poor.'

Liza, Cecil, and myself procured the food, cutlery, delph, and a few pots for the party from our obliging establishment. We had to dip into our own pockets for the sherry, spirits, and beer.

We started off with prawn cocktails; then had farmhouse vegetable soup, poured from the kettle; followed by a delicious Madras curry. Our sweet was fried bananas with lashings of honey, and fresh cream. We didn't bother about coffee, but instead got down to the serious business of drinking, due tribute having been paid to Mr Chuckleworth's culinary skills, the unanimous opinion being that he was wasting his talents as a dishwasher, and should aspire to being a chef.

Drinking parties often get under way on a tame note, with people politely swapping snippets of information, and opinions about the news of the day. Then, as the atmosphere warms up, they cast off their shells, and reveal something of their true selves.

However, at our party, Liza from the beginning, was on for all of us casting off our clothes. The other women, obviously embarrassed, just went as far as casting down their eyes, and the subject was changed to that of true love.

In Liza's opinion it didn't exist. Men were always after the one thing, and the one thing only.

Cecil remarked that sometimes women were after it too.

Angela said that she had been in love several times. Mr Chuckleworth, looking at Rodney uncomfortably adjusting his position on the mattress, wanted to know where those men were now. She nonchalantly shrugged her shoulders, and gave her current boyfriend a sweet smile, and a playful pat on the cheek.

Julia claimed that she was never in love in her life, never intended to be, and was looking forward to dying an old maid, as she'd never trust any man further than she could throw him, but the twinkle in her eyes belied the earnestness of her declarations.

I couldn't draw one word out of either Rodney, or Cecil on the subject, so I sided with Liza, agreeing that the silent ones always prove to be the most formidable handful when they get a woman on her own.

One of the effects of drink on people at parties is that it leads them to believe that they can sing. Not alone that, but they also believe that their captive audience will be enthralled by their performance. Sometimes they're right, either because they do have talent, or more likely because their listeners are too drunk to know the difference.

Liza started the singsong going by screeching her way through the then popular air that begins, 'If I were a blackbird I'd whistle, and sing.' I wouldn't pay a penny to hear Rodney singing, but with me nicely tanked up, and fond of the chap, I thought he was as good as Nelson Eddy, rendering with Angela, 'The Indian Love Call,' and I can still recall with nostalgic pleasure himself, Angela, and Julia harmonising two songs in particular: 'Michael Row the Boat Ashore,' and 'Yellow Bird.'

Everything went well until about 4 a.m., when Cecil declared that he wanted to sing solo. In case you have forgotten, I'll remind you that he was tone deaf.

The first song he chose was 'Danny Boy,' which has some

extremely high notes not suitable for a non-singer.

We all clapped, and cheered as he roared his head off. When we demanded an encore he told us that if we could contain our excitement until he greased his vocal chords with a beer, he'd then gladly dip into his repertoire, and come up with another classic.

The chosen piece was 'Goodbye From The White Horse Inn,' in the course of which uncivilised bawling, there was a loud rap on the door.

Cecil calmly stopped midstream, said, 'Excuse me,' and went over, and opened it.

Our Italian landlord was without.

He informed Cecil that all the other tenants were banging on his door, complaining about the noise emanating from our flat.

'Keep a list of those who are complaining, and I'll deal with them in the morning,' ordered Cecil, who then shut the door in the landlord's face, turned the key, and started into 'Goodbye,' again, with even greater gusto.

The party broke up at about half-six on that Sunday morning after Rodney had gone out, and hailed a taxi for the girls.

For our last five days in London Cecil and I could never be found guilty of sobriety, except when we awoke in the morning - if we did go to bed the night before. He was trying to drown his sorrows because he was leaving a woman behind, and I was trying to drown mine because I wasn't.

Angela and Julia saw us to the train on the Friday evening. The sun was a few hours in the heavens on the Saturday morning when we got our first glimpse of the homeland in two months.

On to Edenstown went Cecil and Rodney, while I travelled home to see my mother, who quizzed me about how I got on in London. She found it hard to credit that I had been paid for two weeks as a builder's labourer, and for six as a dishwasher.

'I don't know what the world's coming to at all,' said she,' when you never did a hand's turn at home in your own kitchen, in all your born life, and yet you'd wash dishes for strangers for six weeks.'

Late on the Sunday night I returned to 'St Jude's,' where Miss Casey thanked me for the delph, and cutlery, which Cecil and I had brought as presents to her. He had already told her that the job-lot had been given to us by the owner of our dishwashing hotel, as souvenirs of our stay there, so that she wouldn't suffer from scruples when she'd read the name of the hotel stamped on the delph.

On our first day back at work Mr Chuckleworth and I didn't turn up, as we were much too excited to consider controlling children when our hearts were set on learning how to control a car.

Accompanied by our policeman friend, Arthur Morgan, we haggled with every used-car salesman in the town, and then settled for an as-good-as-new, nine-year-old, black Morris Minor.

The deal done, Arthur brought us out for a driving lesson, with Chuckleworth making sure he was the first to grab the wheel.

He who was a high-tension wreck with a putter in his hands on a golf course green, was the diametric opposite behind the wheel on the road. During our initial instruction he shoved the needle up to 70 miles an hour on a straight outside Edenstown. That mightn't be a great speed in your eyes, but it was in Arthur's, as he screamed at him to take his foot off the accelerator, shortly before a cow jumped out in front of us.

'We'll test her nerve,' commented Cecil. And he skimmed right past her nose.

'That caps it,' said Arthur as he pulled the key from the ignition. 'Never again am I sitting in this car with a lunatic like you behind the wheel.'

After Arthur cooled down he gave us a summary of the rules of the road; then handed me the keys with an injunction to go easy on the juice. I did a steady 12 miles an hour back in to town. I can still recall the thrill I experienced that first time I was behind the wheel.

Thenceforth we motored to the golf course, and, rain, hail or snow, played right through the winter.

In the Edenstown Golf Club in those days there was a clique who considered themselves to be 'quality' people. They were convinced that they were a step above the rest of the members. Yet, if one scrutinised their respective characters one would find that they had as many frailties as us, and if one examined their near, and distant family history, one would discover that they had more than their fair share of skeletons in their cupboards.

They would love to have preserved Edenstown GC as their own

exclusive, country club, and were disgusted that golf had become so popular that their pitch was invaded by every Tom, Dick, and Harry. Some of the 'ordinary' members - especially if they were in their employment - touched their caps to them, but Cecil, and I did not approve of their snooty attitude to their betters, and gleefully stuck pins in their bubbles of pride every chance we got.

Their self-appointed leader was a haughty hunk of a man by the name of John Byrne. He was in the rag trade in a big way, along with three of his brothers, who were as nice a bunch of fellows as you'd meet in a long day's travel. To ensure that the staff never forgot which of them was the boss of the firm, he insisted that they'd always address him as Mister John, not Mister Byrne.

At the golf club, Mister John, up to his neck in self-importance, was laughed at - behind his back - for collaring all distinguished visitors to inform them that his grandfather was a founder member, and that among the list of past captains his father's name appeared twice, if you don't mind, in gold lettering on the roll of honour above the fireplace in the main lounge, a distinction which had never been emulated by any other member.

Our Mr John was, or had been, chairman of every religious body in the parish, and was also president of the teetotallers' society, so a great source of embarrassment to him was the black sheep of the family, a fourth brother, whose existence he refused to recognise, and whose name was never mentioned in his presence.

All that was wrong with the brother was that he was over fond of drink, and over fond of the opposite sex, as evidenced by the fact that he had fathered children with a few local women out of wedlock. He was better known than the dogs on the street in his latter years, for the pathetic way he hobbled from pub to pub, due to the agony he suffered with the gout.

One Saturday evening Cecil was lacing his shoes in the crowded locker room of the golf club when Mr John imperiously brushed past him.

Mr Chuckleworth called after him, for all within earshot to hear: 'You should lay off the drink, and your gout would get better',

Mr John turned to him, his eyes popping out of his head with rage: 'It's not me you damn idiot. It's my brother that has the gout.'

'I wasn't far out so,' said Cecil. 'It's in the family.'

Some time before Christmas I got word from my mother that cousin Charlie, who had qualified as a doctor years previously, had returned recently from Canada with a wife and child, and had bought a practice in Bellpoint, a village just eight miles from Edenstown. As soon as I heard the news Cecil and I went over to see him. We received a royal welcome from himself and Sheila.

After spending a pleasant hour reminiscing about the escapades of our youth I asked Charlie what he was into when he wasn't working. To my disappointment he had no interest in golf, but they were both keen on a card game called bridge. Unfortunately for them they could find no one in their locality who played it. As four were needed for the game, they pleaded with us to learn it, that they would teach us.

Cecil said that it had the name of being a stuffy hobby, suitable only for stodgy, one-foot-in-the-grave dodderers, and that he'd have nothing to do with it. However, after we had a scrumptious meal, and had emptied Charlie's liquor larder, my friend relented, and we were given our first lesson in the game. It gripped us from the start. We found that it has the bluff, the uncertainty, the thrills of poker, combined with the skills of solo whist, to make it the king of the card games. Regularly after that we travelled to Bellpoint, and played until the small hours of the morning. Charlie, decent fellow that he was, supplied the drink, and we supplied the mouths for it.

In Edenstown there was a branch of the teachers' union, of which Cecil and I were prominent, militant members, ready, willing, and competent to create controversy at every meeting we graced with our presence.

The union was supposed to be above party politics, which noble, pipe dream, we saw as a red rag inviting us to drag politics into every item on the agenda, barring observances of a minute's silence for deceased members.

A subject which always generated intense interest was money. More precisely, how badly the state was paying us for the invaluable duties we were fulfilling for the benefit of the children of the nation.

Cecil, and I used to curse, and castigate whatever party was in power, and call on our colleagues to unite; that the only answer was to get them out at the next election.

Inevitably there would be fierce reaction from a few hotheads with fanatical party allegiances, who would take as personal, our criticism of the government of the day, and would stoutly defend the performance of their party.

Indeed on one occasion a headline seeker, who also happened to be a headcase with ambitions to become a member of parliament, took such exception to one of Cecil's stinging denunciations of his beloved party, that he challenged him to step outside the hall door, and settle their differences in a manly way with a bout of fisticuffs.

My mate claimed that there was no need to waste time going outside, that the scrap could take place there on the spot. The chairperson's call for good sense to prevail fell on deaf ears, and the meeting was abandoned in an uproar after Cecil had given the budding politician one clean clip on his glass chin.

Even though we were a thorn in the side of every person who ever took the chair, and of every secretary who tried to take accurate minutes, the teachers in general in the Edenstown area were well disposed towards Cecil and myself. I guess it did them good to look down on, and pity us - which sympathy we didn't need or want - and say to themselves: 'Thanks be to God we are not in the same boat as those fellows, forever in trouble with inspectors.'

#####

Shortly after we had returned from London Rodney fell for an attractive, red-haired girl, Margaret O'Connor, a typist in a solicitor's office. I thought it strange that he never spoke about the air hostess from the evening she saw him to the train. His body language in her company seemed to indicate that he was keen as mustard on her. Perhaps she had told him that he didn't turn her on.

With Cecil and Julia Mannix it was different. Never a week went by but they exchanged letters. Then I noticed him one evening, after reading his latest billet-doux, putting a ring around December 22nd on the calendar we had hanging on the back of the door in our box of a bedroom. Until the day actually arrived he didn't tell me what the circle signified, and I wouldn't satisfy him to ask. That morning at breakfast - we were due to get our Christmas holidays the following afternoon - he suggested that I might like to take a trip to Dublin with him that night, to meet Julia at the airport, as she had accepted his invitation to come to Ireland for a week.

Not alone did I agree to go with him, but since we had had a long school term, and had never previously enjoyed the privilege of meeting a woman off a plane, I proposed that we should honour the occasion by taking our holidays two days prematurely, and head straightaway for the city, with the abstemious resolution that we wouldn't lower more than one pint in every second pub we sighted as we sped along the highway.

Need I tell you that he jumped at my proposal, and off we went with the pleasant feeling that the rest of the staff were stuck in front of children, and us as free and easy as Miss Casey's cats dozing at her kitchen fire.

We, having arrived punctually at the airport, learned that Julia's flight was delayed by twenty minutes. I took a seat in the waiting area, and amused myself keeping Cecil in my sights, while he wiped his brow every so often with the sleeve of his coat, as he paced up and down, watching the arrivals door like an impatient child at the front gate waiting for Mammy to come home from town with the promised lollipop.

The second she saw Cecil she ran to him, and threw her arms around his neck, and nearly ate him, showing her affection, while he tried to put on an act that he wasn't in the least excited.

He had planned that they'd spend the week in two separate rooms in a city hotel, but I was having none of it.

'A ridiculous waste of beer money,' said I; and insisted that they'd come, and stay with me in my old home. I assured them that my mother would love to meet the pair of them; that she'd give them a warm welcome. Which she did, and we had a happy festive season together.

When we were leaving Julia back to the airport she told us that she'd love to work in Ireland, and asked us to look out for a job for her in the Edenstown area. We promised her we would.

As soon as we returned to 'St Jude's,' I broached the subject to Arthur Morgan, whose sister Brigid was manageress in Edenstown's one and only hotel, 'The Dairyhill Arms.' He promised that he'd whisper a word in her ear that evening. Later he told us that there were no current vacancies, but that the assistant manageress was emigrating to the USA in about two months' time, and for Cecil's heart-throb to send on a few references as soon as she liked.

To make a short story shorter, Julia got the job and landed in Edenstown early in March, much to the pleasure of both Mr Chuckleworth, and myself. We shifted our custom from 'Barney's' to 'The Arms,' - as it was locally known - from the day she started working there.

Barney, himself, took a poor view of us leaving him, not only because we were two of his best customers, but also for the reason that we both had considerable sums on his slate for which by law he couldn't sue us.

Cecil, and Julia went out steady, and I went out steady with them, wherever they went. While it is normal for even the most amiable courting couples to have occasional tiffs, they never exchanged a cross word, nor did they ever make me feel uncomfortable in their company.

Julia had been working in Ireland for about three years, when one night, after Cecil, and I had come back from 'The Arms,' and were sitting on our respective beds, having a chat, as we tackled the half dozen carry-out of export lager we always brought home - to take the sting out of leaving the licensed premises - when he suddenly went silent.

I continued talking. He didn't hear a word I said, and him only a few feet away from me. There he was, twiddling his thumbs, and looking at the ceiling, and then at the floor, and then inspecting the ceiling again.

'Are you wondering if the ceiling needs a coat of paint!' asked I.

He looked at me as if he were going to say something. Then changed his mind. He cleared his throat, and made another attempt to speak, but only got as far as quivering his lips, and swallowing his Adam's apple.

'What on earth's wrong with you Cecil, that you've lost your tongue?'

'I don't know what to say. I don't know how you're going to take the news.'

'What news?'

'I'm leaving the digs. I'm getting married.'

I should have been delighted, but my first emotional reaction was sadness, selfishness, that my best friend was parting from me.

It was I who now went silent, as I thought about the great days, the great laughs we had together, and how lonely it was going to be for me, in this wee room on my own.

'You'll come on the honeymoon with us!' said he.

'You must be joking!'

'I'm not. I'm dead serious. Julia, and myself feared that you might take the news badly, and we've decided that we'll have one last memorable fling together, before I settle down to the married life. What's wrong with you coming with us anyway? Haven't we gone everywhere together up till now!'

'Listen Cecil! A honeymoon is a very private venture, and I'm not going to impinge on your privacy.'

'That's a load of rubbish. Everyone knows what happens on a honeymoon, so I can't see how you can claim that what is public knowledge is private. You're coming with us, and that is that.'

'Cecil! It will be an honour for me to go to your wedding, but I'll not be the gooseberry on your honeymoon. My mind's made up. The subject's closed.'

'Blast you anyway. You were never anything else but a contrary fecker.'

#####

They decided to have a quiet wedding with Miss Casey as the bridesmaid, and me as the best man. Neither Cecil nor I had a quiet time leading up to the event.

The ceremony was due to take place on the day after we closed for the summer holidays, on a Saturday morning in an 80 miles away church in the city. Prior to the nuptials himself and myself took a fortnight's French leave of absence, and went on a binge the likes of which only problem drinkers would identify with, or understand.

We must have had a hectic time because much of our behaviour throughout that fortnight is only a blur in my memory. However, one detail stands out in my mind. Starting on the Thursday evening prior to the wedding, we had an all-night session with the collaboration of the porter in 'The Arms.' When he resumed duties 12 hours later, Mr Chuckleworth, and I were still sitting in the same armchairs, in the same spot from which he had left us to go home to bed that morning. Despite Julia's pleas for us to have some sense, we went round the clock with his assistance again, never stirring from our chairs except to relieve ourselves in the toilet.

The bride came downstairs on the morning of her wedding, saw the groom where she had left him the previous night, was naturally worried that he was not in a fit state to drive the car to the city, and suggested that the four of us should go by train instead.

'Not at all,' responded Cecil, 'give me a couple of pots of black coffee, and I'll be as sober as a judge.'

She ordered steaks the size of dinner plates for both of us, for our breakfast. Having eaten, shaved, and donned our new clothes, we went to the hairdresser's, and collected Miss Casey, who was like a cat with two tails at the prospect of being a bridesmaid for the first time, and her nearer 70 than 60.

However, her mood changed for the worse before we were well started on the journey. She had no previous experience of being in a car with Cecil at the wheel, and to exacerbate her plight, she was in what she subsequently called the suicide seat, as Julia had insisted that she'd have the honour of sitting beside the driver.

She might as well not have had a seat, because, after Cecil had pressed the accelerator to the floor as soon as we had left the town, she didn't sit down at all; instead, stood all the way to the city, with one hand gripping the dashboard, and the other her rosary beads, as she begged him to go easier or we'd all be killed.

He was trying to calm her down by pointing out that a devout Christian like her had nothing to fear about the next life, that she was a dead cert to go straight to heaven, when we screeched around a sharp bend on two wheels to be confronted by a flock of Rhode Island Red hens making their leisurely way across the road.

He ploughed through them as if they weren't there. I looked in the rear-view mirror. All I saw was a cloud of feathers in the air.

'The poor hens,' said Julia.

'Poor me,' said Miss Casey.

'It was either them or us,' said Cecil.

Not another word was spoken until we reached the church. As soon as Miss Casey got out she thanked Cecil for the drive, but vulgarly swore that she'd never sit in a car with him again.

'Maybe you will if we have a christening,' said he, 'because if God blesses us with a little girl we'll call her June, after you.'

That pie-in-the-sky promise brought a weak smile to Miss Casey's lips.

I was long over my initial selfish reaction to Cecil getting married, and I'm sure the ceremony was every bit as joyful for me as for my two dear friends.

Usually brides' and grooms' 'I do,' are uttered in inaudible whispers. Not so with Cecil's. His could be heard ringing around the empty church.

The venue for the feast was a nearby hotel. As none of us were yet hungry we went in to the bar for a drink. Cecil asked Miss Casey what she'd have.

'A sweet sherry would be lovely. Thank you.'

He went up to the counter, and bought a glass of dry sherry for the bride, a large brandy for both himself, and me, and a bottle of sweet sherry for Miss Casey.

'Who's that for?' enquired she in a high-pitched voice, when he planked the bottle in front of her, and her looking at it in horror, as if it was a bucket of blood.

'Sorry! I thought you might like to drink it by the neck. I'll get you a glass.'

'I wouldn't drink all that in a month of Sundays.'

'Don't worry,' said he, 'if you don't feel like finishing it, I'll polish it off myself. Whatever else we do we certainly won't leave it behind us.'

After a few more rounds, excepting Miss Casey who cautiously confined herself to the one glass, we adjourned to a small function room, where we had a sumptuous meal with an ample supply of wine to wash it down.

Then we went on to liqueurs which took Miss Casey's fancy. She had never previously tasted that harmless-looking, highly concentrated, sweetly flavoured beverage. Cecil poured scorn on the midget size of the liqueur glasses, and assured Miss Casey that it was a very safe drink, as the alcoholic content was negligible. After a short time we switched back to the brandy, Julia joining us, while Miss Casey stuck to the liqueurs, the more of which she drank the thicker her tongue swelled in her mouth.

By eight o'clock that evening the four of us were a right merry crew when Cecil jocosely asked Miss Casey would she like to come on the honeymoon with them.

'Of course I would, but only for the one night.'

'Bejapers if she's going I'm going,' said I, and we all set off on the half-hour jaunt down the coast to the seaside hotel, where Julia had made a reservation for herself, and the groom. It crossed nobody's mind on our arrival to enquire about accommodation for Miss Casey, and myself. We went straight to the bar and lay in to the drink again, and were all at various stages of intoxication when the shutters went up at about 2.30 a.m.

Miss Casey was disgracefully blind drunk. The bride was giggling and laughing for no reason at all. The groom was in a wild mood, game for anything. And I was as happy as I'd ever been in drink.

'George! Are you and Miss Casey going to sleep together?' asked Julia.

'Good Lord,' said I, 'where we'd sleep never entered my head.'

I went and found the night porter who was having his supper in the kitchen.

'The house is booked out this two months.'

Back I went and told them that I would have to go elsewhere looking for accommodation for Miss Casey, and myself.

'Keep cool,' said the bride as she went behind the reception counter. She discovered the number of the room into which they were booked, and picked the key off the rack.

'Come on up,' said she, 'and we'll see what our room is like. Everything might be alright yet!'

Cecil and I linked Miss Casey - who didn't know who she was, nor where she was - up the stairs, while Julia led the way.

The room was large, but there were only two beds in it - a double, and a single.

'I'm disappointed,' said Julia. 'I was hoping there'd be three beds.'

'We'll make the most of it,' said the groom. 'I always wanted to have a memorable first night, and now is my last chance. George can take the single bed, and I'll sleep between the two of you.'

'Are you serious!' asked the bride. 'Do you want Miss Casey to die of a heart attack when she wakens up in the morning! The only sensible thing to do is, put her in the single bed, and the three of us in the big bed, with you in the middle.'

'No,' said the well-bred groom. 'In these circumstance the courteous thing to do is put the bride in the middle in case she falls out.'

'We won't argue about it now,' said Julia. 'Let's get Miss Casey in to bed before she keels over altogether.'

As we put her in, shoes and all, and drew the clothes up around her, Cecil expressed the hope that she wouldn't be upset in the morning when she'd find her new, two-piece costume wrinkled like a rag.

While Julia visited the bathroom the groom went downstairs, and returned with the bride's case, a bottle of brandy, and the bottle of sherry which Miss Casey had been too cute to drink.

'We've no glasses,' said I.

'That's no problem,' said Cecil. 'We'll pass around the bottle!'

'Wait now,' said Julia, who had just come back in, 'there are two glasses here, on the washhand basin.'

'Don't worry about me. The two of you use them,' said he.

The three of us sat down around a low-sized table decorated with the two bottles.

'We won't stir out of this,' said the groom, 'until the cargo is all aboard.'

'We'll tackle the brandy, and leave the sherry aside,' said I.

'Are you telling me what to drink?'

'George is only out for your good,' said Julia gently.

'George is not going to tell me what to do on the first night of my honeymoon,' said he, as he pulled the cork from the sherry bottle, and flung it at Miss Casey, who was unaware that it hit her on the nose. Then he took a long draught of the sherry, while Julia and I shrugged our shoulders, and helped ourselves to the brandy.

He wasn't much more than half way down the bottle when, with eyes glazed, he slurred: 'Time for bed.'

The light was turned off, and we all got in, with him in the middle. His head hadn't long hit the pillow when he started to snore.

'Are you awake?' asked Julia after an interval.

'Indeed I am,' answered I, reaching for my cigarettes.

'My husband wanted to have a memorable first night. He has achieved his ambition no doubt, but it hasn't gone the way I had expected it would,' said she with a giggle.

'Will we shift Miss Casey in beside him to keep him warm, and go for a walk on the strand till breakfast time?' teased I.

'Good God no! That would be a dangerous move. He might come to, and mistake her for me!'

Conceding that that could prove to be a situation fraught with embarrassing possibilities, I added that I didn't feel one bit tired, and had no intention of falling asleep, as I wanted to witness my discreet landlady's deportment when she'd waken up in surroundings which had never previously greeted her.

'Perhaps this is the first time in her life she was drunk,' said Julia

'I never saw her with a sign of drink on her,' said I.

'The poor creature didn't know that liqueurs are highly intoxicating,' said she.

'She'll know the next time,' said I.

'There'll be no next time with her,' forecast Julia.

We were chatting away for about an hour when the bride expressed a desire to go asleep.

'Have your rest,' said I. 'I'll keep the vigil.'

It was daylight, and I was down to my last cigarette before Miss Casey made a stir in the bed. Quickly I stubbed out the fag, and started snoring in tune with Cecil. She rubbed her eyes, raised her head a few inches, stared over at the clamorous congregation whose chamber she was sharing, shot bolt upright, let a shout, followed by a moan, fell back in the bed, and pulled the clothes over her head.

She doesn't believe what she saw, she thinks it's a nightmare, surmised I.

After a few minutes she peeped out. We were still there.

Up go the clothes over her head again.

She now suspects that it's not a nightmare, and she's figuring out what she should do.

Suddenly she threw back the clothes; leaped out of the bed; and dashed from the virginal slumber suite down the stairs.

She wasn't fully with it. She forgot both her hat, and her handbag.

I went over to the window. There she was, taking short quick steps, and sometimes breaking into a trot, as she headed in the direction of the distant city.

Having thrown a sup of water against my face, combed my hair and taken the hat, and handbag, I went downstairs, had a fry, caught a bus to the city, and a train to Edenstown.

Miss Casey had not yet arrived home when I went in to 'St Jude's.' I left her hat, and bag on the kitchen table, and went straight to bed, where I slept like a log for 18 hours, after my 15-day drinking spree.

Next morning when I went down to a late breakfast she thanked me for bringing back her hat and bag. I attempted to open a discussion on the exciting time she had experienced on the first night of the honeymoon. She sharply told me that she didn't know what happened, didn't wish to know what happened, and implored me not to tell anyone what happened, or she'd be the talk of Edenstown for years to come.

I promised her that I wouldn't breathe a word to a soul, collected my clubs and case, went home to my mother, and spent the rest of the summer playing golf.

Inspectors are human beings. The proof of it is that some of them have a sense of humour of sorts. I actually saw one of them laugh. After examining a class of mine, the guy I have in mind passed a caustic remark about the low standard of my work, and laughed loudly into my face at the witty way he gave me the downer. I retaliated by telling him that at last he had succeeded in convincing me that he was a fool.

'Why are you calling me a fool?'

'Because, from I was a child, I was told that it's only a fool who laughs at his own jokes.'

He didn't laugh at that little joke of mine. Instead he left the room with his tail between his legs.

Clever and all as they are, they can be hoodwinked. I wouldn't have survived so long only I've managed to do so, even though on occasions I've been hard pressed, with time not on my side, trying to pull the wool over their eyes.

There was one of them, a Mr McGahon, with whom I got on quite well - for a while. He was dedicated to reviving our Gaelic language, more power to him! He used to be under the impression that I half killed myself drilling the language. Nothing could be further from the truth. I did the rock-bottom minimum. By way of introduction to the episode in which I bluffed him I'll tell you how I deal with a second language.

The greatest labour-saving device on the market for teaching children any language is to talk to them in that language. I'm not fluent at Gaelic but isn't it just as handy for me to tell them to shut up in Gaelic as in English!

So, from the day I get a new class, whenever I am in the mood, I converse with them in simple Gaelic, about their toys, comics, games, and what they watched on television the previous night. Initially I have to throw in a fair amount of English to retain their attention. Gradually I use more, and more words of the new tongue, with me sitting there drinking tea, and smoking cigarettes. Little effort on my part. Nevertheless they are learning.

When the time is ripe I start having competitions between the boys, and girls. It's amazing how easy it is to generate, and cultivate rivalry between males, and females in a classroom. I get, for example, five boys and five girls out on the floor, looking at a specified picture in their reader. In their turns each of them names in Gaelic something they see in the picture. As soon as a pupil gets stuck - unable to name a new item - she or he retires. Whichever sex is last standing wins. They love such games, and I find them quite amusing myself - watching the contestants as they ferret in their minds for an answer, with triumph, failure or frustration written on their faces.

Training children to read in a second language is the bane of many teachers' lives. The constant recital of, and harping at the same word again, and again, is a soul-destroying exercise for an adult. I have come up with a satisfactory solution which virtually eliminates repetition - for me.

I spend four or five minutes reading a page from the Gaelic reader into my tape recorder, with the children repeating it after me. Then one of the pupils takes over, operating the recorder - starting, stopping and rewinding whenever necessary - while some of the best readers are superintending the class, to ensure that everyone has their finger under the right word, and is repeating what they should be saying. I often go out for a stroll if the weather is fine, leaving my voice inside, spoon-feeding the children the correct sounds to make when learning their native language, and thus improving the standard of their reading.

One day, Inspector McGahon favoured me with yet another of his invasions. After again expressing his pleasure about how good they were at our ancient tongue, he went on: 'Now for a change I'll examine them in some other subjects!' Which gave me a pain in the pit of my stomach, as I had those kids for four years, and had taught them feck all in any other subject apart from a modicum of English, and their tables.

He examined them in history. No response.

He put geography questions to them. No hands up.

He quizzed them about algebra. Vacant stares.

He ascertained what they knew about geometry. Nothing.

I was watching him all the time, and wondering was there anything to be gained by my hiding under the teacher's desk.

Then he came over to me, and snapped: 'Why do your pupils know nothing about those subjects?'

'Up till this minute I believed that you were a brainy bloke, but now that you have asked me such a puerile question you have put doubts in my mind. Isn't it obviously because I didn't teach them!'

'Seeing you're so smart why didn't you teach them?'

'Because I didn't know they were on the programme,' was the best lie I could think of at the time.

'Four subjects! And you didn't know that it is your duty to teach them! My advice to you is to get a copy of the programme and read it. I'll be back!'

That last sentence, 'I'll be back,' is not a casual throwaway remark, but rather a threat which no teacher likes to hear.

Six weeks later, shortly after the roll call had been droned out, a banging noise on the central heating pipes reverberated throughout the school. That was the traditional way by which the first teacher who spied an inspector coming in the gate warned his colleagues that an enemy was entering the camp.

I had given the children a smattering of algebra, geometry, and geography, but had totally neglected history, and had only seconds left to do something about it before he'd be in on top of me.

I rushed to the blackboard and wrote in huge letters: OLIVER CROMWELL.

I had just finished the last 'L' when Inspector McGahon walked in the door.

He glanced up at the blackboard, saw evidence that I had been teaching history, so he ignored that subject, and examined them in the other three which he had been moaning about.

'That's not a bad start,' said he as he was making his exit. I was tempted to say to him that it was a pity he hadn't examined them in history; that he would have been surprised at how much they had learned in that subject, only my nerve failed me.

The year after Cecil and Julia got married I met her - the woman of my life.

She interested me from the moment I first spoke to her. Within seconds of our introduction she was discussing a poem, the theme of which was how a young man fell in love with an old woman. I had for years believed, and still believe, that age should have little to do with falling in love, with being in love, that lasting love is of the mind, not the body; that those who depend on sexual experience as the oil to maintain the fire of their relationship will too often find that the stove is not burning as well as expected, or that their mate has discovered another well.

However, I was surprised that an 18-year-old girl would enthuse about the subject of a youth falling for an ancient lady.

A USA student she was, due to stay in Ireland for the three months, June to August. Above average height, well busted but not to the point of bouncing embarrassment. Raven hair, naturally curling up and out, as it barely touched her broad shoulders. A milk-white, serious, noble face. A small sensitive mouth. A perfectly shaped nose. Symmetrical, sable eyebrows. Long, glistening, ebony-coloured eyelashes, which framed intense, searching, unsure black eyes.

I expect Miriam that you have long forgotten me, but I you never. I am deeply grateful to you for coming into my life. Until I met you I didn't know what love was. I thought I knew, but compared with what I feel for you, will always feel for you, the love which I have felt for other women pales into absolute insignificance.

I am indebted to them for the kindness they showed me, for the experience they gave me. I am especially indebted to those two of them who made a ball of my affections, and kicked it around for their own amusement. My knowledge of them taught me how to appreciate, how to love you all the more. Only they might misconstrue what I would say, I would write to them, expressing my gratitude for the mercilessness with which they drove knives into my heart, and then twisted them to make sure the job was done right. They do deserve full credit for it, as they did it for their own deliberate sadistic satisfaction.

One of them in particular stands out in my mind for the kindness of her cruelty. She hadn't the courage to tell me out straight that she didn't want me any more, so she gave me the message exactly like the compassionate lady who wanted to cut short the long tail of her wee pup, but was too good-natured to do it all in the one chop, so she just snipped off a little piece every day.

I can set all the women of my past life floating in front of my eyes as I wish, Miriam. You stand miles high above them in the sky. I can physically focus you there in the firmaments, and looking up at you, admire, drink in, the beauty I see in your body, in your mind.

Such scenes as the thrilling light which penetrates, and throws fascinating images on the trunks of the trees in the semi-dark suburbs of a forest remind me of the unique, irreplaceable comeliness I always see in you.

I have wonderful, life-restoring memories which I recall so often, to live again the blissful days we spent together. My eager imagination draws you to me, and I bathe myself once more in the beauty of the only woman I ever loved.

Getting to know you was the most exciting adventure of my life. After you had booked into 'St Jude's,' for your long holiday Miss Casey showed you to the sitting room, and introduced us. No sooner had we exchanged the conventional greetings than you enthusiastically expressed your thoughts about the poem which I mentioned earlier, and then withdrew into your sanctuary of reserve, as if regretting that you had unveiled too much of yourself to a stranger. And so I did all the leading, and most of the talking in our early days together.

Previously you had never been involved romantically. You did allow one, on your side harmless relationship, to develop with a neighbouring male through your common love for animals, but then the calculating pig abused your friendship, and, as men have often done to young girls, gave you a brutish fright.

As a result you were almost hostile, and certainly suspicious, distrustful of all men. Along with that, you thought, you were convinced that you were ugly.

From the start I realised that you had no confidence in yourself. You so much yearned to be loved, yet you believed that no one ever could, or would love you. Your mother used to wonder why you never had any feelings for the opposite sex. You had stifled those feelings through fear of rejection.

I remember telling you Miriam that you could never love anyone else until you loved yourself first. You replied that there was no beauty in you to love. I told you many times that I saw captivating beauty in both your mind, and body. You answered irrationally that if ever you believed that there was beauty in yourself, that that beauty would immediately disappear.

Those dark thoughts which you used to harbour about your future, those fears of insanity which you revealed to me, as your faith in my sincerity slowly built up, used to be to me a tremendous challenge. I wondered how I could help this delicate flower whose petals were so firmly closed against the sunlight. I wondered if I had it in my power; I wondered if my love was strong enough; I wondered if it was the right kind of love to enable you to blossom forth, and enjoy the young world in which you were desperately existing.

Apparently I did offer you the right kind of affection Miriam, because at the end of the three months, during which I had the privilege of being with you every day, you were a transformed woman.

At the end of that, my lifetime of happiness, you were no longer the timid creature, who first walked in to the sitting room of 'St Jude's.' You were now a confident young lady, free of constraint, spontaneously responding to every fond word and look I tendered you.

After you returned to the USA you wrote loving letters to me for some time, with your adorable personality jumping out of every page. I have safe, all your letters, along with carbon copies of those I sent to you. I never need to look at them any more, as I read them so often that every word is mirrored in my mind, but I do often take out your lock of raven hair, and, as I hold it in my fingers, I wonder, 'Has she found the bliss she deserves, the man she deserves!'

I had always believed that eventually you would fall for a younger man than me. Yet, when you stopped writing I was heartbroken for a long time. Then I happened to be reading a book of quotations, seeking to soak in some of the profound wisdom of sages long dead, when I came across the French proverb, 'There is nothing wrong with anything. It is our attitude to it that is wrong.' And so I convinced myself that whether I possess my treasure or not is unimportant. What matters is that I love it.

And I always tried to love you purely, Miriam. I never put my arm around your waist. I never kissed you. I never even allowed you to hold my hand. That was the only way, Miriam, by which I knew that I could prove to you that I loved you for yourself.

I remember one night, as we sat alone in the sitting room of 'St Jude's,' you suddenly got up, and left, saying that you could bear it no longer. You had instinctively desired that I would crush you in my arms, and take you, but you knew that my higher self didn't want it. Then, on our last evening together, we stood facing each other by the side of a river. Your lips were trembling, your whole body was trembling, waiting, eager for me to express my love by physical action, but I had found my angel, and was not going to allow my hands of clay to shatter my heavenly dream.

#####

Cecil always maintained that the true test of a teacher being in command in her or his classroom is never to look up when someone enters. If you look up you are not the master. You are admitting that curiosity has got the better of you, or you're afraid you'll be caught working.

Going on that principle, I didn't look up when McVeigh walked back in to my life. Yes! Mr Samuel McVeigh, who had been on the receiving end of a few thumps from my mother, came in my door one day in his official capacity as the new inspector for our area. The children were in the middle of a composition, and I was in the middle of a crossword.

'Is that how you are earning an honest living?' asked he with a sneer on his face.

'No it's not!' answered I. 'There's no prize for solving this crossword. I'm doing it purely to kill time.'

'You are supposed to be working you know!'

I looked him in the eye, and said, 'I'm surprised at your crass ignorance. My job is to make sure that the pupils are working.'

Apparently he wasn't anxious to develop an argument as he chose to ignore my reference to his ignorance, and went down among the children, taking up their copies, and examining their essays. It seems that he could find little wrong with them, as he left the room without a word, and in to Cecil with whom he had many.

Mr Chuckleworth had given his pupils two hours worth of sums to do, and was sitting at his desk, busily engaged studying the horses. Unfortunately all the children had finished their sums or had done as much as they had felt like doing, and were creating a rumpus when McVeigh entered the room. He was not impressed, and conveyed sentiments of his displeasure to Mr Chuckleworth, who also was not impressed, and continued looking at the racing page, while, with a frost-inflected voice he put the query:

'Who are you?'

'I am Mr McVeigh, your new inspector.'

'You are lacking in politeness.'

'I am what!'

'You had not the common courtesy to knock before you came in.'

'I beg your pardon! I certainly did knock.'

Cecil carefully closed the paper. Slowly stood up. Casually strolled to the middle of the floor. Then, standing facing the class with McVeigh at his rear, asked the pupils:

'Hands up those of you who didn't hear him behind me, knocking on our door?'

Then he mouthed the word 'up.' All hands obediently went up. Cecil looked at McVeigh. Said nothing.

'Are you trying to make out that I'm a liar?'

'You have summed up the situation accurately.'

'Nobody heard me because there was such a din in the room that it would be impossible to hear a knock.'

Cecil consulted the children about the matter. Not a single witness came forward to substantiate McVeigh's allegation.

'It seems Mister Inspector that you were hearing things,' said Cecil. 'You'll have to go outside, and politely tap on the door. Then wait to see will I admit you.'

'You're the most impertinent teacher I ever met. You are not fit to be in charge of children!'

'Is that so! Well then you take charge of them!'

With that Cecil walked out the door, and didn't reappear at work for a fortnight. Meanwhile, the morning after my mate had abandoned ship, McVeigh sent to the school a letter giving Mr Chuckleworth a week's notice to the effect that he would be undergoing what every natural born idler of a teacher dreads, a general inspection. As my friend didn't turn up on the appointed day, the inspector wasn't quite able to inspect him.

Shortly after Cecil had resumed occupancy of his chair in front of his class the determined McVeigh arrived again, and again gave a written notice, this time personally delivered in to the hand of the reluctant recipient, stating that a general inspection would take place on the following Tuesday.

The Tuesday came and so did McVeigh.

Considering that Chuckleworth hadn't done a tap from the day he had received his 47 pupils eight months previously, his fifth class was reasonably well prepared for the inspection. Himself, Rodney, and I had decided that the best way to up the standard for the duration of McVeigh's visit was to export Cecil's twelve worst pupils to Dillon's sixth class, while a like number of the smallest, and brightest from there, were temporarily imported, and strategically scattered around the venue for the inquisition. As any teacher who has used that ploy will tell you, it brings about a near miraculous improvement in the all-round answering.

Another matter to which we had given some thought was the time factor, the reasoning being that the more distractions that were flung in the face of McVeigh, the less time he would have for tracking down the skeletons in Cecil's cupboard of inefficiency. So plans were laid accordingly, with a dependable little orphan lad, Donal Carr, assigned to play a small part in the proceedings.

The second McVeigh came in the door - after knocking loudly thereon - Donal, sitting in a back seat, behind a big girl, emitted in a stage whisper:

'Will you look at the ould bags back again!'

McVeigh chose to pretend he didn't hear the impudent comment, and continued on his way to the teacher's table, on which he placed, and opened his briefcase.

'He's going to sell us shoelaces!'

Admirable restraint shown by Sam, who goes to take out his notebook.

'What's the skunk doing now!'

Explosive roar from McVeigh: 'Who said that?'

As nobody squealed on Donal, there poured forth from his mouth a string of cliches about the gross bad conduct of the youth of today. Indeed he showed the depth of his insight by forecasting what every harbinger of doom has said since God made man, namely, that the way things were going nowadays, the next generation of children would have no respect for anything. He put the roof on his slating by placing the blame squarely where it belonged, on the shoulders of the negligent teachers who shirked their responsibilities with no thought for the consequences.

Not having run out of steam yet, he switched to the topic of hygiene, observing that some of the children had uncut fingernails, dirty noses, and unpolished shoes. Next he pointed out to them the state of the filthy floor, where bits of paper, butts of pencils, orange and banana skins were virtually knee-high.

The mention of the litter problem was Mr Chuckleworth's cue to shove McVeigh from the centre of the stage. He apologised for the condition of the floor, and volunteered to remedy the situation at once, whereupon, as good as his word, he went down between the rows of desks, and busied himself gathering up papers, and skins, and stuffing them into his various pockets.

'Why can't you get the children to do that?'

'Example is better than precept. Maybe you'll give me a hand yourself!'

'Mr Chuckleworth! I did not come here to pick dirt off the floor.'

'Mr Inspector you have thrown enough dirt at me, and the children already, to keep us going for the rest of the day.'

'I'll have none of your lip. I came her to examine the children.'

'I thought you came here to examine the floor.'

'You'll cut out your backchat if you know what's good for you.'

'Alright so. I'll do anything to keep you in good humour,' said Cecil, who then gave orders to the class to pick up everything within arm's length of them. When they had a good bundle apiece held against their chests he marched them out to the yard, to refill the rubbish bins which himself, and myself had emptied in the room the previous night.

Meanwhile, McVeigh had been prancing around in circles, consulting his watch, impatiently rubbing his hands, and breathing deeply.

As soon as they were all back sitting at their desks he went to begin his interrogation.

'Wait now,' said Cecil, 'when I do a job I like to do it properly.'

And he grabbed a brush, and started to sweep the floor at a furious pace in the precincts of McVeigh, who was quickly enveloped in a cloud of dust.

'What are you at now! Trying to drive me out of the room! Well you won't succeed!'

The floor swept, McVeigh initiated another attempt to question the class.

'Hold on,' said Cecil. 'I'm just after remembering. We forgot to say the morning prayers.'

The pious scene which followed might impress even a religious maniac. He ordered the children to say separate sets of 'Our Fathers,' 'Hail Marys,' and 'Glory be's,' for all the deceased of the parish who had died within living memory. 'Who else has a granny dead?' he'd ask every so often with a defiant look at McVeigh, who tried to put a halt to the farce, which prompted Cecil to lead his bored pupils through five decades of the rosary for the conversion of the pagan inspector who begrudged them the little time they gave to talking to God.

That done, he turned to Sam, and with a magnanimous wave of the hand said, 'They're all yours.'

McVeigh set out to prove that Cecil hadn't done his work. Much to his disappointment, to his disgust, there was hardly a question he put, but there were at least a dozen in the class able to answer. He went off that evening in a disgruntled mood with no choice but to write a 'satisfactory,' report about my lucky friend Mr Chuckleworth. However, subsequently, sad to relate, he got the upper hand of Cecil, but not in the classroom!

#####

When, in my early thirties, I started full golf - as distinct from pitch, and putt, which I had been playing since I was a child - I spent many happy hours indulging in delightful daydreams. I had succeeded in deluding myself into believing that international fame would inevitably come my way when I'd master the art of getting the ball off the tee.

Gradually, reluctantly, I was forced to come to the conclusion that I had begun golf too late in life, and would have to lower my sights to a more practical objective. Thus it became an obsession with me to win the local captain's prize.

In Edenstown the event has always been decided by match play. Neither Cecil nor I, in our first six attempts, managed to get beyond the second round. Indeed Cecil had earned a distinction in which he took no pride. He had won only one match in his miserable career. Even that would not have happened, but for the fact that his opponent, who was giving Cecil a roasting, received word that his wife had dropped dead elsewhere on the course, which caused him to graciously concede, to make the necessary arrangements about the removal of the remains.

Yet again, in our seventh annual attempt, Cecil went under in the first round, this time to that man McVeigh, who was, it must be said, a splendid golfer who played off six.

Smirky Sam annihilated him nine, and seven. That in itself was hard enough to take, but what we both intensely resented was the way he rubbed it in. When it was obvious to him, after he had won the first three holes, that Cecil was a bag of nerves not capable of putting up a fight, he bubbled over with sarcastic good humour as he damned with faint praise my friend's timid efforts on the greens to edge the ball nearer the hole.

I could almost hear him purring, in between his humming, as we walked from shot to shot. I resolved that if fortune favoured me to the degree that I'd meet him in the final - we were in opposite halves of the draw - by fair means or foul, I'd give him a match that he'd remember for the rest of his life.

Morning, noon, and night I practised my swing. In the classroom, on the course, and in the bedroom - where I had installed a full-length mirror and used the handle of a brush as an imaginary club - I twisted, and contorted in an effort to imitate Ben Hogan's rubber man convolutions as illustrated in his bestseller, 'Power Golf,' the nett result of which was that I never knew whether I was going to hit the ball or miss it, when I proceeded to perform my genuflections on the tee.

Against Cecil's dogmatic advice I even went so far as to take lessons. He was convinced that there was no point whatsoever in going to the local professional, insisting that if that gentleman knew how to play perfectly he'd let nobody in on the secret, but instead, would go out, and win everything himself.

Anyway, I did reach the final. Granted, I was in the weaker half of the draw, yet only I stood on my opponents' balls in the rough

116

whenever I got the chance, I'd never have scraped through to the ultimate round.

McVeigh skated home in his section, beating tiger after tiger, without ever having to go beyond the fifteenth, and he was a cocky pain in the neck pup, on that sunny summer evening, as we walked down to join battle on the first tee.

Captain's prize finals in Edenstown always attracted large galleries, a percentage of which no doubt came only because they couldn't resist the smell of the two free drinks they'd get after the presentation - one from the captain, and the other from the winner. There was an even bigger crowd than usual, not because either of us was extra popular - which we were not - but for the simple reason that every member of the club was aware that McVeigh and myself were bitter enemies. They came along hoping for fireworks, which Cecil, my eager caddy, did his best to provide. (Yer man was too mean to either invest in a caddy car or pay someone to carry his bag).

I was off 16, so he had to give me eight shots - four in each nine - the first of which was to come at the first hole.

As McVeigh addressed the ball, and was about to drive off, Mr Chuckleworth broke the customary silence, and addressed me in a loud voice:

'You've a shot here, George. You should win the hole!'

Sam stood back from the ball:

'Are you going to start shouting every time I go to hit the ball?'

'Time will tell,' answered Chuckleworth with an evil grin.

McVeigh glowered at him, and then went through the ritual of addressing the ball again, before banging a screamer 280 yards on to the middle of the green.

I connected well with mine, and sliced it 170 yards in to the light rough on the right.

Again in a loud voice for all to hear:

'It's within your distance, George. He thinks he's going to win the hole, but you'll give him a nasty shock, won't you!'

I took out my nine iron, and pitched it within a foot of the hole. His putt for an eagle stopped on the lip. I tapped mine in for a win. First blood to me!

'How right I was, George. Didn't I tell you, you'd put one over on him!'

Which gloating remark earned Cecil a contemptuous look from

117

Sam.

The second was another par four, this time 410 yards with a dog-leg to the left. As I stood on the tee about to hit the ball, I was idiotic enough to let doubts into my mind by thinking along the lines that he was a big hitter, and I had no stroke here. And what did I do but try to whiplash it a mile. I paid the penalty by having my first fresh air of the round. Then, to make up for lost ground, I tried to drive it further the second time, and missed it completely again. All flat!

Going to the short third tee Cecil pulled a half bottle of whiskey from his hip pocket.

'Have a mouthful of that, George. It will do you a world of good.'

Even though I didn't know at the time that Cecil had a plan up his sleeve to give Sam the runs, I took a long slug before planking the ball on the green, well inside McVeigh. His bold downhill putt went four feet past, and I sank mine to go one up again.

The next was a long par five at which I had my second stroke. If I win this one I'll have him worried, thought I, before I ballooned the ball to the sky, for it to come to rest within spitting distance of where I stood. My stroke's gone now, and it looks as if I'm going to lose the hole as well, was my negative attitude. I did lose it, and the next three along with it, to be feeling down in the mouth, as I shaped up to hit my pitch to the 110 yards eight, with him well in on the green.

'Hold it a minute, George,' said Cecil. 'Have another drop of this first.'

As he handed me the bottle he whispered, 'You're a brilliant pitcher. You're well able to get in near that hole.'

I took a draught. Then shaped up again. Lo, and behold! I hit a nigh perfect shot which just stopped rolling two and a half feet from the cup.

'Aw haw,' cried Mr Chuckleworth, 'I knew it. I knew it. That's miracle water I'm giving you. Miracle water!'

'Here,' said he, proffering what everybody thought was the same bottle to McVeigh, 'to hell with begrudgery, and to show I'm a good sport, take a sup of this but don't take it all.'

Sam was so surprised to hear Cecil speaking civilly to him that he fell for the bait, and took a greedy slug, remarking as he handed back the bottle, 'It's working wonders for your friend. It will hardly do me any harm.'

'Divil a bit,' said Cecil. 'It'll make you feel like a two-year-old.'

It was only then, as we were walking up to the green, that my pal confided in me that he was carrying a second bottle, doctored with a reliable, rapid-acting laxative. Julia it was who had come up with the idea, and procured it from a chemist, after spinning him a yarn that she hadn't gone for a month.

Laxative or no laxative, he sank a six-yard putt to halve the hole, and remain three up.

Then as if inspired by the purgative he rattled off a string of birdies, and pars, to leave me five down with five to go - even though I had made use of my strokes, but merely to get halves. Cecil kept telling me, 'If only you can keep the match alive until the quick-fire urge hits him, you'll come out on top.'

However, he betrayed his own doubts about nature coming to my aid in time, by setting off the alarm clock in his trousers pocket, when yer man was at the top of his backswing on the 14th tee. The ball went out of bounds, and he went for Cecil.

'Sorry!' said Cecil. 'A freak accident. How was I to know when it would go off!'

'Give me that clock! You're not going to get the chance to use it again.'

'Certainly. Keep it as a reminder of the day you threw away the captain's prize.'

Some of the crowd condemned Cecil for his unsportsmanlike behaviour. The majority were amused by his cheeky tactics.

McVeigh, after putting the clock in his bag, let fly his longest drive of the day, but the two shots he had lost enabled me to win the hole.

Four down with four to play looked a bleak prospect, but one should never give up. At the short 15th I hit the thrilling pitch of which I had often dreamed. My ball landed three feet beyond the pin, and spun back into the cup for the only hole in one I've ever had. While the gallery clapped, McVeigh muttered for my benefit, that it was the fluke of the century.

When he was sticking his tee in the ground to try to emulate my feat, Cecil couldn't resist saying to him, 'You've that for a half!'

'Will you go to hell!'

'Sorry Mr Inspector. I won't open my mouth again until George has won the match.'

Almost needless to say I won the hole, but I still had a lot to do if I was going to pull the game out of the fire. However, I had a stroke coming at the next, and the last, that is if I could keep the match alive till then.

I hit a nice drive down the 16th fairway - a 490 yards par five - and was stone dead in four, but he was on in two, and after a well-judged fourteen-yard approach putt, had a tiddler to finish me off. It's all over bar the shouting, thought I, as he carefully took up his stance to knock it in to the cup, but I had not reckoned on Cecil's resourcefulness, as once more he came to my rescue.

At the critical split second when McVeigh had drawn back his putter Mr Chuckleworth flung himself forward on to the green. Crash went my bag, and rattle went my clubs, for yer man to give it a beautiful jab three inches wide of the hole.

'Who shoved me?' shouted Cecil, in case Sam would try to saddle him with the blame.

'You did it deliberately! You did it on purpose!' screamed Sam coming towards Cecil.

'He did not,' said Arthur Morgan, who had been standing behind Cecil. 'You're blaming an innocent man in the wrong. Looking over his shoulder I lost my balance. It was completely my fault. Please accept my apology.'

As we were walking away from the green Cecil said under his breath to me, 'If that shock to his system doesn't set the medicine in motion nothing will.'

I had driven what was for me a first-class 180 yards drive up the middle of the par five 17th, which was bounded on the left by a river - a graveyard for many balls - and he was on the tee about to strike off when suddenly he stopped, and ran in to the shrubbery.

'It will be interesting to see how he'll play now that he has a bee in his bowels,' commented Cecil.

Eventually he emerged obviously embarrassed.

'Gamesmanship at its best,' censured Cecil. 'Keeping your opponent waiting for five minutes, and you two up with two to play. I wouldn't do it to my worst enemy.'

'You don't often get the chance,' retorted Sam.

For the second time in the round McVeigh hit a poor shot - a lovely quick hook into the river. Then he over-corrected with his third off the tee, and found whin bushes waiting for him with open arms, in the deep rough on the right.

As I scanned the faces of the gallery it was plain that many of them were enjoying his misfortune, not for my sake, but human nature being what it is, rabbits find it encouraging to see tigers playing tripe. One down with one to go.

The final hole was a short par four with the green situated on an island of a plateau. We both struck satisfactory drives, and were walking away, with McVeigh as usual well in front, when Cecil ran after him, and handed him his tee, remarking, 'You forgot this you'll need it for the 19th!'

Sam bit his lip, and told him to feck off.

Each of us got on in regulation with him well inside me, a mere four feet from the pin, while I was a good twelve yards away. Even though I had a stroke at the hole it looked odds-on that I needed to sink mine to keep the match going. I allowed a shade too much borrow on the left, and missed by a whisker.

Once again McVeigh had a putt for the match. As he was addressing the ball all present tried to keep one eye on him, and the other on Cecil.

As he was about to take his stroke he dropped his putter, and scurried to the clubhouse.

'I fear he has mistimed his departure,' said Cecil to me. 'It's always advisable to answer nature's call, rather than try to postpone the inevitable.'

'What's up? Where's he gone?' asked an old lady of Mr Chuckleworth.

'Have you ever had a pressing desire to powder your nose, Mam?' was the delicate reply.

In due course he returned, and got down, to the putt again. A hush once more descended upon the scene, broken only by the striking of a match by Cecil as McVeigh tapped the ball towards the hole. It ran round the rim, and came to rest, hanging over the lip, to a chorus of 'ohs,' and 'awes.'

As we were walking down to the 19th McVeigh coldly remarked to me:

'I'm sure you feel the tension. You look a nervous wreck!'

'I don't feel a bit,' answered I, even though my heart was pounding dreadfully as the possibility of victory frightened the wits out of me.

I mounted the tee, and hit a mediocre 160-yards drive.

'Nothing to worry about,' comforted Cecil. 'It's well within your reach, and don't forget you have a stroke.'

No more than me, McVeigh didn't connect properly. Nevertheless he finished beyond the 200-yard mark.

My mishit second shot sailed into a deep bunker on the left of the green. The crazy thought immediately crossed my mind that I'd have to get down in two from there or else it was bye-bye to the captain's prize for me.

McVeigh strode as far as his ball. He then rubbed his chin, and scratched his head. Next he slowly walked up to the green, and looked back, as good golfers do when there's a lot at stake. Then he made his second dash for the clubhouse, much to the amusement of the gallery at large, even the most innocent of whom had by now diagnosed his dire complaint.

'Feeling better?' asked Cecil when he returned.

'No,' said he, 'I'll feel better when I pitch this ball stiff.'

With that he had a socket in to a clump of trees away wide of the green.

'That would have been a great shot if only it had been straight,' commented Cecil, inducing a general titter.

Stymied by a grand oak tree, it was still Sam's turn to play. He went for death or glory. It was music to my ears listening to the branches crackling as he failed to make it out. However, he now had a clear gap. Using his three iron, he ran the ball along the ground right up within an inch of the flag, to loud applause from the crowd.

I flung his ball back to him, and went down into the bunker. I had three shots from there for a win, and four for a half. As I hadn't a stroke at the next I felt it was now or never.

'Get it out first time,' said my anxious caddy.

Over eager to act on his sound advice, I exploded right across the green in to another bunker. Down I went again. This time the opposite extreme. I barely got it out on to the cut surface - twelve yards from the pin. I studied my putt, and said a little prayer that God would guide it in to the hole. He must have taken over from me, because it didn't go along the curved line that I had intended. Instead it went like a rocket straight for the cup, hit the back, hopped up in the air, and then fell down into the hole, for me to shed tears of relief.

To my surprise, the first person over to congratulate was

McVeigh. I found in my hour of glory that my hostility towards him had temporarily evaporated. Even Cecil bought him a drink at the subsequent festivities.

#####

I mentioned earlier that Cecil, and I took up bridge with cousin Charlie and his wife Sheila as our tutors at their home in Bellpoint. After my friend got married, Julia often accompanied us there, though she refused to take up the game, giving as her reason that she had heard that most husband/wife addicts often have fierce rows when playing together. Indeed she said that she read about a wife who shot dead her husband because he called her a bum bridge player. She didn't want to run the risk of having to shoot Cecil.

Be that as it may, after some years Cecil and I progressed from fireside bridge to join the Edenstown Club. We weren't long there when we realised that we could hold our own with the best of the members, and so decided to try our luck further afield.

In Ireland congresses or national championships are run over long weekends in various hotels in rotation throughout the country for most of the year.

It took us a while to find our feet on the circuit, and to get to know all the players. When we did, we livened things up for them, and managed to get ourselves barred from a few hotels.

One Saturday night in the early hours of Sunday morning, himself and myself found that everybody else had gone to bed, and we were there, left to our own devices, drinking in the foyer of the hotel.

'The devil always find work for idle hands to do,' remarked Cecil, as he went behind the reception desk, pulled open a few drawers, rooted around in them, found the register, and the morning-call book, and brought them to where we were sitting.

'Those people don't know what they want,' said he, as he ripped out the old call-sheet, and proceeded to write a new one, with my assistance.

We first dealt with a woman who had every sign that she was growing both a beard, and a moustache. We left instructions for her to be supplied with a raw egg, and hot water to shave at 7.30 a.m.

Then we did our bit to try to reform a dirty old bachelor, who never darkened the door of a church or a chapel, but was big into pornography, and had the lazy habit of lying in bed till lunch-time on a Sunday. For him we requested a 6 a.m. call, and a copy of the bible.

Two keen, early bird, golfing brothers had ordered a full breakfast for 8 a.m. Opposite their room number we put: 'Under no condition to be disturbed.'

A devout Jewish lady who had asked for lemon tea, and toast, received instead, bacon, sausage, and black pudding with a jug of chilled orange juice.

The previous night we had seen a greedy glutton going around the dining room, stuffing his gob with the leftovers from other people's plates. He had ordered 'a hearty Irish breakfast,' for 10 a.m., with two heavy lines under 'hearty.' There was delivered to him at 7 a.m. a glass of cold milk.

In short, we gave all the guests as far as possible, the opposite of what they wanted, the early risers a rest, and those who never got up to go to church or chapel, an unexpected rude awakening.

There was chaos the next morning. Managers were called, waitresses were abused, and receptionists accused.

We slunk out of the hotel after paying our bill, having made one slip. We forgot to disguise our handwriting, which was compared with our signatures on the register. Three days later we received a letter stating that if we visited that town again we would be doing them a favour if we took our custom anywhere except to their establishment.

We were barred from the second hotel for a different type of exploit.

Cecil had helped out now and again in busy times at 'The Arms,' where Julia had retained her position as assistant manageress, and so had become familiar with the intricacies of a switchboard.

Again we were off for a weekend with the bridge-playing fraternity. And again at about three in the morning they all had disappeared to bed. The only sound that broke the silence was the night porter hoovering a carpet away in the distance, as we finished our drinks.

Having done so, we were staggering up the stairs when Cecil did an about turn, in the process of which he nearly sent me tumbling back down to the foyer.

'Sorry George! I'm after getting an interesting idea which should break the monotony of our drab lives.'

Down he went to the switchboard, and made some adjustments.

As he climbed the stairs for the second time he told me, 'I've taken it upon myself to keep the guests happy. You can be my assistant.'

He explained that all calls were going to come through to the phone in our room.

We didn't get our first bite until 20 past 5. On the line was a dapper little dentist, who spent a fortune on drink, never had a civil word for his wife, and was impossible to play cards with, always blaming his partner for everything bar the weather.

'Yes, can I help you?' said Cecil soothingly.

'Bring me up a glass of Scotch.'

'A lot of good it would do you. Go back to sleep at once or I'll go up and flatten you in the bed.'

'What! What did you say?'

'You heard what I said,' answered Cecil, and my friend slammed down the phone.

He didn't pluck up the courage to call us again for over an hour.

I answered: 'Yes. Night porter here.'

'Thanks be to God it's a different voice this time!'

'What on earth are you talking about?'

'Some time ago I rang down for a glass of whiskey, and some madman threatened to come up, and flatten me in the bed.'

'I'm that madman's father, and if you don't stop annoying us, the two of us will go up, and beat you in to pulp.' And down I put the phone.

Unknown to us at the time, within ten seconds he had his clothes on, grabbed his overnight bag, and flew out by the fire escape.

Our services were not sought again until seven o'clock. It was this puritan-minded, sixteen-stone, keep-your-distance woman, who had herself convinced that every man who glanced up or down her body had a desire to feast his eyes on her in the nude.

'Yes madam,' said Cecil, in a deep sexy tone.

'I'm just after wakening with a dreadful headache. Would you by any chance happen to have a couple of aspros handy?'

'What aspros you want! What you need is a good massage. Leave the door open. I'll be up in a minute.'

All was quiet then until coming up near eight o'clock, when the phone, once it started ringing hardly ever stopped, with clients who hadn't bothered ordering their breakfast the night before, now demanding it, as if they were the only people in the house we had to look after.

'I want grapefruit segments, bacon, eggs, and tomato, brown bread, red jam, and coffee. And make it snappy.'

'Certainly sir. I'll send it up to you in two shakes of a lamb's tail.'

'May I have two hard-boiled eggs, tea and toast please.'

'What about trying some of our porridge? The porridge we serve here is delicious. You never tasted the likes of it.'

'Right so. I'll have a bowl of it.'

'Would you like us to sugar it for you, or will you sugar it yourself?'

'No, no. I don't take sugar at all on porridge, but make sure it's good and hot.'

'It will be that hot it will burn the lips off you.'

'Fresh grapefruit please, liver, bacon, and sausage, and a pot of black coffee.'

'The sausages are gone off. I wouldn't advise you to have them.'

'They're what!'

'They're gone off. I'm just after coming through the kitchen. The smell of them nearly turned my stomach only I held my nose.'

'That's disgusting. And what about the liver?'

'It's not great either, but I don't think it will make you sick, unless you have a delicate constitution.'

'What kind of a dive did I book myself into at all! Yet the meal last night was alright.'

'Huh! You must have been one of the lucky ones. The night porter told me that he spent the whole night carting up bread soda to half the house. I'm fed up telling them to get rid of the mice in that kitchen.'

'Listen. Forget about me and my breakfast. I'll go out and have it somewhere else.'

'You're right too. I wouldn't eat here if you paid me.'

Next we received an outside call from an elderly American gentleman touring Ireland for the first time.

'Have you any rooms available for this coming Thursday night?'

'Wait now sir till I check it out! Ah, we have, yes.'

'Will you reserve a twin-bedded one for myself, and my wife?'

'With or without bath?'

'Without please.'

'You dirty divil.'

'What did you say?'

'I was saying that I presume you don't mind fleas.'

'Fleas!'

'Ah yes, we've had a lot of complaints lately about fleas. I'm telling you in advance so that you'll know what you're in for. What did you say your name is, sir?'

'No. It's alright. We mightn't hit that part of the country at all.'

Back on the home front things began to hotten up for us, as the guests became irritated, with no sign of their breakfasts arriving. They supplied us with interesting facts about what they had ordered, with great emphasis on the time they had originally ordered it. We were both patient, and sympathetic, and guaranteed them that it was on its way.

However, when they were ringing for the third time some of them went outside the bounds of decency in their protests. We gave back as good as we got. We stood up for the staff of the hotel, defended the standard of the hotel, and when they swore they'd never come near the place again, we assured them that it didn't make the least difference to us.

The more contrary among them demanded to speak to the manager, whose role one or other of us acted, while explaining that there had been a lightning strike in the kitchen, and that they'd be lucky if they got any breakfast at all.

Suddenly! During an exchange of blue language the line went dead. Shortly after that there appeared in our room a muscular gentleman who was both the manager, and owner. He adopted a threatening attitude, gave us five minutes to vacate his hotel, and warned us never to step inside the door of it again.

We asked him could he not take a joke.

He confessed that he couldn't.

#####

Remember that time you lent me the price of the bottle of brandy, my dear reader, my only reader, my most lovable reader! You got the money two days later in the post I presume!

You didn't!

I sent it to your home address!

That's not your address at all!

That explains it. I'm very sorry. That was an inexcusable mistake for me to make. I hope you'll forgive me. I promise you that I won't do that again.

No. It wasn't a cheque! It was hard cash in a brown envelope. In fact I put in a few extra bob just to show my appreciation of the way you obliged me. Some low-down son of an unscrupulous basket is after going and drinking it. It kills me to think of it.

Tell me! How are you off for money at the moment?

Once bitten twice shy, you say. That's not fair! You're not going to blame me because it went astray in the post are you?

You'll give me the price of one pint! That would only make me worse! I never drank one pint in my life. There's no logic to drinking a measly pint. I'd sooner drink vinegar. I wouldn't have as bad a thirst after it. I'll tell you what: I'll save you money. Just give me the cost of a bottle of vodka. That's cheaper than brandy.

I'm not honest you say! I'm not dependable! I'm not trustworthy!

If you don't retract those accusations this very minute, I'll sue you for slander. I'm not joking either. I'll have you climbing the big steps.

I told you myself that I owe money rings round me! Might I ask you when I told you that?

Just a while back!

I must have been blind drunk and thought I was in confession. I always like to keep the priests happy by telling them terrible things about myself, and promising them that I'm going to mend my ways, and me with no ways to mend.

You still don't believe me! You still don't trust me!

Well I'll tell you what, and this might be the last chance you'll ever get of obliging me, I'll make you two promises - Number One: I'll never ask you for money again if you lend it to me now. Number two: I'll guarantee never to pay it back to you!

Isn't that honesty for you? I bet you're surprised to meet a man as truthful as me.

You're going to give it to me!

Well words fail me! I feel so grateful I don't know how to thank

you! Maybe you'll throw in the price of a few smokes as well?
   Thanks! I'll be off now.

#####

(Spasmodically I kept a diary. As I continue my autobiography I'll intersperse edited extracts from it to give you some idea of the trauma Cecil and I went through because of our addiction to alcohol.)

As I said some time ago, I didn't start drinking until I was 32 years of age. Now only eight years later I realise that I have one hell of a problem. Friends knew it long before me. Arthur Morgan told me a few months after I had started, that I didn't know how to drink, that I was a gulper, and should slow down my pace. In my ignorance I believed that he was the one who didn't know how, and took pride in being able to drink himself, Rodney, and everyone else bar Cecil, and a local fellow nicknamed 'Lan-yah-wan-yah,' under the table.

I have to admit that I'm now totally dependent on drink. I can't live without it. I see no point in living without it, as I feel I might as well be dead if I couldn't have it.

One Sunday afternoon not so long ago I had a chat with Arthur, and us warming ourselves at the sitting room fire in 'St Jude's,' with all the others gone off for the day. He held up Lanyahwanyah as an example to me, and told me that I was making good progress on the road to his hapless hell.

Poor old Lanyahwanyah! At one time he was on the top of the world, a professional man whom every girl of the day in the town of Edenstown had her cap set for. A strikingly good-looking chap then, with a great interest in sports cars, rugby, and racing. Too generous he was when he had the money, splashing it around as if it were going out of date.

Look at him now! No matter what hour of the day or night you go through Edenstown you're nearly sure to see him staggering along the street, or sitting in a doorway with a cheap bottle of wine clasped in his hand. He sleeps in an old hay shed hard by the cemetery, which he visits every night, rain, hail or snow, to kneel down, and say a drunkard's prayer at the tombstone of his ill-starred wife, whom he sent to an early grave with a broken heart.

Arthur, as I was saying, told me that if I didn't do something about it soon I'd end up another Lanyahwanyah. Had it been anyone else who had spoken to me in that vein I would have intensely resented it, and would have told them to mind their own business, whereas I had been eight years in digs with him, and he had proved to be a salt of the earth policeman, who, with some collaboration from the station sergeant - a great man for his pint - had got Cecil, and myself out of a number of scrapes we had been involved in through drink.

Friends on the bridge circuit now and again concernedly ask me, 'Why do you drink like that?' My stock reply is, 'I drink to forget.' Then they might say, 'You'll kill yourself in two years,' or 'You'll kill yourself in three years.' Why the dickens don't they pick six months, and not have me waiting around so long!

The morning is the worst time for me. First of all I've to make the decision whether or not I'll get up. I notice lately that I'm absent from 'work' much more often than I used, and I certainly never go to the school on a Monday. When I do go about getting up I've no heart in it. I've no heart in facing the day, in facing people. And I hate, I dread entering the classroom. Rarely do I talk to the children now, but just let them belt away with their comics and toys, as long as they don't annoy me. The inspectors are breathing down my neck. I'm worried that I'll have a general inspection soon.

When I got into the habit of bringing my dog, Lazarus, along with me to the school nobody passed any remarks until the day McVeigh laid his beady eyes on him. He ordered me to get him out of the room at once. I told him that I wouldn't, that the parents had raised no objections, that the children loved him, and that as long as I was in the school he'd also be there.

'What will happen if he bites one of them?' asked he.

'There's not the least danger of it,' said I, even though there was an admirable wicked streak in him since he had grown to manhood.

I got him as a pup from one of the kids the Christmas before last. I hadn't a bull's notion what breed he was, nor did I care. All I saw was a winning little black fellow. Later I was informed that he is half greyhound, half Labrador. I was surprised at him growing to be a fine strong size. I'd love you to see him leaping gracefully over a three foot wall as spectacularly as any steeplechaser.

One night when Cecil and myself were walking home from a

pub a gang of teenage hooligans got the idea into their heads that they'd mug us. I set Lazarus on them. In five seconds he had them scattered. From that day to this they haven't come next or near us.

Cecil went over the moon about the businesslike job that Lazarus did, and ever since he brings to 'St Jude's,' at least once a week, a pound of the best steak, not for me, but for Lazarus. I think that the dog is as fond of him as of me.

To come back to my own story: when I awaken is the most dreadful part of my day. It's worse still when I don't get up, when I don't go to 'work.' I sink into deep, lonesome depressions.

I have written on the wallpaper beside my bed: 'Lord teach me how to laugh again, but don't let me forget how I cried.'

How I wish I could get off this accursed drinking! Last week I was speaking to an alcoholic who is off it four months. That seemed like a lifetime to me. Four months without a drink!

I asked him how he did it. He told me that, 'There's no secret attached to it. I stay off it one day at a time. Every morning I make up my mind that I might drink tomorrow, but I won't drink today. That may sound silly to you but it has worked for me.'

I tried it for three days, staying in bed. Most of the time I was shaking like the steering wheel of a badly balanced car. On the third night I said to myself: I'm better drunk than this way, and out I went, and got plastered. Maybe I should have gone instead, and got tablets for my nerves.

Every morning I make up my mind that I will give up drink. At night the craving takes over, and I decide to have just one more go. I'm alright then. I can relax somewhat after I've had a fair few down. I can manage to dismiss to the nether regions of the subconscious the fierce pangs of remorse which I had felt on that very morning.

Cecil is far worse than me. His health has been deteriorating steadily for the past year. Julia is worried sick about him. He hasn't eaten a decent meal for ages, she tells me. He used to be quite fond of reading. Now he never takes up a book. He can't concentrate. When I meet him in the morning - if the two of us happen to be at work on the same day - he can hardly talk. He starts a sentence. In the middle of it he forgets what he was going to say.

However, there is a kick in the old dog yet! Before that recent spell of mild weather broke, we had one great session with a priest, a Father O'Halloran, home from the mission, and recently appointed as a temporary curate in Edenstown. We weren't long in his company when he gave us reason to suspect that he was in the same boat as ourselves - an alcoholic. Subsequently we learned that he was liable to suffer blackouts of an interesting nature.

It was on a Saturday morning that we bumped into him going to the first tee, and he on his own. Cecil asked him would he like to make up a threeball, which invitation he gladly accepted. We were only going up the second when he produced from his bag a bottle of the best Irish, and asked us would we care for a drop.

'Manna from heaven,' declared Mr Chuckleworth before drinking to the priest's health, and then passing the malt to me.

When I handed it back to his reverence, after treating myself generously, he good-humouredly remarked:

'It's obvious that this not the first time you fellows have put a bottle of whiskey to your heads.'

'The first time today,' conceded Cecil.

After the game was over and the bottle ready for the bin, we adjourned to the nineteenth where the three of us settled in for the evening before settling in for the night, at a late hour of which - we being the last patrons on the premises - Father O'Halloran wangled Gerry, the steward, into keeping the bar open by persuading him to have a glass with us. He hadn't a hope of motoring along at our speed but instead, after a few circuits of the course, retired permanently to the pits, and us only revving up our engines to get our second wind.

We put him lying on a couch, and placed two armchairs against it to prevent him falling on the floor.

Having performed our Good Samaritan deed, we resumed our obligation to keeping the juice of the barley industry in a sound state of health at the expense of our own.

Up towards 6 a.m. Cecil suggested that we'd better be going home, as Julia, alone in their rented flat, might be wondering where he was. I reminded him that Father O'Halloran had mentioned earlier that he had to say the 8 o'clock Mass, and that we might as well wait, and take it in on our way home.

'You're right,' said he, 'if we don't go to bed it'll save us getting up later.'

So we continued as barmen cum customers until it was time to head for town. Cecil and I were going to leave a tip for the steward.

Then we thought that he might take offence, so we stole a bottle of whiskey instead, and gave it as a present to his reverence, and him outside in his car companionably waiting for us.

We, in our old crock, led the way in, with Mr C. as usual driving. We had to come to a sudden halt at a shut railway gate near the town. His reverence mustn't have been watching where his car was taking him, because he banged into us as the train whistled by. A broken light, and the back bumper bent a different way was the only damage done, yet he was extremely upset.

'Are you certain you're alright, or will I bring the pair of you to hospital?'

We did our best to convince him that there wasn't a bother on us, but whatever got in to his head, he couldn't seem to accept that fact as we walked in to the church.

All went well until he mounted the pulpit to preach the homily. He gave a to-the-bone sermon on the evils of drink, called out the routine announcements, and finished off by appealing to the congregation to pray for the repose of the souls of the recently deceased Cecil Chuckleworth, and George Ryan, who tried that very morning to beat a train across the railway line but were stopped dead in their tracks.

Every head turned towards us. We, who seldom smiled in public, felt obliged to flash them a simper, and a shrug of the shoulders, to let them know that one shouldn't believe everything one hears.

After Mass we went to the sacristy - where his reverence was unrobing - passed no remarks about him being under the impression that we were dead, instead invited him to join us for breakfast in Cecil's flat, my friend casually mentioning that Julia wouldn't be ten minutes getting ready a fry.

'Great,' said he, 'I'll eat you out of house, and home. Do you realise that we haven't had a bite bar a sandwich for 24 hours!'

'To be honest I didn't notice,' said Cecil.

Another woman wouldn't have let us inside her door, but Julia, more than relieved to see her husband home, welcomed us warmly.

She had just placed an appetising fry in front of Cecil when he got a pain in the upper right side of his stomach. He said that he'd go and lie down for a while, and for us to go ahead with our breakfast.

While we were eating Julia brought up the subject of his health.

She said that it wasn't the first time he had that pain, that his legs were slightly swollen, and that he sometimes vomited even with no drink on him. Father O'Halloran said that he must see a doctor at once. Julia sighed. She had been trying for months to get him to let my cousin Charlie examine him. He wouldn't hear of it. He'd be alright in time!

Knowing well that there was no point in asking me to advise him, as his quick retort would be, 'It's yourself that should see a doctor,' Julia went, and asked Rodney - for whom Cecil had a great smack since our trip to London - to try to talk him in to going to Charlie. Rodney - who was married for some years to a farmer's daughter, and had two lovely little girls - implored him to have some sense, and look after his health. His pleas fell on deaf ears, and he went so far as to say that he believed Cecil had a death wish.

Having heard the background to the situation Father O'Halloran said that he'd go into Cecil, and see could he talk some sense in to him. He spoke firmly to him, telling him that if he really loved his wife, he'd look after his health for her sake if not for his own.

To our surprise, to our delight, he agreed to see Charlie. I immediately rang my cousin, who too was amazed that he had agreed to be examined, as the mention of my friend's health had always been taboo when we were over in Bellpoint for our game of bridge.

Having given him a thorough examination, Charlie persuaded him to go into hospital without delay, and arranged there and then on the phone in the flat, to have him admitted to the Redbarns Psychiatric Hospital, above in the city the next day - Monday.

I wanted him to let me drive him up - along with Julia - but no, stubborn man that he was, he wouldn't let us. We were making too much of a fuss over nothing. He'd go by train.

We saw him off from the station, and promised that we'd go up to visit him on the following Saturday, but we hadn't to wait until the following Saturday to see him, because he walked in to my wee room in 'St Jude's,' the very next evening, and me just lying on my bed looking at the ceiling, after having the boiled egg for my tea.

'What on earth happened, Cecil! Is it that they can't cure you?'

'Ah no. I didn't go in at all.'

'You didn't go in!'

'It would seem that way. Wouldn't it?'

'Listen Cecil, I've told you often enough that I don't like you being sarcastic with me, and I know bloody well by the peculiar glint in your eye that something queer happened.'

'Nothing queer happened. I just signed another fellow in in my place.'

'You signed another fellow in in your place!'

'That's what I said.'

'Might I ask: who did you sign in your place!'

'The taxi driver.'

'Charlie didn't make any arrangements about getting a taxi driver a bed there!'

'Tell me something I don't know. I signed him in in my name.'

'In your name! And who were you supposed to be when you were doing that?'

'The taxi driver's son.'

'Will you come off it, Cecil! You're keeping me on tenterhooks, feeding me scraps of information, like a teasing youngster throwing crumbs from a stale loaf to a starving dog...'

The train having reached the city, Mr Chuckleworth dismounted, and went to a taxi rank, where he engaged a decrepit looking wreck, by the name of Jim Hartigan, a former sailor, who, on the way to the hospital, boasted to my friend about all the women, black, white, and yellow, whom he had thrilled in his day. He also claimed that he was now keeping two houses going, his third wife in one, and a slip of a girl in the other - a flat not one mile from his own door.

Cecil didn't believe the half of what he said, but merely remarked, 'You'd never think to look at you that you have such astonishing stamina.'

Then Mr C suggested that they'd go in for a drink. The great lover was reluctant to enter a pub as alcohol was the one thing that didn't agree with him; that he couldn't hold drink; and that he'd be languors drunk after a few.

('Good,' said Cecil to himself).

'Come in for a lemonade so. It will only take a few minutes.'

When Cecil got him inside up against the bar counter, he revealed to him that he himself was an author who had written numerous bestsellers. He expressed intense disappointment on learning that Jim had never read even one of them, but then Jim didn't read books, good bad or indifferent, because he was illiterate, which admission inspired Cecil to suggest that the two of them together should write the story of Jim's life, as everybody was interested in sex.

'I can't spell.'

'We'll buy a pocket dictionary.'

'Will my name be on it?'

'No. It will be on your book. In banner headlines on the front cover. We'll stick it at the bottom of every page as well... Barman! As soon as you're ready there, two large brandies, please.'

'Ah no. No. I'd sooner have a lemonade.'

'Don't you know that it's customary to launch a book with large brandies?'

'Oh is it! No. I never heard that.'

'You have a legitimate excuse. You never wrote one before.'

'That's true, but I'm very excited at the idea of writing one now.'

'A natural reaction my good man. Let's honour the occasion properly with the brandies!'

'Alright so.'

As they tackled the brandies Cecil continued, 'Before I start taking down notes so that I can lay out the general structure of your bibliography...'

'What's that?'

'A bibliography is the technical name for the story of your life.'

'I'm learning fast. You would have made a great teacher.'

'Whether I would or not, don't interrupt me again, unless I ask you something. You're breaking the thread of my thought.'

'Sorry! What were you going to ask me?'

'We'll have to discuss the royalties. What way do you think they should go?'

'I don't know what you mean by royalties.'

'Royalties are the cut you get from the publisher for writing the book.'

'I see. Aye.'

'Would you think it would be fair if you got 99 per cent, and I as the ghost writer got one per cent.'

'That would be alright with me. It sounds fair. What's a ghost writer?'

'A ghost writer is the mug who does all the work, while the other fellow gets all the credit.'

'Well then I'll let you put your name on the book as well, but in smaller writing.'

'Are you sure you won't be jealous?'

'No I won't, as long as my name is twice as big as yours.'

'Okay so. I'll start taking notes while you tell me more about yourself.'

Cecil produced a pencil, and pulled from his pockets all the used envelopes and unpaid bills he had available, while Jim, who had only been waiting for wind of the word to blow his trumpet again, resumed his bragging about all the women he had bedded.

As he bullshitted away, my friend industriously scribbled down a string of full stops, commas, and exclamation marks.

'What's that you're at?'

'Did you never hear of shorthand?'

'Aye. I've heard tell of it alright.'

'Well then you go on with your story, and leave the writing to me.'

Hartigan wouldn't budge to take another large one until Cecil came up with the conviction that there was too much material for the one book, that they'd have to write two, and they duly launched the second one, after which Jim's barriers of self-preservation broke down, and he himself bought the third round.

However, he was safe in the caring hands of Cecil, who saw to it that he received proper medical attention by driving him in his own taxi to the psychiatric hospital, where he booked Hartigan in instead of himself.

'You were expecting to admit my father, a Mr Chuckleworth, earlier today, weren't you?'

'I'll check it out... Yes, we were.'

'I'm sorry I'm so late with him. I have him outside in the car.'

'Bring him in so.'

'It would be more practical if you used a stretcher. I don't think he knows where he is at the moment. He got away on us this morning, and went off on another skite. He has our hearts broken. This is his fourth hospitalisation in the past six months. And the poor man, he becomes so bad that he doesn't even know his own name. You'll have to put him in a straitjacket for a few days to see will he settle in.'

#####

137

Mr Chuckleworth, the last train long gone, booked in to a hotel for the night, next day left the taxi outside the station, caught the train for Edenstown, came into my room, and brought me up to date about his escapade.

'It was an interesting adventure Cecil. That aside, what are you going to say to your poor wife? She was full of hope when you went off on the train yesterday morning. She's going to get a terrible shock when you walk back in to her!'

'I have been thinking about it all the way down on the train. I don't know what to say to her, but I do know that I've my mind made up that for love or money I'll go near no hospital. With the help of God I'll be alright. Come on now. You run me to the flat.'

He wasn't alright! I drove him home, and, as was to be expected, Julia was dumbfounded. However, she pulled herself together, and threw her arms around him. I left them on their own, and went to 'The Arms.' I wasn't there an hour when I got a ring from her. She sounded desperate. Cecil was after taking another turn with the pain in the same place. She couldn't get through to my cousin. His line was engaged for the past 20 minutes.

I told her that I'd try once more for Charlie, and that if I didn't get through I'd drive over to Bellpoint, and find him. The line was still engaged, so over I went posthaste, to find his wife still on the phone, granting an audience to a friend who never knew when to stop talking, while Charlie was listening to the wireless.

He didn't even wait to throw on his jacket, and was at Cecil's bedside within 12 minutes. To our relief Cecil wasn't as bad as we had expected. The agonising pain was gone, and he, ghastly pale, was sitting up in the bed, sipping a cup of tea.

When Charlie said that he'd again arrange to get him in to hospital he told him to forget about it, that the look of the Redbarns institution was enough for him, that surely he had the right to choose where he'd die, and he'd prefer to die in his own home.

'Don't be talking about where you're going to die, Cecil. Aren't you full of life!' said I.

'I am, at times.'

Charlie then told him that he'd have to stay in bed for at least a fortnight. He didn't want to go by the medical advice. Julia looked at him with pleading eyes, saying nothing. I suppose he thought about how he had bitterly disappointed her by reneging on his promise, and returning home. Reluctantly he gave in. Charlie said that he'd visit him twice every day.

#####

Two days after Cecil had come home unexpectedly I received my anticipated notice of a general inspection to be held on the following Wednesday.

About six months previously I had put the wind up Inspector McVeigh. I advised him that if he had a genuine interest in his own physical wellbeing he'd for evermore give my classroom a miss when he'd visit the school.

He didn't pay any heed to my advice, except that after that he was always accompanied by his boss, Mr Peter O'Keeffe, who, on the first day I met him, tried to poke his nose into my private affairs in a way that would vex a saint, never mind an unreasonable man like me.

Wherever he heard it I don't know, but he told me he was aware that I had an alcoholic problem, that his father had suffered from the same disease, and that he knew the measures I should take if I'd have the commonsense to listen to him!

Hadn't he one hell of a neck putting himself up to be a doctor, and wanting to give me advice completely beyond the boundaries of his job of spying on teachers. I told the two of them that I'd sooner die a roaring alcoholic than have it said that an inspector cured me.

He never mentioned the subject again, but every time they came to me after that, my first greeting to them was, 'How is the good doctor, and his assistant today?'

I'm sure that they both thought I was half mad, but I was only playing a game with them, and did I put on a show or did I not, to cut short my general inspection when the Wednesday did arrive!

On that designated morning for the exploration of my talents as an unconventional teacher, the two of them entered my classroom, each bearing a briefcase, the carriage of which did not prove to be necessary, indeed an encumbrance, in the light of what subsequently transpired.

I fired my first shot across their bows by saying, 'Let's get this straight! The only subject that I'm going to allow you to examine is singing.'

'We'll start with that so,' said O'Keeffe, trying to humour me, as I well knew.

'We won't start with it. We'll finish with it,' said I.

'Go on so,' said he, believing in his cunning little mind that I wasn't going to get my own way.

'I'm only going to do the one song for you.'

'Is that all they know?' butted in McVeigh.

'Are you finding fault with me before I even start!'

'Go on! Go on! Let's hear the song,' said O'Keeffe.

I started up the tape recorder, and out came the golden voice of Harry Secombe filling the room with that moving hymn, 'How Great Thou Art.'

The children automatically joined in, and I proceeded to give an exhibition of conducting the likes of which was never before seen on this planet. Using a humble wooden ruler as my baton I twisted, and twirled, I convolved, and convulsed, as I worked them right through the high notes, and low. Then, as I was gyrating full circle on the tips of my toes, with my right arm outstretched to bring them through an extremely long note, I deliberately collapsed on the floor, to guffaws from O'Keeffe, and shrieks of glee from McVeigh.

Up I sprang, and roared at them, 'How dare you pair of ignorant louts, gloat, and laugh at my misfortune! Get out! Hist Lazarus! Go for them Lazarus! Hist!'

With his teeth bared, and a constant throaty growl, which put the shivers up their spines, he had them shifted from that room faster than they had entered therein. As they tried to rush out the door together, with my dog snapping at their heels, McVeigh's briefcase caught in the handle. Wisely he let go the bag and pulled the door shut. I opened it, and threw the bag after him, telling him that maybe now he'd think twice before annoying me again.

#####

I was hardly in the door of the digs that dreary December evening when I was called to the phone. It was Charlie, at their flat. Cecil had taken a sudden turn for the worse at midday, was dying, and mightn't last an hour.

140

I couldn't believe the words I heard. Stunned, I sat down, and looked in to space trying to come to terms with the fact that I was going to lose the closest person in the world to me, my mother apart. Though far from religious, I always had great faith in her prayers. I rang our neighbour, Mrs Murphy, and asked her to pass on to Mammy a message: that my best friend barring herself was on his deathbed, and to say a prayer that God would spare him.

Next I went to the kitchen, broke the news to Miss Casey, and told her that I was going immediately to see him. Tears welled up in her eyes as she asked me could she go along with me.

'Why wouldn't you come with me! I know he thinks the world of you in his own peculiar way, even if he did use you as a cockshot now and again for his own entertainment.'

Lazarus, as usual jumped in and sat on the back seat of the car. Off we went on that depressing drive to their garden flat.

He had been in a coma for a while but was conscious, though his eyes were closed, when we arrived. Father O'Halloran had a feather in his hand putting water on his tongue.

'Do you know who this is?' asked I.

'Why wouldn't I know that voice,' answered he in a barely audible whisper, without opening his eyes, but raising his hand languidly towards me.

'Take my other hand Julia.'

'You'll pull out of this Cecil.'

'Indeed I won't, George. I'm finished... finished.'

'Cecil! Where there's life there's hope. I need you. Julia needs you even more than me. Hold on to the will to live. You were always a fighter. Don't throw in the towel now!'

'Thanks for trying to lift me, George... How did you get on with the inspectors?'

'I set Lazarus on them, Cecil. I ran them.'

'Good man yourself! Some of those fellows will never learn that we are human beings doing our best no matter how bad it is.'

'Miss Casey is here, Cecil.'

'Hello, Miss Casey. It was good of you to come. Will you ever forget our honeymoon? Hadn't me and you a great night in that bedroom!'

'You were always having me on Mr Chuckleworth! Always having me on.'

Then he expressed a wish to speak to Rodney, and Arthur, and also asked me to bring in Lazarus if I had him outside in the car.

I contacted the two of them, and brought in Lazarus, who went straight to Cecil, put his front paws on the quilt, and licked his face. Then sat down at the head of the bed, never taking his eyes of my mate.

Before the lads arrived Cecil had relapsed into a coma, and Father O'Halloran gently signalled for us to go on our knees, to say a decade of the rosary for the soul that was about to leave us.

How I prayed! How I begged God to work some miracle to allow him to live for another while. Just another while! How I said with such meaning those words which a thousand times previously I had so thoughtlessly muttered:

PRAY FOR US SINNERS NOW AND AT THE HOUR OF OUR DEATH. AMEN.

In her hour of sorrow Julia didn't forget that she was hostess. She plied Miss Casey with cups of tea until it should have been coming out her ears, and made sure that our glasses were never empty.

Cecil didn't go as quickly as Charlie had expected, but put up a long-lasting fight, was still fighting for his life as the freezing, dark dawn broke, and, need I tell you, every single one of us stayed through the night by the bed of death. Then, the struggling breathing, to which we had been so keenly listening, seemed to stop. The same thought, the same fear crossed our minds simultaneously. But no, he wasn't gone!

Suddenly he came to! He regained full consciousness, and spoke to us all!

'Goodbye to each of you... Goodbye Julia... Goodbye George. Don't grieve for me. I'll meet you again in heaven, please God.'

Back he went into the coma.

Half an hour later he gave a slight shudder. No warning. No death rattle. Just a slight shudder.

Charlie went over, and pronounced him dead.

As soon as I learned that my mate was gone from us I wanted to get off on my own. Away from everybody. To share my grief with nobody. I called my dog Lazarus, who too had kept the long vigil. He refused to budge from the head of Cecil's bed.

Out from the garden flat I trudged, and headed for 'The Arms,' where I spent the day unsuccessfully trying to drink myself senseless to deaden the pain at the loss of my friend.

With Lazarus walking between us, Julia and I headed the mourners, following the hearse to the church, on that bitter, cold, winter evening. The prayers over, the priest announced that the burial would be after the ten o'clock Mass next morning. When we were leaving, Lazarus, who had been waiting outside during the brief ceremony, refused to come with us, instead stood sentinel at the church door.

Poor Julia, noticing that I was in a bad state, begged me to go back to the empty flat for a meal. Ignorantly I refused, explaining to her that I was going to go for a few to 'Barney's' - the pub where I first drank with Cecil. There I resumed my solitary drinking until I was thrown out at closing time.

Armed now with a bottle of whiskey I got a crazy urge to go and have a look at Cecil's grave. On my way there I saw Lazarus still at the church door. He wouldn't leave to come with me.

After dragging open the creaking cemetery gate I went in and searched around. In the moonlight I descried the heap of ice-clad clay, and stones that were going to pound upon the coffin of my mate. I staggered over, and stood looking down at the open grave, hacked out of the unwilling ground.

I opened the bottle of whiskey, and flung away the cork. The more I drank the more morose I became until suddenly my mood changed. The thought struck me that Cecil must be in heaven; that he didn't want me to be sad; that he wanted me to enjoy my bottle of whiskey. So I drank to him in heaven again, and again. I held the bottle up towards the sky, and shouted, 'Cheers, Cecil! Good luck, Cecil!'

I went over in my mind all the droll remarks he made, and the crackpot deeds he did, such as setting fire to his own bag of straw in the van. Then I went into a fit of hysterical laughing, during which I stumbled and capsized into the grave. Six feet down. On my back. I tried to get up, but couldn't even get as far as a sitting position! I lay there. Helpless. Feeling the cold biting me, freezing me. Every so often I shouted, 'Help.'

Then I heard steps approaching. Coming nearer, nearer. Unsure steps. Pausing steps. Yet coming nearer. I wasn't afraid. 'Help,' I shouted. 'Help.'

Then! Surveying my situation with his mouth open, as if surprised, I saw the down-and-out, Lanyahwanyah.

'Get me out of here will you? I'm frozen stiff.'

'Who do you think you're trying to fool! You should be sweating after kicking all that dirt off yourself. Goodnight!'

He turned on his heels, and tottered off in the moonlight.

Gradually fatigue took over, and I conked out, into a deep, drunken sleep.

Hours later I awoke, and saw Cecil directly above me in the grave, staring down at me.

He said: 'Come up out of that or there'll be no room for me!'

#####

When first he came out of the coma, Cecil believed he was in his own bed, and that it must be night-time, it being so dark, but when he attempted to scratch his head he struck wood.

He tried to turn around in the 'bed', but again touched timber.

'Why the hell did they shove me into a wardrobe!' wondered he as he gave the lid of the coffin a strong push

Then he felt all around him, and the more he felt the more his terror grew.

'God,' said he, 'it can't be true that I'm dead, and buried.'

Logic, however, took over. He realised that whatever about being buried, he wasn't dead; but he might as well be, as he'd surely die of starvation unless there came to his rescue an earth tremor of sufficient power to throw him up out of the grave, and burst open his coffin.

'God,' prayed he, 'I don't want to be too demanding. I'm just asking you to send me an earthquake that will merely give people a bit of a jolt and a fright, yet violent enough to enable me to get out of this predicament in which my would-be friends have placed me.

'No God! I've had second thoughts. Please cancel that request! Give them a good shaking when you're at it. It won't do them a bit of harm, and maybe it will discourage them from sticking people into coffins before they're half-ready for the grave.'

At that very moment the church clock boomed out the hour of 2 a.m.

'The drunken bousies! It's in the chapel they have me. Thank you God for not letting them bury me. I'll promise you this much God: I'll scare them stiff when they gather around me in the morning to pray for the repose of my soul. In the middle of the ceremony I'll rap on the lid once, to attract their attention, and start them wondering if they're hearing things. Then I'll lie low for a while. Just long enough for them to convince themselves that they only imagined they heard a noise. Then I'll let an agonising moan that will tighten the skin on the napes of their necks, and I'll follow up with a bang on the lid that will have them quaking at the knees. Thus he continued to amuse himself with terror-scheming thoughts to while away the long hours as he waited for his own funeral.

#####

To some degree Julia was to blame for the fatal mistake, as she, with the best of intentions no doubt, had made sure that our glasses were never empty at her dying husband's bedside, and consequently all of us had become sozzled out of our minds.

It didn't matter about the lay people present, but if Charlie hadn't got sloshed he would never have deemed Cecil to be a coffin case.

Father O'Halloran too, would, I presume, normally be able to judge if a person is in the land of the living. If a priest hasn't the gumption to know whether or not a soul has left a body, how the hell can he be expected to assist it on its way to heaven.

So Julia, who dished out the drink, must shoulder some of the responsibility for the medicine man, and the minister of religion becoming maggoty drunk, to the point where neither of them knew the difference between a coma and a corpse, and as a result, my poor pal paid the penalty by being awarded a death cert - a gift which no man in his full senses would accept with equanimity.

#####

Back in the box Cecil was wondering had his person been treated with the respect due a living body being placed in a coffin; or had the undertaker dumped him in like one would throw the carcase of a chicken into a dustbin.

How he'd have loved to have awoken at that split second when

145

the undertaker, armed with the lid, was about to plank it on top of him!

'Excuse me sir,' he would have said, 'are you sure you're doing the right thing?'

No doubt the undertaker would have tried to bluff his way out of the situation by hiding the lid behind his back, while telling Cecil that he was delighted to see him looking so well.

Cecil would have told him that he too was looking well, but mightn't feel too well after Cecil had taken him to the cleaners for attempting to bury him alive, as there had to be some law against such carry-on.

If the undertaker then waved the death cert in his face, and claimed that everything had been legal and above board, Cecil would have threatened to beat the life out of him, as that too must be legal and above board, since no court of law would find a dead man guilty of giving a corpse collector a hammering.

Cecil chortled to himself at the idea of being the first customer to attack an undertaker, and as the night wore on, he gradually settled down so well that he went, and did something foolish. Something which you or I would never dream of doing in a coffin. He fell asleep!

He was still deep in slumberland when being wheeled down the aisle, and out into the hearse after the Requiem Mass the following morning. The transfer job was done so quickly that my dog didn't get a chance to go near the bone box then. Later, when the coffin was placed on the ground near the open grave - in which, I as yet lay unnoticed, out to the world in my drunken stupor - Lazarus went over, and sniffed along the edge of the lid. He started wagging his tail, and barking nonstop.

Everyone, of course was horrified at the profanity of the hullabaloo he was creating. He was duly shooed away. Everyone, that is, except Cecil who didn't consider it unseemly to be wakened up rather than put down.

One blow he gave the lid, then cocked sideways his head listening for reaction, which came in the shape of Father O'Halloran forecasting that his remains would return to dust.

'I'll dust him alright, if I get my hands on him,' hissed he, as he gave the walls of the coffin a double thump on the right, and a rat-tat on the left, which prompted the prayer book to jump from the priest's grip, while every mourner within earshot was stuck to the ground like a tree.

'It's safe to assume that I've won their undivided attention,' concluded Cecil, as he paused for a short interlude to give them a chance to allow their imaginations run riot. Then he let a low, spine-chilling moan, which aroused terror among the majority of them, and inspired Miss Casey to proclaim with a shriek, that the end of the world must be nigh, as the dead were showing signs that they were about to cast off their shrouds, and come forth from their coffins.

A bloodcurdling screech from Chuckleworth lent credibility to her prediction, and caused three of those present to go into a faint, among them being Doctor Charlie.

The only one with the presence of mind to do something practical was Arthur Morgan, who beckoned to the dumbstruck undertaker to help him unscrew the coffin cover.

Julia was alongside at the joyful moment when the lid was pulled off for her husband to make his official return to the land of the living. Unlike some spouses who would take a dim view of their mates coming back from the dead, she was thrilled to look once more on the countenance of the man who had never allowed her to experience the peace and quiet of one dull second from the day she married him.

After Cecil had been helped from the redundant prison, Father O'Halloran whipped off his cassock, and shoes, and insisted that he'd put them on, which he did, but not before Julia's affection exploded into eager squeezes, and passionate kisses.

'Easy there,' said he. 'Easy! Was it you that dressed me for this party? You forgot to put on my trunks! Were you not afraid that I'd catch a chill in my kidneys?'

Someone then noticed that there was an occupant in the grave, but I had to play second fiddle to Cecil, as they considered him the star turn of the show. However, when he was told that I was in the hole dug for him, curiosity got the better of him, and he had to see for himself.

By this time, with all the commotion, I was gradually coming to, wondering where I was, and what the hubbub was about.

I looked up and saw him, directly above me in the grave, dressed from neck to ankle in black, and him as white as a ghost.

He said: 'Come up out of that, or there'll be no room for me!'

Convinced that he had come from the next world to haunt me I let an unearthly back of the throat scream. I calmed down somewhat when other faces, smiling, and laughing popped into vision.

'Cecil! Is it really you or am I imagining you're there?'

'It's me alright. I just dropped by to see how things are going with you.'

'I was sure you were dead.'

'I'm dead sure you're wrong.'

'How did you get out of the coffin?'

'Lazarus it was who saved me. Lazarus warned me that they were about to bury me.'

'Come on home out of that before you get your death,' interrupted Julia. 'You can tell him all about your resurrection later.'

'You're right, Julia. I'm petrified with the cold.'

As I scrambled out of the grave he scanned the faces of the late mourners, looking for the gentleman whom he forevermore addressed as Doctor Quack. He failed to pick him out lying prone behind a headstone.

'That bum Charlie's not here! I suppose he couldn't spare the time to come to my funeral because he's too busy writing death certificates.'

On being told that Charlie fainted flat on his face when he heard Cecil's bloodcurdling yell, and hadn't yet regained consciousness my friend was on for sticking him in the coffin, and screwing down the lid tight, just to give him a taste of his own medicine, but the idea wasn't feasible as his wife, Sheila, was standing guard over him.

Arthur Morgan had rushed out to the road for his car, and drove it right up to where we were assembled, so that Cecil would suffer the minimum delay in being brought back to the flat, but Mr Chuckleworth rejected the offer, claiming that he was a man of high principle, who, whenever he travelled anywhere, always returned by the same transport. So, as he had come in the hearse, he'd go home in that vehicle. In to the driver's seat he sat, having given the undertaker a hand to put in the first coffin ever carried out of the Edenstown graveyard.

As they went through the town, people stopped on the streets, to open their mouths, and bless themselves, while staring in disbelief at the corpse who drove himself home from his own funeral.

Getting out of the hearse Cecil confided in the undertaker that Julia and himself had never got around to furnishing properly their flat, and that maybe he'd give him a present of the coffin as it was a lucky one, which would look posh, standing in a corner of their sitting room, with it showing off a hand-painted flowerpot on a tripod. The undertaker granted him his request after making him promise that he'd never breathe a word to a soul about his generosity, as he didn't want to be pestered with people coming rapping at his door looking for free coffins just to stick flowerpots in them.

#####

About six weeks after Cecil had won the toss in his dice with death, Father O'Halloran was recalled to his own diocese of Dublin, and appointed parish priest of Rockmallen, a fashionable, recently built-up, seaside resort, some seven miles from the city.

We were all sorry to learn that he was leaving us. In his early fifties, with a shock of curly, black hair, greying at the temples, he was a tall man with a heart of corn, and a constant faraway look in his pale blue eyes. Like ourselves he had one particular failing: he was allergic to sobriety. Yet he had managed, by his example, entreaties and total identification with our common problem, to steer the convalescent Cecil and myself clear of booze right through the Christmas season. That was some feat, considering that with us one drink was too many, and a thousand not enough.

He was only a month gone when he arrived back in Edenstown to tell us that he, as manager, would soon be opening a new school, and asked would any of us like to go on his staff. Both Cecil and myself hated the sight of Mr Samuel McVeigh, the inspector. As there was little hope that he'd accommodate us, by jumping head first into a cesspool, we decided to make the move.

When his reverence asked was either of us interested in the headmastership I told him that it was boring enough having to put in the day in school, without also having to investigate petty complaints, such as parents claiming that their darling child had brought home nits in his hair.

Cecil, however, who never previously had been offered the post of headmaster - and never would be again - accepted, though he did regret that being the boss would remove the enjoyment of sending in ridiculous excuses whenever he decided not to turn up for work.

To our surprise and delight, Rodney Dillon also wished to get a job in Dublin, as he expected that the day would come when his children would be attending university, and being on the spot would save the expense of paying for them in flats. Father Paddy appointed him as second-in-command to Mr Chuckleworth.

When Cecil called to the hotel where Julia worked to suggest that she should hand in her notice, as they would be moving to Dublin, where he would be donning the mantle of headmaster, she burst out laughing as she was sure he was pulling her leg.

'I'm not joking I really mean it.'

'You have no interest in teaching, never mind being a headmaster.'

'I didn't say I had.'

'Well then, why are you taking on a responsible job like that?'

'Julia dear! Don't you realise that for the first time in my life I'll be in a school where no headmaster can look down his nose at me.'

'You'll miss George.'

'No I won't.'

'Why? Did you fall out with him?'

'No. He's coming too. He's going to work under me.'

'Work under you, my eye! The only work he ever did was how to get by without working.'

'Won't it be a good idea to have somebody in the school worse than me. Won't it help to keep the heat off me!'

'Fair play to Father O'Halloran! He has more faith in you two tulips as teachers than I have. I hope the pair of you don't let him down.'

'Of course we will. We've every intention of doing so! Rodney's coming too.'

'Thanks be to the good God that there'll be at least one stable character in the school.'

'Are you implying that Rodney is a donkey?'

'I am because he'll have an ass as a head,' said she with a beaming smile, before asking would she have much trouble in getting a job in a Dublin hotel.

'Not at all. They're always looking for staff. You've only to read the ads in the daily papers to see that. Anyway, I've already asked Father Paddy to keep an eye out for you.'

'That's great. Will your promotion mean much extra money to us?'

'Not that much Julia, but I think enough for us to consider buying a wee house.'

'I'd love us to have a house of our own, instead of making somebody else rich, paying rent all our lives.'

#####

They sank themselves up to their necks in debt by buying a three-bedroomed bungalow looking straight out at the Irish Sea, with the golden strand only the breadth of the road away from their garden gate.

I asked them to accept my dog, and me as lodgers, because I'd sooner give money to them than to a landlady. Cecil said that he knew bloody well that I had no intention of paying them a brass farthing, but he was prepared to put up with me for the pleasure of having the company of Lazarus, but he'd have to find a second lodger to pay for the expense of having me as their first.

So, he drafted out the following ad which appeared in one evening paper, the other having refused it:

'Wanted - gentleman willing to pay exorbitant rent for room in fashionable, seaside district. Comfortable bed supplied - solely for sleeping on. Breakfast, and evening meals provided free of charge. Use of toilet: cover charge. Hot water for shaving will cost the current price of whiskey. Apply in person between the hours of 5, and 7 p.m. to Mr C. Chuckleworth, 'St Gerard's,' 19 Soldiers' Point, Rockmallen, Co Dublin.'

While we were having a cup of tea in the kitchen on the evening it was published I told him that none but a madman would reply to such a farcical ad.

'You've hit the nail on the head. That's exactly what I'm looking for. He'll want to be mad to pay the rent I'm asking.'

'And how much are you asking, assuming that you do get an interested client?'

'That's between me and Julia, but I'll tell you this much: it exactly equals the monthly repayments on the mortgage. Wouldn't it be great to hook a sucker to provide us with a free house!'

'We'll be in clover Cecil, if it comes off; but why did you put in those clauses about charging him for shaving, and relieving himself in the toilet?'

'Don't take them seriously. They're only there as a safety play. I've no intention of applying them unless I'm landed with someone who turns out to be a nasty customer, and I want to get rid of him. I'll shift him quickly when I go demanding an outlandish fee every time he sits on the weight-reducing seat.'

Just then there was a knock on the hall door.

'Don't tell me I've a bite already,' muttered Chuckleworth to himself as he went out to answer it.

On the doorstep was an immaculately dressed man, in a dark blue, double-breasted suit, and black shoes. He had long legs noticeably out of proportion to his short body, from the front of which hung a potbelly. His head was as bald as a goose's egg. He had a round, shiny face, lively, blue eyes, a distillery fan's nose, and an infectious grin.

'Hello! I called about the ad in this evening's paper. Do you happen to be Mr Chuckleworth?'

'I don't happen to be Mr Chuckleworth. It wasn't an accident. It was a planned conception.'

'Good! I'm glad to hear that you weren't an unwanted child. My name is Reynolds, Sylvester Reynolds. I'm pleased to meet you,' and he proffered his hand, which Cecil ignored.

'I don't know yet whether I'm pleased to meet you. Is that your Mercedes at the gate, or did you hire it for the evening to impress me?'

'Of course it's mine.'

'Show me your driver's licence and insurance!'

Mr Reynolds, obviously amused, produced the requested documents, which Mr C. solemnly inspected, and then handed them back with the lips of his hatchet-face pursed in thought.

'Have you plenty of money?'

'That's a very personal question,' answered he with a smile.

'No more personal than me letting you in under my roof to sleep in a bed next door to my wife. What's your occupation?'

'I am an editor. The editor of 'The Irish Chronicle.''

'Why do you want to live in my house? Can you not afford one of your own?'

'Indeed I have a house of my own, a fine big one at that. It's a long story. My family's reared. My wife has left me. She claims that I drink too much, that I prefer the bottle to her.'

'Do you?'

'I'm not sure. I thought I wouldn't miss her when she went. A house can be lonely when you're living on your own.'

'Why don't you keep a dog?'

'That wouldn't be fair. The dog would be lonely when I'd be out, as I am, most of the time.'

'Come on in! Come on down to the kitchen, and have a cup of tea...'

'This is George Ryan, a psychiatrist friend of mine.'

'That's very interesting, Mr Ryan. Delighted to meet you. My name is Reynolds, Sylvester Reynolds. I spent yesterday morning with a psychiatrist myself.'

'That too is very interesting,' remarked Cecil.

'Nothing serious. My doctor talked me in to going to him as he's convinced that I've a drink problem.'

'Don't mind him,' said I. 'I'm no psychiatrist. And I wouldn't try to fool anyone who has a drink problem. They spend enough time trying to fool themselves. That fellow there, Cecil, nearly met his death over drink. And I was a nervous wreck, a stuttering fool over drink. We both gave it up together a few months ago, with the help of a friend.'

'I must do something about it myself - soon,' said Sylvester, in the typical alcoholic's fashion of dismissing to the vague future that which should be tackled without delay.

While Cecil was making a fresh pot of tea for the visitor, I kept him in chat, and then, when it was ready, excused myself, to give them a chance to discuss their business.

Lazarus and I went for a walk along the beach. On our return the car was gone, and Cecil was in high glee.

'A decent man, a very decent man. I wish there were a few more like him in this world. He's after giving me a cheque for a month's rent in advance. Money's no object to him.'

'That's great news indeed, Cecil. There'll be no need for Julia to work now at all.'

'You must be joking! Why do you think I married her! Is it for her to be sitting on her backside all day, wondering how much she should spend on perforated lace curtains, and out of date antiques!'

'It's only natural for her to want to have her house nicely furnished.'

'She'll get twice as much satisfaction out of furnishing her house nicely if she earns the money for it herself.'

'There's a lot in what you say. Besides, Father Paddy did go to the trouble of getting her the job. I wonder what she'll think of Sylvester. He strikes me as being a lonely kind of a person.'

'That's what has brought him here. Seeking company he is. He told me he doesn't know what to do with himself when he goes home at night. Most nights he doesn't go home at all. He stays in hotels. He's browned off with them. They're too impersonal.'

'Well Cecil, we'll provide the company free of charge, as long as he pays the mortgage.'

'Aye indeed. He told me he liked my ad; that I've a good sense of humour. I might try my hand at the writing sometime.'

'If you were as good at writing stories as you are at writing cheques for the bookies, you'd make a fortune.'

'You needn't talk. You didn't back a winner this three weeks.'

Julia arrived home then from her job in the nearby 'Annaverna Hotel,' and had to be told all about the new lodger. She was glad that he wouldn't be taking up residence for a few days, as it would give her a chance to buy the bed, and get the room ready.

#####

Having appointed six of his friends to teaching posts in the new school, Father Paddy sought candidates for the last post via the press. Snowed under with applications, he decided to set up an interview board consisting of himself, down-to-earth Rodney, and less than enthusiastic Cecil, who claimed that one might as well judge a cock by the way he crows as a teacher by the way he talks.

So Mr Chuckleworth took little or no interest in the proceedings as the various candidates drifted in and out of the interrogation office, until there entered the last applicant, one bottle-shouldered, pudding-faced individual by the name of Dick Sharkey - a man whom Cecil immediately recognised as a bluebottle from the ointment of his past life; a man for whom he harboured a deep resentment; a man who, according to my friend, was blessed with the ideal qualities to be elected permanent president of 'The Irish Hypocrites' Club.'

They had soldiered together - very much apart - in the same

school in their early teaching days. Cecil had fourth class which each year was passed on to Sharkey in fifth. 'Sham' - as Sharkey was derisively known to both his colleagues and pupils - used to tell Cecil to his face that he was extremely pleased with the standard of the annual class he received. Behind his back he would inform the headmaster, the parents, the parish priest, and the inspector, that Chuckleworth's class always knew less at the end of their year with him than when they initially went under his control.

Tales used to be carried back to Cecil that Sham was forever running him down in relation to the ignorance of his class. Chuckleworth didn't waste his breath tackling him about his backbiting, instead nursed a resentment for the toad. Eventually Cecil moved on to another school, and for some twenty odd years never laid eyes on Sharkey, but he heard from an acquaintance of his that Sham had got two young girls into trouble before marrying a widow woman twice his age for her self-confessed creditable bank account, which turned out to be an overdraft.

'Hello, reverend Father. It's a grand day, reverend Father. It was very good of you to call me for the interview. Ah me ould segocia, Cecil! it's great to see you! I hear you're going to be the new headmaster. An excellent choice, reverend Father.'

'Don't ould segocia me! To you I'm Mr Chuckleworth. Get that straight before you tell another lie, Sham.'

'Sorry, Mr Chuckleworth. I thought with us being old friends you wouldn't mind the familiarity.'

'We were never friends, old or young, you walking hypocrite.'

While Sham's mouth was opening in painful astonishment Cecil continued:

'You heard that I'm the new headmaster. That's true. I heard that you were unlucky both in love, and in marriage! Is that true?'

'Cecil! You are totally out of order,' declared Father Paddy. 'This is supposed to be an interview to help choose an assistant for the school, not a meeting convened for you to work off your resentments on the applicants.'

'Sorry Father! Sorry Sham! I won't ask you any more personal questions. It's just that I felt like vomiting the moment you crawled across the saddle of the door.'

Sharkey turned appealing eyes towards Father Paddy, who commanded Cecil to behave in a Christian manner or else leave the room.

'I won't leave the room. You and Rodney asked all the questions up till now. It's about time I got in on the act.'

'You'll have to be fair, Cecil. That's that! You can ask all the questions you wish as long as they're relevant.'

'Alright Father. Leave me to it! And now Mr Sharkey, why did you apply for this job? Is it because your present parish priest has at last realised that you are a fraud?'

'I have excellent references from that reverend gentleman.'

'That's true,' said Father Paddy. 'They are first-class references, the best I've seen.'

'A sure sign that he wants to get rid of him,' asserted Cecil.

'He doesn't want to get rid of me. He'll miss me very much if I leave. I'm his right-hand man in all his parochial affairs.'

'It's a teacher we want - not a craw-thumper of a parish beadle,' countered Cecil.

'Would you be willing to take the church choir?' asked Rodney, who suspected that he himself was going to be landed with that unre-munerative, time-consuming job.

'I'd be delighted to. I love music.'

'Would you take it every day?' enquired Cecil.

'I would, yes. No problem.'

'I mean including Saturdays, and Sundays?'

'Yes, yes. I'd have no objection.'

'And what about every night?'

'Ah now, Cecil!' said Father Paddy, who was trying to smother a grin, by working his face into a solemn contortion.

'Alright Father, I'll skip the night-duty aspect of the job. You didn't tell us yet, Mr Sharkey, why you want to get away from where you are. There must be some reason. Did you leave a bun in some oven?'

'Mr Chuckleworth I'll treat that question as a joke.'

'It would be no joke if you did.'

'Mr Chuckleworth! I'm originally from Dublin, and my sole rea-son for applying for this job is because I'd like to get back to my native city.'

'I suppose you didn't ask the natives do they want you back!'

'Don't put any heed in him, Mr Sharkey,' advised Rodney. 'How would you deal with disruptive pupils in your class?'

'I'd send them to the headmaster for punishment.'

'You have a nerve,' snarled Cecil. 'Do you think that I was born to solve your problems.'

'Sorry Mr Chuckleworth, but that's what's usually done in other schools when children get out of hand.'

'You can take it as certain, Mr Sharkey, that what's done in other schools won't be done in ours,' which remark caused Father Paddy to raise his eyebrows.

'Well then Mr Chuckleworth,' said Sharkey playing it foolproof as he thought, 'I'd do exactly as you'd advise with disruptive children.'

'Supposing I told you to kick the arse of them! Would you follow that advice?'

'No! I would not!'

'Why?'

'Because then I'd have to deal with disruptive parents.'

'Sound reasoning,' remarked Father Paddy, as he and Rodney smiled at Cecil getting the wrong end of the stick for a change.

Then his reverence asked Mr Dick for his views on the teaching of religion.

'Of paramount importance to me.'

'Are you a practising Catholic?' asked Rodney.

'Of course I am. First things first with me.'

'What do you practise?' asked Cecil.

'Christian charity.'

'Does that include your tongue?'

'I never said a bad word about anyone in my life.'

'Not within their hearing,' was Cecil's final shot.

'Alright Mr Sharkey. That will be all,' said his reverence. 'Thanks for coming.'

When Sham departed a discussion started about who was the most suitable candidate. Cecil claimed that they were all ideal bar Sharkey. However Father Paddy plumped for him, pointing out that he had the best references, and the best inspectors' reports. As Rodney - with the church choir in mind - backed him, Cecil had no chance.

Thus Sham Sharkey was appointed to the last post in Rockmallen National School.

#####

On a showery April afternoon Sylvester Reynolds, the editor, arrived to take up residence in the Chuckleworth's bungalow. After our evening meal we spent the night sitting around the kitchen table, chatting, getting to know each other by exchanging views, and swapping experiences.

From the start Julia, Cecil, and myself took to him, a man after our own hearts, who placed no value on material things, only out to knock the maximum enjoyment out of the NOW moment. Yet, underneath his hard-man, roguish sense of humour, he was a sad, serious person.

He revealed a lot about himself.

Even before he was married, his wife-to-be used to have frequent clashes with him re the amount of liquor he stowed away at a session. This despite the fact that she herself could knock pints back like a darts player.

The nuptial noose wasn't long around his neck when he realised that she was even more unreasonable than he had anticipated.

'Imagine,' said he, 'she wanted me to buy a carpet for the flat! To spend good money on something for people to walk on! and me a junior reporter, barely earning enough to fulfil my drinking commitments!'

Seldom did she go to the pub with him, and if she did agree to go, she always prefaced the venture with a lengthy lecture on the merits of sobriety.

'Yet as sure as you're sitting in this kitchen, she'd always be the first drunk. Was that fair?'

Cecil declared it to be a travesty of justice.

She didn't become really contrary, however, until after the first child was born. She expected him to stay in now and again to mind the baby, as if he had nothing better to do.

One Saturday morning she rose early, told him that she was going off for a few hours to visit her sister, and that she wasn't bringing the child, that he, for a change would have to mind it.

To show that she was in earnest, she planked their one, and only in the bed beside him. To prove that she didn't trust him, she had already, while he was fast asleep, removed all his trousers to the custody of an understanding neighbour across the street.

Sylvester played with that child for a full 20 minutes before the drought came at him.

He did then what any genuine drinking man would do: got up; went to dress himself; was puzzled that his trousers weren't in their usual parking place; searched the house from top to bottom, including under the kitchen sink, and the coal bunker; found nothing but an odd sock that had been missing for months.

Undaunted by the setback, he put on a clean pair of trunks; the sock he found, and its brother, plus suspenders; a blue shirt with a tie to match; polished his shoes; threw on his jacket; donned his soft hat, with the brim as usual dipping down over his eyes; tied the child in the pram; gave it a pound of butter to play with; and wheeled it out the hall door without looking up or down.

He did confess that he was a tad shy when passing by people on the street. Some of them seemed to be embarrassed. What should he have done! Stay at home in bed just to please the neighbours!

One timid old lady, who had never let a male near her in her life, was heading towards him, thinking that it was a grand morning for that time of year, when she noticed that he had no trousers on him. She stopped to double check her facts; then scurried at a dangerous speed to the far side of the street.

A bright young thing approaching him went into a fit of the giggles. The giggles stopped when he asked her was she in the mood.

Having tied the pram to a lamppost, he was about to go in the pub door, when who came along but 'Scruples' Spicer, the self-appointed watchdog of the morals of the parish. Spicer wanted to know why Mr Reynolds wasn't wearing his trousers. He was told that Mr Reynolds wasn't wearing them because it was his wife's birthday.

Spicer next wanted to know had Mr Reynolds just escaped from the local lunatic asylum. The opinion was expressed that saner people than 'Scruples' were in there already.

Then, when Spicer was asked would he provide Mr Reynolds with a few pounds to get drunk, he stated that he was going straightaway to report the scandal to the parish priest. He was advised to go to hell instead.

In the pub itself Sylvester got nothing but sympathy for the dreadful deed his wife had done in her attempt to deprive him of the pleasure of a few jars on a Saturday morning.

Offers to obtain a pair of pants for him on loan were made, and rejected, Sylvester being of the belief that the more embarrassment his wife suffered, the less likely she would be to run off with his trousers again.

As he had anticipated, on her way home from her sister's, she recognised the child in the pram parked outside the pub, and concluded that he must be inside. As he had also foreseen, she popped her head in to find out if he was wearing one of her frocks.

'Ah, there you are Edwina! I'll be with you now. Good luck lads. And thanks again for the offer of the trousers. It was much appreciated.

As soon as she got him outside the door she went on the attack.

'You've made a public disgrace of yourself. You'll be the talk of the parish.'

'I won't be the talk of the parish. You'll be the talk of the parish. They'll all be saying: "What kind of a woman is Sylvester Reynolds married to! She won't even let him wear his trousers."'

'I might be the talk of the parish, but only because they'll all be saying that I was an awful eejit to marry a buffoon like you! Will you look at the state that child's in! Both himself, and his clothes covered in butter!'

'What did you want me to do! Bring him in to the pub, and have him sitting on my knee, while I'm holding a pint with one hand, and him with the other. Anyway, surely you don't want me to break the law. He's under the age for entering licensed premises.'

'You've always an answer, haven't you! Well you can go back in to that pub and stay there till you rot. I'm not walking down the street with you.'

'Go ahead. I'll walk behind you. I wouldn't want to embarrass you for the world.'

After further argument and vain pleas for him to go back in for another pint, while she'd go, and get his trousers, they set off down the squinting street in Indian file, with her wishing the ground would open, and swallow her, and him respectfully doffing his hat to every woman gifted with the boldness to stare at his lower regions.

'That was a mean thing you did to your poor wife,' said Julia.

'How would you like if I collected all your panties, and gave them to the postman to mind?' asked Cecil.

'I wouldn't care as long as the weather was warm,' answered

she.

'I'd pick a cold day,' said Cecil.

Everybody laughed. Then Sylvester asked Cecil to tell us about the most embarrassing experience of his life.

'Asking me to do that, Sylvester, is in effect an admission that you were embarrassed merely because you walked down a street half naked!'

'Of course I was. Wouldn't you be!'

'I'm not so sure about that,' answered Cecil. 'More often than not I enjoy the excitement of being in an embarrassing situation. I remember being at a wedding where I should have been ashamed of my life of what I had done, but it didn't cost me a thought.

'I'll give you the background to the catastrophe. After qualifying from the training college, for various reasons, I failed to get a teaching post for some months, so I was delegated to step into my father's hairdressing shoes while he went visiting relations in Canada.

'As ours' was the only barber's shop in the village there wasn't a slump in business on my appointment as temporary hair-chopper, and face-ripper.

'On the eve of the wedding I decided to shut the shop, and go drinking with the groom, Andy Lawless, and his friends. A good day we had. And too good a night! We were all as drunk as a fiddler's bitch when we parted at about three in the morning.

'Ten minutes after me going in home a rap came on the door.

'It was the groom himself.'

'What's wrong Andy?'

'Cecil! I completely forgot to get the haircut, and shave for my big day tomorrow.'

'Today Andy - if you want to be accurate. Come in. I won't let you down.'

'At the best of times I was useless as a barber, but on this particular occasion everything was against me.

'When I went to light the Tilly lamp I found there was no oil. So I had to make do with a candle sitting on each side of him.

'The scissors were nowhere to be found. So my mother's big sewing shears had to be called into service.'

'That's a great growth of hair you have,' said I to put him at his ease, as I lopped a lump out of it.

161

'I let it go too long, Cecil.'

'Don't worry about that,' said I, as I took a huge clipe from the other side to balance things up. I kept on balancing, and rebalancing until there was only a wisp of hair sticking out here, and there. I left it at that or else he would have been as bald as a coot.

'Now,' asked I courteously, 'would you like a sup of oil to give it a good sheen?'

'No. I don't use the stuff.'

'Andy, it's not worth my while lighting the fire to get hot water for only the one shave. Won't cold water do you?'

'It will do me rightly,' said he obligingly.

'I soaped him up. Honed the cutthroat razor, and then set about stropping it. As he watched me cutting the strop to ribbons he anxiously asked:

'Are you sure you're sober enough to shave me?"

'Are you sure you're sober enough to sit still there, in the one spot, while I'm at you?' asked I, as I waved the open blade in front of his face.

'I am,' said he shifting uncomfortably in the chair.

'I nicked him here. I'm nicked him there. I'm nicked him everywhere. As a result the bride was only in the halfpenny place throughout the nuptial festivities, as everybody was talking about the botched haircut, and shave I gave the groom for his big day.

'The most vexed person there was my mother. She was nearly foaming at the mouth with anger, and got the parish priest to confront me.

'You'll have to take the pledge for life,' said he.

'I won't take it for life, Father. I'll take it for 40 years."

'Did you actually take the pledge for forty years?' asked Julia.

'I certainly did not, Julia. I said 40 years to get my mother off my back, but I made the mental reservation that I really meant 40 minutes. And what's more I kept it for the 40 minutes.'

'You're not going to tell me Cecil, are you' said Sylvester, 'that you were not embarrassed at that wedding, with everybody talking about the notorious job you did on the groom?'

'I was not in the least embarrassed. It did me good to look at him. I was highly amused. I'll admit that I was annoyed at my mother for coming the heavy on me, but I was well used to that all my life.'

'Changing the subject, Sylvester,' said I, 'and going back to your escapade in the pub with no trousers, it seems to me that you would not have done what you did that morning unless you were dependent on drink even as a young man. Despite that you rose to being the editor of a national newspaper. No mean feat!'

'Perhaps I was lucky in a way, in getting in with the right people, but in the newspaper business nobody passes any remarks about how heavily you drink as long as you're able to do your job. Anyway, did you ever yet meet a journalist who wasn't fond of the bottle?'

'Not many,' I conceded.

'You didn't tackle your garden yet,' remarked Sylvester to my mate, as he stood up, and walked over to look out the kitchen window.

'Ah no. That's true. I haven't got around to it yet,' answered Chuckleworth, who hadn't the remotest interest in gardening, and couldn't care less if the weeds were growing a mile high over his house.

'I'm very fond of gardening. A most satisfying hobby,' declared Sylvester.

'Is that so!' said Cecil.

'I love it. Nothing more relaxing. I love to watch things growing. I'll do the garden for you if you like.'

'Oh that would be great,' enthused Julia. 'I'll help you with it, when the rough work is done.'

'Wait now,' said Cecil, 'I was going to do it myself, but seeing you are so fond of gardening, Sylvester, I won't be selfish. I won't deprive you of the pleasure of digging it; but, as you well know, every man has to pay for his pleasures in this life. How much are you prepared to pay me per week for letting you do it?'

'I might look like a cabbage, but I'm not that green,' replied Sylvester with a grin.

'Don't mind him,' said Julia, 'we'll do it together, but as sure as God made little apples, when it's finished and looking lovely, he'll claim all the credit for himself.'

#####

On the morning the new Rockmallen national school opened for the intake of pupils everything went smoothly for the maiden head-master, Mr Chuckleworth, for the first few minutes. He was standing at the main door, twirling a bunch of keys in his hand, and discussing with his staff the merits of the champion jockey, Lester Piggott. While he was passionately proclaiming that Piggott could continue riding winners until he was ninety, unless he lost his nerve, a woman with a four-year-old in tow, came up behind him, and tapped him on the shoulder.

'Excuse me! Are you the headmaster?'

He turned his cross-eyed, hatchet-face towards her.

'What made you think I'm the headmaster?'

'A woman pointed you out to me.'

'Tell that woman to point the finger at somebody else.'

'I only wanted to ask you about my son.'

'What do I know about your son! I never laid eyes on him till this minute.'

'I only wanted to ask you about the money for his books.'

'I'm not going to give him the money for his books.'

'I didn't ask you to pay for his books. I just wanted to know the price of them,' said she with her temper rising.

'That's a commercial question. I only discuss business matters when I'm in my office.'

'And when will you be in your office?'

'Never! If I can help it. Good day to you Mam.'

He left her there incredulously gaping at him, and ordered us to bring in the pupils, and lock all the doors.

Sham Sharkey deferentially mentioned to him that many of the parents had come specifically to consult Chuckleworth about their children starting in the new school. Cecil told him that he had better things to do than be gossiping about children, and that Sham too, if he didn't get in quickly, would be locked out with the rest of the rabble.

It took the whole of that day to sort out the 321 pupils, and allocate them to their classes. Cecil allowed most of us to have our say in the dividing up of the classes. As he himself put it, he wanted 'to be seen to be democratic.' His only proviso was that he was to have the smallest class and Sharkey the biggest because he had the biggest mouth. After that he didn't care what happened.

As matters were manipulated there were only 11 in Cecil's sixth class, whereas there were 64 in Sharkey's infant class. Sham was so incensed that he tore off his bowing and scraping mask, and berated Chuckleworth, telling him that he was breaking every rule in the book by giving him six times as many pupils as he himself took.

Cecil enthusiastically agreed with him, and suggested to Sharkey that he had sufficient grounds to resign on the spot. Furthermore he informed Sharkey that he'd accept his resignation without shedding a tear. Sham failed to come up with an answer to that cheerful admission, and went off slobbering to himself that there was no justice in this world.

#####

On moving to Rockmallen, Cecil, and I had discussed inspectors, and resolved to do enough work to keep them off our backs. I had had enough of pressure from them to do me all my life. So, for my own peace of mind, I followed through with my resolution. Whereas Cecil proved that he had not the willpower to muster up the motivation to do anything in school except solve cryptic crosswords, and study the horses. Therefore he was ill-prepared, when, within two months of him becoming a headmaster, Inspector Vincent Ward invaded his pitch.

It didn't help matters, that Cecil, after their introductory exchange of identities, expressed the opinion that Ward, with his thin-faced, hawk-nosed, eagle-eyed features, should never be let in to a school, as the children might take fright, and run home to their mammies.

'You're asking for trouble making personal remarks about my appearance.'

'I never had anything except trouble from the likes of you.'

'That's because you're a loafer.'

'You're guilty of prejudging me. How do you know but that everything in the garden is lovely?'

'Before I came here I checked up on your record as a teacher, and unless there has been a miraculous change wrought in your capacity to work, I'm sure I'll quickly find out that you haven't done a tap from the day this school opened.'

Then he asked Cecil what the total number of pupils on the rolls was.

'321.'

'You've dealt yourself a good hand so. You've only seven in your class unless I'm not able to count!'

'You're not able to count, because there's one out in the toilet, and three didn't come in today.'

'I'm not surprised that they didn't come in. Nevertheless you have eleven out of 321. That leaves 310 allotted to the six other teachers. Don't you know that the first duty of a headmaster is to see that there is a fair distribution of the numbers among the staff?'

'That's news to me. When I started first I had 63 in two classes, and the headmaster had none in any class.'

'He was a walking headmaster I presume,' said Ward.

'I didn't ask him to walk,' cheeked Chuckleworth.

'Maybe you'll be getting your own walking papers sooner than you think,' threatened the inspector, who then ordered Cecil to show him his weekly note, his monthly progress records, and his yearly schemes.

My dear reader, in case you are lucky enough not to be a primary teacher, I should tell you that before each school year begins, each primary teacher is expected to set out in writing a general plan of all he proposes to teach in each subject in that year. Then, before each week begins, he is supposed to write out in detail all that he intends to teach in each subject during that week. At the end of each month it is his duty to enter in a special book all he has taught for that month. Need I tell you that Mr Chuckleworth had no weekly notes, no progress records, and no yearly schemes.

'I left them at home,' said Chuckleworth.

'Go home for them! I'll wait here,' ordered Ward, with the nostrils of his bird nose twitching.

'Now that I think of it: the wife accidentally lit the fire with them yesterday morning.'

Ward twisted his face into a sneer of disbelief, and stared at Cecil.

'If you don't believe me I'll go home, and bring her in to you. She'll swear that there is no word of a lie in what I'm saying.'

'I've no doubt that she will,' said Ward in a tone dripping with sarcasm.

'Are you insinuating that my wife is a perjurer!'

'I'm not insinuating anything,' answered Ward, who felt that

Chuckleworth was working him on to unsafe ground.

'Well then, you had better watch what you're saying about her!'

'I'm not interested in your wife...'

'She's not interested in you either,' interjected Cecil.

'I'm not interested in your wife,' repeated Ward, 'but I am interested in what you have taught these seven pupils for the past two months.'

'Go ahead, and examine them,' said Chuckleworth defiantly, while hoping that Ward would hit on something taught them by their previous teachers, but Mr Hawk-Nose was too clever by half to be fooled that way.

'What have you learned since you came in to Mr Chuckleworth's class?'

They looked at each other, and began laughing.

'So that's the way it is!' commented Ward as he glared over at Cecil, who at that moment was vowing vengeance on those charges who had betrayed him with a snigger.

Ward then launched into a series of questions on the fundamentals of every subject on the sixth class programme. Even Cecil was surprised at their ignorance.

He stormed out of Cecil's class in to mine where he was also expecting to find a long list of shortcomings, but I had realised that after the to-do I had had with the inspectors back in Edenstown I'd be a marked man, and had done enough for him to declare my work 'satisfactory.'

When we were all comparing notes after he had left the school it was no consolation to Cecil to learn that the other teachers got on famously with Ward, and considered him to be a fair-minded man. Sharkey asserted that he had shown great sympathy to him 'with his exceptionally large class.'

'You and your large class ought to be tied together, and thrown in the river,' was the only retort that Cecil could come up with in retaliation for that dig.

At home in the bungalow that evening the atmosphere was funereal thanks to Cecil's melancholic mood. He, normally a voracious meat eater, refused to touch the steak and onions that Julia put in front of him. Both of us did our level best to cheer him up, but we might as well have been talking to the wall, as he was still deep in depression when at half-ten Sylvester breezed in nicely jarred.

Cecil spouted out to him the happenings of the day.

Having listened to his harangue about children, parents, and above all inspectors, Sylvester said to him, 'It's blatantly obvious that you were never cut out to be a teacher.'

'Tell me something I don't know,' said Cecil peevishly.

'Is there any chance that you'd give him a job with "The Irish Chronicle,"' asked Julia.

'Certainly! I could manage to fit him in somewhere,' answered Sylvester warmly.

'That's great,' declared Cecil, his face lighting up, and him sitting up straight in his chair. 'I always had a yen for the writing, and a hatred of teaching, but before I surrender my job as headmaster I'll have a go at knocking a pension out of the department of education.'

'You haven't a hope,' said his wife. 'You haven't enough service.'

'Julia dear, don't underestimate my ingenuity.'

'Cecil dear, what do you mean?'

'Did you never hear of teachers being retired on a disability pension?'

'That only applies to people who go blind or deaf or something.'

'And what about the unfortunate teachers who go mad?' enquired he of his adoring wife.

'You're not mad,' laughed she.

'Maybe not at the moment, but I've an uneasy feeling that I'm going to be afflicted with a temporary bout of insanity.'

From that night until the day he stopped teaching, Chuckleworth, in public, was a changed man - a confirmed lunatic.

The first sign of his personality disorder was evident the following morning. On his way to work he called to the local post office, and - permission having been granted - he pinned to the notice-board the following item:

WILL ANY PERSON GIVE A GOOD HOME TO A SEX-STARVED TOM-CAT (ONLY ONE PREVIOUS OWNER). APPLY WITH REFERENCES TO MR. TOM CHUCKLE-WORTH, HEADMASTER OF ROCKMALLEN NATIONAL SCHOOL.

On his way home that evening he parked his car on the crown of the road in the middle of the busy main street, got out, accosted an elderly nun, who was window shopping, abused her about the outrageous behaviour of her twin daughters, and warned her that if she didn't exercise more control over them he'd have them drummed out of his school, and sent back to Ireland.

And so within one day tongues were wagging that the headmaster had gone off his rocker.

A smart aleck gentleman, by the way wanting to buy the cat, but in reality intending to poke fun at Cecil, called to the school, and enquired about its breed.

Mr Chuckleworth informed him that the cat had escaped from his clutches, and asked him would he rush to the post office, and change the notice to the following:

LOVESICK TOM-CAT HAS STRAYED FROM GOOD HOME. DO NOT APPROACH HIM IN DAYLIGHT. ANSWERS TO THE NAME ELVIS. SUBSTANTIAL REWARD FOR INFORMATION LEADING TO HIS DETENTION.

Signed: Tom Chuckleworth.

Next he had the school playground ploughed up, and drilled for a potato crop. When Jack Rabbite, the farmer who did the job approached him for his fee Mr Chuckleworth told him that he had had second thoughts about the scheme, and would prefer a crop of onions instead, and asked him to convert the drills into beds for onions. Mr Rabbite told him that that was a crazy idea, and he again demanded the few pounds due to him.

Cecil dug in his heels, and said:

'No beds, no fee!'

'If you don't pay me, I'll tell every soul in the parish that you're the meanest man I ever met, and that you're as mad as a hatter.'

'I defy you, to do that,' challenged Cecil.

'You'll soon find out whether I will or not,' said Mr Rabbite, before he turned, and walked off in disgust.

As you will remember, Cecil hated the sight of Sharkey. He never made any effort to hide his hostility; nor did he ever enter his classroom. So Sham was surprised when one morning the headmaster landed in to him with a lollipop stuck in his mouth. He was even more surprised when Cecil offered him a suck, while the children exploded in laughter.

'No thanks. I don't eat between meals.'

'Ah go on! Have a suck. You'll love it.'

Sharkey yielded to his superior's wish, and took a suck. He declared that it was delicious. Cecil told him to finish it, but ordered him to return the stick to him when he had bared it to the bone, because he was going to bring it home to beat the lard out of his wife, as she was getting too fat.

Sham ignored the domestic titbit, and remarked that it was a lovely day, which prompted Cecil to tell him that he was a lovely man. Sham beamed with delight as he graciously accepted the compliment. Cecil then expressed a wish to hold Sham's pudgy hand, to which request Sharkey reluctantly agreed, as he shyly looked around at the children. However, he withdrew it quickly when the headmaster accused him of being a child molester, and asserted that he was not fit to be in charge of infants, even worse, unless he put a brake on his animal urges, he was doomed to roast in hell for most of eternity. Sharkey ventured the view that Chuckleworth was being unreasonable, with which opinion Cecil concurred, and then walked out of the room.

That evening Dick Sharkey wrote to both the bishop, and the inspector, colourfully describing his headmaster's bonkers behaviour that morning, and telling them that they could rest assured that Chuckleworth was now as nutty as a fruitcake.

After roll call one morning, a parent, named Ignatius Dooley, who was regarded as the most fervent christian in the parish because of the hours he spent daily on his knees in the church, called to the school to consult Cecil about his only child - a son.

A son on whom both the mother, and he doted. A son who could do no wrong. A son, who, despite the over-protective attitude of his parents, remained a solid, sensible, likeable chap, with brains to burn.

That son, the previous evening, at prayers before dismissal, had thoughtlessly blessed himself with his left hand!

Chuckleworth was 'horrified.'

170

'Where did this pagan come from! Was there no religion taught in his home! What kind of parents had he! What evil influence were they working on him that he couldn't even bless himself correctly! When did they start practising voodoo! Drastic action would have to be taken! Atonement would have to be made to God for the dreadful deed which was almost as unholy, almost as obscene, as girls coming to school in ankle socks!

'Nothing but a written apology addressed to God, signed by the mother, and countersigned by the father, would prevent the conscientious headmaster from having him barred from the school for a year, and a day!'

The unkind references to the parents' religious deficiencies were repeated word for word to the mother, and again to the father when he came home from work.

The mother was on for thrashing Cecil. As the father was of a light build, and Chuckleworth was not unlike a gorilla in both the body, and the arms, he declared that he was a man for peace at all costs.

Thus, as I said earlier, he called to the school to 'consult' Cecil about his son.

'I'm no consultant. I wouldn't have the cheek to charge their fees.'

'Well then, Mr Chuckleworth, maybe you'll advise me about him.'

'The only advice I'll give you is to produce the apology before I wring your neck.'

'Now Mr Chuckleworth, a reasonable man like you wouldn't use force!'

'I won't use more force than is necessary,' promised Cecil as he took up a boxer's stance, with his left fist tapping Dooley on the nose.

'Mr Chuckleworth what exactly do you want me to do?' cried the terrified Dooley.

'Calm down,' roared Chuckleworth into his face, 'there's no need for the two of us to go mad.'

'Yes Mr Chuckleworth. You're right Mr Chuckleworth.'

'Where's the written apology?'

'I'll do it for you this minute.'

'And what about the wife?'

'She won't sign it. She refused point-blank.'

'That being the case, you'll have to do a public act of penance. In you must come to my classroom to promise my pupils that your family will give up the practice of witchcraft.'

While Cecil went to open the door Dooley twisted, and made a beeline for the gate. The headmaster didn't go in pursuit as he reckoned that he had done enough to earn another letter to the authorities.

#####

In case nobody had yet thought of complaining to the Minister for Education about him, Cecil, himself decided to contact that august personage -

Rockmallen National School,
County Dublin.
Date as postmark.

Dear Minister,

I wish to refer to your blackboard policy. Why do you choose black! Don't you know that black is associated with dirt, with anger, with death?

Don't you know that staring at empty blackboards all day cannot be good for the mental health of the inmates of your schools?

Consequently, I demand a supply of white blackboards.

To save carriage fees, compel that useless inspector, Ward, to carry them out on his back. It will be the first honest day's work he ever did.

Incidentally, I don't want to give scandal, but I saw him sneaking in to a public toilet the other day with my tom-cat under his arm.

Your obedient servant,
Cecil Chuckleworth.

As Cecil knew there was no chance that the minister would answer his demand for the white blackboards, he decided to take matters in to his own hands by that night painting all the school blackboards white, which caused consternation the following morning among most of the members of the staff. They gathered in the corridor to discuss the sanity of the magician who had caused their black blackboards to vanish.

'What's wrong! Why are you not working?' asked Chuckleworth, as he stuck his head out his door after hearing the commotion in the corridor.

They explained that their blackboards were now useless as they had nothing but white chalk, and so they would be severely hampered in their work.

He lent them a sympathetic ear, and told them not to worry about it, that he'd solve their problem.

Straightaway a telegram was sent to Ward, the inspector:

'Urgently required in Rockmallen National School a bucket full of black chalk.'

#####

The headmaster next turned his spotlight on the parents, to see could he unearth any juicy facts about their private lives, by issuing to each pupil the questionnaire hereunder printed, with instructions to fill it in that night, and bring it to the school on the morrow:

MARKET SURVEY ON MARITAL RELATIONSHIPS IN THE PARISH OF ROCKMALLEN

When your Mammy is out does your Daddy often fix the fuse for the nice lady next door?

When Daddy and Mammy are fighting what do they throw at each other?

If glassware who picks up the pieces?

When they have made up, do they send you a long distance on a message?

If you had been at the wedding ceremony would you have advised them not to get married?

Give a full description of the stolen goods in your house.

Signed: Chuckleworth (Mr)

The majority of the parents were less than happy with the questionnaire. That evening, a local councillor, Ray Gunne, who had made several fruitless attempts to become a member of parliament for the constituency, decided to cash in on their disquiet, by calling a public meeting to be held that night in the local hall. He toured the parish with a loudspeaker urging all parents to attend.

Cecil, gifted with enough insight to know that people often tore him apart behind his back, felt that it would make a nice change to have them doing so to his face. So he went along to the thronged hall.

He was challenged at the door by Gunne.

'You've no right to come in here, Chuckleworth! This meeting is only for parents.'

'What proof have you that I'm not the father of half the children of this parish?' said Cecil, before giving him a disrespectful shove as he walked past him.

Prior to Cecil's arrival, the hall had been alive with the clamorous chatter of angry parents discussing the questionnaire, and the author thereof. His entry caused a deathly silence to descend upon the place. One could sense the hostile tension thrilling the air as he casually walked up the centre aisle.

When he was halfway up, a heavily-built woman, with a low-slung arse, who was beside herself with indignation at the nerve of Chuckleworth coming to the meeting, jumped to her feet, and screeched at him:

'Well you have a cheek!'

'No, I have four - the same as yourself - Mam.'

'You're a vulgar unmannerly tramp,' yelled her husband, who had a face like a shaven monkey.

Chuckleworth stared him in the eye for a full twenty seconds before admitting:

'You have dispelled all my doubts about Darwin's theory of evolution.'

'We'll throw him out,' shouted Monkey-Face's drinking buddy.

'You will not. There'll be no breach of the peace while I'm here,' stated the local sergeant - a happily married man with two children at the school. He was one of the few to see a trace of humour in Cecil's questionnaire.

At this point the councillor mounted the stage, and called for order. The meeting was about to begin. The headmaster made his way to a vacant seat in the middle of a row, whereupon those on either side of him stood up, and went elsewhere.

'How did you know that I like plenty of elbow room! Thank you indeed for your consideration,' remarked Cecil.

The self-appointed chairman began his speech:

'It saddens me to look at you people...'

'I don't blame you!' commented Cecil in a stage whisper.

Ignoring Chuckleworth, the small-town politician started again:

'It saddens me to look at you people gathered here tonight, when you could be, when you should be at home relaxing in the bosom ('Here! Here!' shouted Cecil) of your family; but you considered it your duty, and I considered it my duty, to take steps to put a stop to this raving lunatic's mad antics in our midst'.

Cecil stood up and bowed to the four points of the compass.

Dramatically Gunne pulled the questionnaire from his trousers pocket, and waved it high above his head.

'Never before in the history of my existence did I read such a scurrilous document. Even a madman, and I have no doubt that he is mad ('Here! Here!' interjected Cecil); even a madman cannot be allowed to get away with this obscene attempt to invade our family privacy.'

'Don't forget that he ploughed up our children's playground,' shouted a voice from the back.

'That madman cannot be allowed to continue as headmaster of our school,' yelled Monkey-Face.

'How will we get rid of him?' asked a small woman with a large family.

'We'll form a committee,' answered Gunne.

'With you as the chairman,' proposed Cecil.

That's what they did do. They formed a committee. And Chuckleworth went home quite pleased that so many people were willing to help him get a disability pension.

Throughout his teaching career Cecil had borne an intense dislike for inspectors. Now for a change he was anticipating with relish the inevitable visit of one of those gentlemen who look at life through a keyhole.

As luck would have it, on the day that Hawk-Nose Ward arrived at the school, the headmaster was attired in his green slippers, blue pyjamas, brilliant red dressing gown, and yellow nightcap.

'Why are you wearing those gaudy garments?' asked the inspector in a querulous tone.

'To cover my nakedness,' answered Chuckleworth.

'I don't like them,' snapped Ward.

'Which colour do you not like?'

'None of them.'

'Obviously we have different tastes. I don't like anything you're wearing either.'

'I didn't ask you to comment on my attire.'

'I don't remember asking you to comment on mine.'

'You should be properly dressed in your working clothes?'

'My wife, Julia, claims that my pyjamas are my working clothes.'

'I'm glad to learn that you're not always idle,' retorted Ward before opening an attack on a new front.

'Show me your weekly notes, and your yearly schemes.'

'You're a very thorough inspector. Ha, Ha.'

(Chuckleworth had planned to go 'ha-ha' now and again, like the local looney often did as he wandered along the promenade).

'I told you to produce your weekly notes, and your yearly schemes,' barked Ward.

'Patience is a virtue Mr Ward. Seldom in a woman but never in a man.'

'Don't force your luck too far, Mr Chuckleworth. Give me the notes, and schemes!'

'Certainly.'

The headmaster rummaged through a load of rubbish on his desk, while Ward glared at him.

'Ah here we are. No, that's not them. Yes. Yes. Now I have them. No! I'm a liar, I haven't.'

Then, with an exclamation of triumph, Chuckleworth pulled out from under a heap of old newspapers a greasy copy, and handed it to Ward.

'Very impressive,' commented Ward sarcastically.

'You're easily impressed. Ha Ha.'

The inspector opened the copy. Started to read. Suddenly stopped.

'What is the meaning of this! You propose to do a hang-gliding course with the children!'

'Ah yes,' said Cecil enthusiastically, 'we'll take off from the church tower.'

'You'll what!'

'We'll take off from the church tower.'

'I don't believe what I'm hearing. You'll do no such a thing!'

'Have you thought of a better place to take off from so?'

'I certainly have not! What put it into your head to do this hang-gliding course?'

'The most noble of all the virtues is courage. What better way to teach children to be brave than to have them jumping off church towers!'

'Was that why you had the playground ploughed up?'

'Yes. It will give them a soft landing place if anything goes wrong.'

'Why did you inform the minister for education that you saw me going in to a public lavatory with your tom-cat under my arm?'

'I was thinking since that that was a case of mistaken identity. It must have been your brother I saw.'

'I've no brother.'

'Well then it must have been his double.'

'What about the white blackboards?'

'What about the bucket of black chalk! Did you bring it with you? The teachers are held up waiting for it, and they are blaming me! I've shifted the responsibility over to you.'

'And I'm thinking of shifting the responsibility from you; the responsibility of being the headmaster of this school.'

'Why would you do such a thing as that to a hard-working teacher like me?'

'Because of what I've seen on this visit, and the previous one. Not because of the numerous complaints the department has received about you, including an 18-page report from a local committee listing strange deeds done by you in the name of education, in the short time you have been headmaster of this school.'

'Give me a look at it, till I see who signed it, and I'll tear them apart!'

'You'll tear nobody apart. My advice to you is to see a doctor.'

'Why should I! Never felt better in my life. Fit for anything I am.'

'Fit for anything is right,' repeated Ward.

At this point a child by the name of Peter Savage approached the headmaster with his hand up.

'Please sir! May I go to the toilet?

'Go down out of that! Didn't you go yesterday!'

'Mr Chuckleworth!' admonished the inspector, 'no teacher should ever deny a child the right to relieve himself.'

'I'll have to get a jug in the corner so, or the carpet will be worn to a thread with them tramping in, and out.'

Overruling the headmaster, the inspector told the child to go to the toilet.

'Sit down Peter Savage if you know what's good for you,' shouted Cecil, who then walked out, turned the key in the lock, and went to the bookie's, leaving the inspector with the only pupil who had attended Chuckleworth's class since the parents' meeting, almost a fortnight previously.

They scrambled out through a window. Young Savage went home, while the inspector headed for the school manager in the parochial house.

Father Paddy, who had been away on holidays for three weeks, arrived home the previous night to find two copies of the parents' report in his mailbox. The one from the parents' committee included a covering letter baldly stating that they wanted my mate sacked without delay. The other, from the bishop, instructed him to investigate the contents of the report, and if they were found to be true to set about getting rid of Cecil as discreetly as possible.

This put Father Paddy in an awkward position. As he saw it, he was the one who had invited Cecil to leave Edenstown for Rockmallen. He was the one who had offered him the position of headmaster, and thus walked him in to a hornet's nest. What would he do at all!

Not for one moment did he doubt the veracity of the report, signed as it was by many reasonable parents. Besides he had already been aware of some of the incidents described in the report. He had turned a blind eye to them, firstly because he had been amused by them, and secondly because, having read a lot about the disease of alcoholism, he knew that most alcoholics, even at the best of times, are a bit daft, but otherwise harmless, and so he - an alcoholic himself - had made allowances for Cecil's eccentricities.

However, it was clear that while he had been on vacation Cecil had gone a step too far, and that it was his distasteful duty to obey his bishop, and do the job of hatchet man or else there would be a revolution in the parish.

So, he was relieved, delighted, to learn, when the inspector called the next day, that he wouldn't have to actually sack Cecil. There was a more humane solution, revealed Mr Ward.

After exchanging the conventional greetings, and pouring a whiskey for the visitor, Father Paddy and he sat down in the presbytery parlour.

'Well now, to what do I owe your visit?' (As if his reverence didn't know).

'Do you realise that you have a madman on your hands; a madman in charge of over 300 pupils?'

'He's not very mad is he?'

'He's mad enough to come to school in his night clothes. He's mad enough to have the children jumping off church towers. That's mad enough for me.'

'What then do you suggest we do with him?'

'Even though he has been obnoxious to me, and hates the sight of me, it is my duty to be fair to him. He's sick. Very sick. Not at all fit to be in charge of children. Normally a person in his mental state would be brought to a psychiatrist. He's so contrary that we'd never get him near one. I believe that if you wanted him to do something you'd have to beg him not to do it, and then he'd go and do it for spite. To come back to the point: he's as mad as a March hare, and drastic action we'll have to take. This evening I'm going to recommend to my superiors that he be put out immediately on an ex gratia pension, and that he be debarred from ever again teaching in any national school in the Republic of Ireland.

And so Chuckleworth earned a pension, and turned to journalism.

#####

Some months later the four of us were in the kitchen sitting around a roaring coal fire - Sylvester with a half bottle of whiskey beside him, and the other half inside him. He had gone through a phase of controlling his drinking, pints instead of shorts, but was now back on the small ones. Julia was sipping a rum and blackcurrant. The teapot was, as always, on the hob, for Cecil and myself.

We were discussing Chuckleworth's contributions to "The Irish Chronicle." Sylvester had told him to do a light-hearted, weekly column on any subject he wished - let it be an article or a short story. He had chosen to do a series of political essays which Julia acclaimed as masterpieces, and the editor deemed them to be drivel.

'All you have done so far,' said the editor, 'is trot out trivial observations. You don't seem to have the ability to transfer your sense of humour to paper.'

'Oh yes I have,' asserted Cecil.

'Well then, show me that you can by writing a short story with a bit of humour in it!'

This was Chuckleworth's answer to the editor's challenge:

THE DOG'S MIRROR
By Teddy Coleman

Did you ever wonder how a lunatic's mind works? The best way to explain it is to tell you about myself. I, Teddy Coleman, a small man, not graced with good looks, live on my wits - what's left of them - in a Dublin tenement. My large room is on the fourth floor. On my left lives my best chum, John O'Hare, a casual labourer, a drunkard, a grand fellow. On my right is Miss Maggie Hughes, an elderly angel, who, when I'm out, minds my dog, 'Dash' - an Irish terrier, with a wiry, reddish coat. I mentioned those people and the dog because we should never forget our friends.

I'm often drawn to women, but, whatever is wrong with me, they usually want to get rid of me quickly, though I did live with a gamey, middle-aged lady, Sharon O'Dea - for the best part of a day.

I found her to be attractive from the moment we struck up a conversation, that Saturday morning in Bewley's Cafe, Westmoreland Street, Dublin. With my pot of tea, and bun I boldly sat down opposite her, without asking was there someone sitting on the empty chair - as I didn't see anyone there.

She didn't look up. Continued doing the crossword. A shy woman, thought I, as I nibbled at my bun, and peered to see how much she had done - three words to go.

I poured myself a second cup. Delayed over it. One word to go.

Finished my second cup. No sign of her getting it.

Unexpectedly she looked up, and caught me trying to read the clue upside down.

'Sometimes neat under a calf!' said she, wearing a puzzled look.

'Has to be ankle,' said I, in a tone which implied that any fool would know that.

'You're a clever little man. Obviously you do crosswords yourself.'

'I don't! I earn my living composing them,' lied I, to let her know that I wasn't a nobody.

'That is indeed interesting. I never before met anyone who earns their living that way. Which paper do you do them for?'

'A syndicate in the USA. They appear in a daily every day of the week in all of the 49 states.'

'You must be making a fortune.'

'I am, but I live frugally. I'm putting by my money. Being a bachelor I feel insecure about my old age.'

'Really,' said she, pushing out her bust a fraction more than was necessary.

'I don't think I'll ever marry now. I left it too late,' said I, in a regretful tone, with a mournful look on my face.

'One never knows what the future holds for us,' said she.

'Maybe we'd do ourselves in if we did.'

'What a morbid thought,' she exclaimed, and then confessed that her favourite hobby was solving crosswords, and that she'd love to see some of those I had set.

'I'll be delighted to show them to you. Before coming out this morning I put the finishing touches to 13 weeks' supply. I've them in an envelope ready to send off. Come back to the flat with me now, and I'll give you a glance through them before I stick them in the post.'

She looked at me suspiciously.

'Don't think for one second that I've an ulterior motive,' said I.

'I don't know you from Adam.'

'I don't know Adam either, though I've heard a lot about Eve.'

'You could be a con man!'

'Well now, it was very pleasant meeting you,' said I, rising from my chair, 'and I hope you continue to enjoy solving crosswords as much as I enjoy setting them.'

'I didn't mean to be offensive.'

'No need to apologise. I know well that there are chancers knocking around. I've met them myself, and a woman can't be too careful who she takes up with. All the best.'

'Some day we'll meet again,' said she, getting up to go out along with me.

'Is that so! Since you're able to see in to the future why aren't you backing horses?'

'You're vexed with me!'

We stood facing each other outside the exit door. I looked her in the eye, and paused before saying:

'You're judging the book by the cover. I'm aware that nobody will ever stop me on the street, and ask me for my autograph, mistaking me for Gregory Peck. I'm merely an old fool making a lot of money, and not knowing what to do with it. Goodbye!'

'If you promise not to lay a hand on me I'll go to your flat.'

'If you promise not to lay a hand on me I'll let you in to my flat.'

'It's a bargain,' said she with a nervous laugh, and then asked me my name.

'Teddy Coleman. What's yours?'

'Sharon O'Dea. Did you bring your car, Teddy?'

I hadn't even a bicycle pump, never mind a bicycle, so I told her that my car had a flat tyre, and that I was too lazy to change the wheel that morning.

'We'll go in mine so. It's around the corner on the quays. Where do you live?'

A facial twitch revealed that she wasn't impressed by my address.

As we got in to her Wolseley 16/60 I asked her where she lived. She had her own luxury apartment in posh Ballsbridge.

After I had collected my dog, Dash, from Miss Hughes, and he had finished fussing over me, we entered my humble abode. Miss O'Dea enthusiastically asked to see the nonexistent crosswords.

'Of course I'll show them to you. Would you like a drink first?' said I, producing a bottle of whiskey.

'Only a drop,' answered she.

'That's all I intended giving you,' said I, barely covering the bottom of her glass.

She looked at the thimbleful; then at me in astonishment.

'Water it to your own taste,' I advised, as I flash flooded my own

182

tumbler.

Having held hers up to the light to see had it yet evaporated, she meaningfully looked at the amount in mine, and let loose an artificial laugh, remarking that I was not the perfect host.

'If I had offered you a large whiskey you'd have suspected that I was trying to get you into bed. To prove that I'm not, I did the opposite, and you accuse me of being mean. I can't win.'

She went into a sulky silence, broken only when I asked her was she fond of drink.

'I wouldn't want to be if I were depending on you.'

'Here! Help yourself.'

When she had treated herself magnanimously she again asked to see the crosswords.

'Certainly. This very minute. I'll get a great kick out of showing them to you. I hope you won't find them too difficult.'

I tore the place apart searching for them. I looked under the bed, under the mattress, then up the chimney, while explaining that I had the habit of hiding them in the most peculiar places, in case I was burgled.

'Have another drink while you're waiting.'

Which she did.

As I was opening, and shaking my considerable collection of paperbacks I begged her not to worry that I wouldn't give up till I found them. After much shaking in vain I stopped, and looked up at the ceiling for inspiration.

'Now let me think. Where could they be! Blast it. I'm an awful idiot. I remember now. Didn't I post them in the letter box beside the bus stop this morning. I can never trust my memory Matilda!'

'My name is not Matilda. It's Sharon.'

She reached for the bottle again, while remarking that she found all highly intelligent people to be absentminded. Having replenished her glass, the mellowing guest went to put her arms around me, while telling me I was a wee dote.

'Wait now. We came here for you to see my crosswords. I'll demonstrate how I set them. Mention any word, and I'll make up a clue about it.'

She picked words at random. It was no trouble to me to supply cryptic clues almost immediately, because that's a hobby of mine to kill time when I've nothing better to do. She was impressed.

'I love intellectual men.'

'It's the drink that's talking.'

'It's not, Teddy. I genuinely find you're enjoyable company, and I have a suggestion to make. Let's go over to my apartment where we'll be more comfortable. Please don't take offence at me saying that!'

I'm getting places, realised I, but I wasn't going to jump head-long at the offer.

'I'll go on one condition.'

'What's that?'

'That I bring my dog! My babysitter, Miss Hughes, always goes to town on a Saturday afternoon, and Dash would be fretting for me if he were here on his own.'

'No problem.'

From the moment we entered her apartment she went hard at the whiskey again. I stayed with her until we both reached the stage where our inhibitions didn't curb our inclinations.

'It's ages since I had a man.'

'Flattery will get you nowhere.'

'Come on,' slurred she, pulling me towards the bedroom.

'I'll go only if you let Dash in along with us.'

'There'll be plenty of room for him.'

In we got between the sheets.

Dash jumped up beside us.

We put our arms around each other as some people do in bed.

Dash looked at us, and then looked in the large mirror at the end of the bed. He started barking at a hell of a rate.

'Dash is upset,' said I. 'He thinks you're mugging me.'

'Don't mind him. It's the other dog he's annoyed with.'

'There's no other dog,' said I.

'He thinks there's a dog in the mirror.'

'Dogs don't think. They work by instinct.'

'We'll work by instinct too,' said she.

'No. We'll take down the mirror.'

'No. We'll put out the dog.'

'We won't. If the dog goes I go.'

'We'll turn off the light so.'

'No,' said I. 'I want to see what I'm at.'

We continued arguing, but failed to reach a compromise.

Meanwhile, Dash kept on yelping nonstop at the other dog. Eventually the dog and I got on her nerves. She was stricken with a touch of hysteria, and threw the both of us out.

On our way home Dash didn't bark once - not even at a cat he observed sitting on a high wall.

#####

The editor's verdict was that the story was reasonably good. However he pointed out what he considered to be a flaw.

'Maybe I'm nit-picking, Cecil,' said he. 'You introduced a character, John O'Hare. Then he played no part whatsoever in the story. Every character, especially in a short story, must have a purpose. Otherwise he's superfluous.'

'You're a hard man to satisfy, Sylvester. Next week, just to humour you, I'll have John O'Hare writing the story. If that doesn't please you I don't know what will.'

THE SHOPLIFTER
By John O'Hare

One Friday morning Teddy Coleman and I were chatting in his tenement flat. Due to financial difficulties, neither of us had suffered the luxury of a sore head for months. We moaned about how lucky those were, who, at that moment, were nursing hangovers. We surmised that they didn't at all appreciate the dryness in the throat, the splitting headache, and the shake in the hand. How we wished that now and again we could afford the pleasure of such pain.

He suggested we should bang each other's heads with a claw hammer, and then we'd feel as good as them. I said we should instead go, and look for work. He ruled that out because, he claimed, we then wouldn't have enough time to drink.

'We're stumped so, Teddy, doomed to a life of temperance.'

'No. We're not. We'll search for women to live with us. We'll mind the home, and let them be the beerwinners.'

'And where will we look for these women?'

'We'll go to a dance tonight, John.'

'A dance! You need money to go to a dance. Where will we get it?'

'Go in next door, and ask doting Miss Hughes. Tell her your

185

mother's after dying of a tumour on the brain, and that you need the money for a Mass card.'

'Why don't you ask her, Teddy?'

'It's too soon for me to take advantage of her again. Last week she gave me the price of a Mass card for my third mother!'

Miss Hughes, God bless her, is the easiest touch in Ireland. She came up trumps, and off to the dance we went.

On our way there, Teddy warned me that we shouldn't get ideas beyond our station, that we'd have to visualise ourselves as women see us, that I looked like a greasy barrel of fat, and that he looked like a dwarf who had survived the horrors of the Belsen concentration camp, and that our best bet must be to go for the ugliest ladies in the hall.

I was useless in the beerwinner quest. With no drink on me I became tongue-tied as soon as I put foot to floor, whereas Teddy, always fluent with the words, had no problem in bullshitting nonstop - telling each of them that she was the only one in the hall with the electromagnetism to switch him on. He told small-busted ladies that heavy bosoms turned him off, and he confessed to those endowed with hoppers that he was a big boob fan.

While all but the prudish were amused at his spiel not one woman would give him a second dance, and as the night wore on it looked more and more likely that we'd be seeing each other home until Teddy gave me a dig in the ribs.

'Do you see that wee woman with the short hair over there! sitting on her own in the corner. She didn't get a dance all night. I'll surely score with her. I hope to God she's not on the dole.'

'She's lovely, Teddy,' said I, by way of encouragement, and her with a face that would make an ass bolt.

He did get off his mark with her. So I left them to it, and came back to my room.

On his return he reported to me:

'I think I've struck gold, John. She's trusting, she's sex-starved, she's bird-brained, she's a kleptomaniac - the ideal woman for me.'

'What's her name?'

'Lily White.'

'Where does she work?'

'When not in jail, in city centre shops. She was only released from prison this morning.'

'What was she in for?'

'Shoplifting.'

'Where does she live?'

'I don't think she lives anywhere.'

'Don't tell me you brought her home with you!'

'She's within in my bed impatiently waiting for me to foist my affections on her.'

'She'll lift everything and do a bunk.'

'Do you take me for an idiot! I've her locked in.'

'Well Teddy! I don't think much of your grandiose plan to get a woman to provide us with money for drink. All you've accomplished is you've provided a jailbird with a bed for the night.'

'That's where you're wrong, John. She has promised to do a stint at the shoplifting tomorrow. Saturday's the best day she said, when the shops are crowded.'

'That's great news so, Teddy. Things are picking up for us.'

'I hope she's not picked up, or we'll have another dry Saturday night.'

'Will she have any problem turning her assets into cash?'

'Not at all. She knows an honest receiver.'

'You better go back to her so, and humour her, Teddy.'

'You can humour her instead, John! The light's off. She won't know the difference. I've a dread of getting the pox.'

'I suppose it's the least I can do for you Teddy You've done all the work up till now.'

'Here's the key. Don't utter a word. Come back before daylight. I'll nod off here in the chair.'

When I returned Teddy was sleeping like a child. I didn't disturb him, but set the alarm for 7.30 a.m., at which time he awoke, and asked for his key.

'It's there on the dresser, Teddy. Try to get in without wakening her.'

The turning of the key did waken her.

'Where were you, Teddy? I missed you in the bed.'

'I went out for a ride on my bicycle. I always do every morning. It keeps the calves of my legs in shape. You were a topper last night, Lily. The best I ever had.'

'I'm not too bad if a man is patient with me. Would you like it again now, Teddy?'

'I'd prefer to wait until after your shoplifting spree.'

She came back that evening with eleven pounds odd

'Give me the half of it,' said he with his hand out, 'that'll be fair.'

'Willingly,' said she passing over six pounds. 'Will we hop in to bed for a few minutes now, Teddy? It would clear my head after being stuck in town all day.'

'I've an admission to make to you, Lily. You're the first woman I ever slept with. My conscience is flailing me. It's not right what I did outside the bonds of matrimony. I'm going straight to confession to purge my soul. You probably don't understand.'

'I do understand. I used to have a conscience myself. I'm sorry for being the one that took your virginity, Teddy. I'll say a prayer for you.'

'Do! Go now or I won't be able to resist pulling you into the bed.'

'We'll have one more go so, Teddy, and then I'll leave you in peace.'

'You'll leave me in pieces if we have another go.'

'Alright so,' said she with a sigh. 'It was nice knowing you, Teddy. Goodbye.'

He shut the door gently after her.

I, myself, met her going down the stairs, and me coming up with a half pound of sausages. She stopped. Stared at me. I was sure she had copped on to me!

'Weren't you at the dance last night with Teddy Coleman?'

'That's right.'

'Had you any luck?'

'No. No woman would have me.'

'That's a pity. Teddy, and myself had a great time.'

#####

As that story went down quite well Cecil decided to feature Teddy Coleman again the following week:

A FISHY TALE
by Teddy Coleman

Long years ago I wangled my way into sharing a house with two young policemen, Mike Glennon and Ambrose Williams, in Howth - a fishing village, near Dublin. They accepted me for what I was, a scrounger, on the fringe of sanity. Many's the wine, and wild women escapade we three were party to in that same house, but it wouldn't be ethical for me to divulge the scandalous behaviour in which they indulged, in case they might track me down, and beat me up.

However, I will tell you about an episode which began one Saturday night when we went women hunting, and met up with three delightful damsels - Eithne, Cliona, and Sheena.

We talked them in to bringing us back to their flat for supper. None of them was interested in me. I was just tagging along, feeling, as usual, that I'd get more notice from women if I had cauliflower ears, and a beetroot nose. Two of them had their eyes on Mike. The other obviously fancied Ambrose.

As marriage-bent women often do to new male acquaintances, they slanted searching questions, to which they were given imaginative answers, being led to believe we were medical students - with which they were suitably impressed.

I invited them to come out in our boat on the morrow to do a spot of fishing in Dublin Bay.

We hadn't got a boat. We knew as much about fishing as a pig does about a clean shirt, but Dublin Bay was definitely there at the time to which I refer.

Eagerly they accepted the invitation. Nor were they daunted when Mike, scratching his head, trying to put them off, asked were they good swimmers. They admitted that they couldn't swim a stroke.

'Won't we be safe in the hands of two fine big men,' said Sheena, who then, remembering I was present, added 'and one brave little one.'

I smiled at her, as if pleased that I had been given a mention. I then suggested that they should bring plenty of beer and grub, as we medical students were short of money, but when we qualified at the end of the term, they'd be the first we'd invite to the celebrations. Along with that I promised we'd give them all the fish we'd catch.

'At what time should we set off?' enquired Eithne.

'A 7 a.m. rendezvous on Howth Harbour pier,' firmly announced I.

The men put on a show of inscrutability.

Cliona, having consulted her watch, declared such an early rise to be ridiculous on a Sunday morning; that it was now ten to two, and they'd have to be up at six, as their flat was some distance from Howth.

'The fish will bite better before they've had their breakfast. That's why an early start is essential,' said I.

Reluctantly she gave in.

Sheena pointed out that they wouldn't be able to bring beer as no pubs would be open at that unmerciful hour.

'Bring the money instead, and we'll have a few jars when we complete the voyage,' said I.

No sooner were we in our taxi for home than Mike wanted to know:

'What the hell are you after walking us in to this time?'

'Aren't the both of you able to row! Didn't you tell me you were in the Garda Rowing Club for a while, or were you spoofing?'

'Who'd need to spoof with you around!' said Ambrose. 'We can row alright but I think we'd need a boat.'

'That's no problem.'

'No problem!'

'Aren't there plenty of boats always tied up in the harbour. Who'd miss one.'

'Maybe the owner might,' said Mike.

'Even if he's not around,' said Ambrose, 'somebody would surely see us taking it.'

'Why do you think I insisted on seven o'clock! There'll be few afoot then. Anyway, if we are challenged, we can say we heard a shout for help out at sea, and that you policemen are going out to investigate.'

'How are we going to catch the fish! With our bare hands is it?'

'There's nothing to fishing. You put a bit of bait on a hook, and throw out the line. The greedy fish tries to gulp it down, and you haul in your net. That's all that's to it.'

'Where are we going to get the lines, and the bait at three o'clock in the morning?'

'Isn't our closest neighbour, Frank Byrne, a fanatical fisherman. He'll give us anything we need.'

'He's an old man, not in great health. He'll be fast asleep in his bed now.'

'What difference does that make! As long as he's there is all that concerns us,' said I.

'I wouldn't like to be the one to rouse him. He's a cranky hoore. He'll curse you to Kingdom Come,' said Ambrose.

'One should not greet emotion with emotion,' said I. 'When I knock him up I'll be pleasant about it. I'll ask him for a sup of milk - that we ran short - and, when I get it, I'll casually mention the loan of a few lines, and a bit of bait. He might even give me a few tips.'

'A tip on the arse is what you'll get,' predicted Ambrose as the two of them went in our front gate.

Strolling up the road to Byrne's bachelor residence I looked forward with relish to the diabolical reception I was certain to receive.

Frank, a God-fearing, daily Mass-goer from the time he had given up the trawler fishing some years previously, was white-haired, mustachioed, round-shouldered, and hollow-chested. He had a recurring, consumptive cough, and a peevish shell, under which was hidden a generous streak.

My trump card was his being indebted to Ambrose and Mike, who, a couple of weeks previously had come on daylight robbers in his backyard loading their stolen van with every valuable he possessed, and him only a few hundred yards away, standing on the pier with a rod in his hand.

The next evening he walked in to our kitchen, slung four sea trout on the table. 'Eat those if you feel like it; or throw them in the dustbin.' Didn't say another word. Walked out.

I banged the brass knocker once.

No reaction.

Two harder bangs.

Pause.

Upstairs window opens.

Head comes out.

Roar comes down.

'Who's there?'

'It's only me - Teddy.'

'What the feckin hell do you want at this hour of the night?'

'Frank, it's not night. It's three o'clock in the morning.'

'Feck off, or I'll go down and put a hatchet in your head.'

Window bangs shut.

Knocker bangs once.

Pause.

No reaction.

Knocker double bangs three times.

Bare feet heard thumping downstairs.

Bucket heard rattling.

Water heard gushing.

Door chain heard clanking.

Door seen being chucked open.

Bucket of water thrown at observer.

Satisfied man, in long nightshirt, glowers at saturated victim.

'Take a good look at what you're after doing. All over a sup of milk. Ambrose and Mike won't like it when I tell them you refused to oblige us. The old saying is true, "Eaten bread is soon forgotten."'

'What the hell do you want, you fecker you?'

'All I want is a sup of milk that would do a cat.'

'You've no cat.'

'I didn't say we had. It's to make a drop of tea.'

'Don't be telling me lies. None of you magpies ever drink anything bar alcohol.'

'Well then, it's for the porridge in the morning if that'll please you.'

'Blast you! I'll get a sup of milk to get rid of you. Come in!'

I sat down on a chair in the kitchen whistling, 'The Bonny Shoals of Herring,' while he was pouring the milk from a dirty jug into a cup.

'Is that milk alright?' queried I in a doubt-casting tone.

'If you think it's not, there's no one asking you to take it.'

As he handed it to me, on account of the beer I drank with the lads, and then the onion sandwiches in the girls' flat, I unintentionally released a high-sounding blast of gas.

'How dare you fart before me!' said he angrily.

'Sorry Frank. I didn't know it was your turn.'

'Get out this second. The next time you waken me at three in the morning it's a jug of piss I'll throw on you.'

'Thanks, Frank. There's no doubt about it. You're the salt of the earth. Oh! Just one simple question before I go.'

'What!'

'Would you mind lending us a few lines to go fishing?'

'Surely to God you're not going fishing at this hour of the night!'

'No, but we'll be heading off soon.'

'There's lines round in the shed. Take whatever you want, and

192

get as far away from here as possible.'

'Great Frank. Would you mind lending me your bicycle lamp for fear my hand might catch in a hook.'

'Why you're not locked up is a mystery to me. You've me wide awake now. I won't sleep again. That's for sure. I'll put on my clothes, and go round and get them myself.'

While he was upstairs cursing, and dressing, I wrung out my shirt in the kitchen sink, stuck it in my coat pocket, then began singing at the top of my voice, 'Oh what a beautiful morning, oh what a beautiful day, I've got a beautiful feeling that everything's going my way...'

Down the stairs he tramped - a cunning cigarette lit.

'Frank, would you lend me a cigarette? Mine are waterlogged due to the accident.'

'Next you'll be asking me for bait.'

'You can see in to my head, Frank, and I'm not in the least surprised. I overheard an old man in the local, last night, saying that you're the smartest man in these parts, and also the most naturally gifted angler. He even said that you can smell them out.'

'Why wouldn't I be good at fishing, and me at it all my life, and my father before me.'

'Frank! Where's the best place to catch fish?'

'Water.'

'I know that much, but the three of us are going out in a few hours time, and we haven't a notion of how to fish or where to find them.'

'You divil out of hell, sit down there in that chair! Keep your mouth shut, and your ears open.'

'You forgot to give me the cigarette, Frank. You put your hand in your pocket, and took it out again absentmindedly.'

'Here!'

'Frank, my matches are wet too. Could I please have a light?'

'Here!'

'I don't suppose you have any drink in the house, Frank, or is it too personal a question?'

He looked at me. Reflected.

'Teddy, I'm 71 years of age. And in all my born life I've never before met a man with your nerve. Only I know you're half mad I wouldn't put up with you.'

I shoved my shirt deeper into my pocket, sat up perkily, looked him in the eye, and said, 'As long as you don't call me cheeky I won't take offence.'

'Well I will call you cheeky.'

'You're an exceptionally ignorant man, Frank. It's not cheek. It's faith.'

'How the hell could brazen impudence be faith!'

'Because I've faith in Holy Scripture, which says, "Ask and you shall receive."'

'This time you won't receive.'

'You're a foolish man to deny the Word of God, and you with one foot in the grave.'

'You feckin scourge! I'm not denying the Word of God. I'll give you a drop of Jameson, and then out you'll go. And I never want to see your face again for as long as I live.'

'You mightn't have long to wait, Frank. You're not looking the best,' said I, while he was going to the cupboard to fetch the whiskey, and two glasses.

'Here! As soon as you down that, you'll get out the door.'

'You're forgetting something, Frank.'

'Forgetting what!'

'Before you started fussing over the cigarette, and the drink you were going to tell me how to fish, and where to fish.'

'Right! Right! Would you and the lads fancy catching a conger eel?'

'We certainly would.'

'My mate, Sean Power, and myself were fishing off the rocks at the end of the Bull Wall yesterday. There's a monstrous conger eel lurking there. It would be one hell of a coup to nail him. We had him on the line. Damn it didn't he get away on us. He looked to be up on eight feet long.'

'Eight feet! That's nearly twice as tall as me. There'd be an awful lot of eating on him.'

'If you weren't careful it would be the other way round.'

'What do you mean?'

'Congers are a vicious fish. They've teeth as sharp as razors. They'd take the arm off you as quick as they'd look at you.'

'That's great Frank. We'll have women with us. They'll be thrilled to bits, if they're not scared out of their wits. What kind of

194

bait did you say you were going to give me?'

'I didn't say I was going to give you bait.'

'Well, if you had said you were going to give me bait, what kind would you have given me?'

'Can't you catch your own bait!'

'You're talking in riddles to confuse me. What kind of bait will I use to catch my own bait?'

'Throw out your lines with bits of a rag on them. You won't have long to wait for the mackerel to take. The bay's alive with them these days. Come on, and I'll get you the lines.'

After handing them to me, shutting the shed door, he said, 'Don't forget to bring a hammer.'

'A hammer! Are you advising me to catch eels with a hammer?'

'Not even you could catch a fish with a hammer. Though I wouldn't put it past you to try.'

'Quit needling me, and tell me what the hammer's for.'

'If you catch a big conger you never let him in to the boat while he's conscious because he could do you an injury. When the chap with the line hauls him as far as the gunnel, the other fellow, standing by with the hammer, bangs him on top of the head. In case you're lucky enough to catch the big one that's out there - and it's the likes of you that would catch him - don't let him in to the boat alive. Remember that. Now Teddy! Good morning to you, and good fishing, and never waken me again in the middle of the night. It's not right nor fair.'

'I know that. I shouldn't have done it. I'm genuinely sorry. Just one last favour, Frank!'

'What!'

'Would you ever lend me a hammer?'

Resignedly he shook his head, re-entered the shed, and threw me the conger banger. Closing the gate after me, to cheer me up, he told me that it was one hell of a long distance to row from Howth to the Bull Wall, and that whatever about us making it there we mightn't make it back.

Some hours later when we three men reached the harbour there were more afoot than I had expected. They put no heed in us, being engrossed as they were, in getting ready to go out themselves.

We picked a purple painted skiff, 'The Christine Keeler,' and sat in, waiting for the girls, who arrived on the dot of seven, with their sandwiches, and flasks, all three looking beautifully sensuous in their cotton dresses.

The girls on board, we set off. After hours of exhausting rowing we took a break. Sheena was persuaded to sacrifice her silk stockings, which, with a nail scissors, were cut in bits, and used to catch the mackerel.

It was amazing how readily the scavengers took the bait. Soon there was a thick, blue-green slimy carpet of fish covering the floor of the boat.

Rowing was resumed. Late in the afternoon we hove to on the river Liffey side of the breakwater - the stretch of rocks which runs from the Bull Wall to the North Bull lighthouse.

Ravenously we partook of the sandwiches and tea.

Then we blew the whistle for what we hoped would be a ding-dong dice with the devil of the deep in the shape of Frank Byrne's escapee - the monstrous conger eel.

For more than two hours we were casting our lines along the rocks, getting the little nibble, nothing much, until suddenly, dear God, I got a bite which sent a shock through my body.

I gave a jerk, for which I was punished by being almost dragged from the boat.

'We have something here,' shouted Ambrose. A rather silly remark in the circumstances.

I kept tugging, and tugging. Our craft moved nearer, and nearer the rocks.

Until unexpectedly, like the pop of a cork, whatever it was came clear.

Moments before that, the big B & I passenger, and cattle boat had passed up the nearby river channel. There was a heavy swell coming from its bow wave. Meanwhile, the three girls, out of their minds with excitement, were balancing, and falling on the oily mackerel. Mike was on my left urging me to keep cool. Ambrose was on my right, hammer in hand.

I hauled away for all I was worth.

Then the memorable moment arrived.

Up appeared the cruel mouth of the eight-foot conger.

As I dragged him across the gunnel Ambrose made to bang him on the head. In that split second the steamer's swell hit our skiff, and he missed his mark.

In came the conger, with the help of the wash, biting in all directions.

We made a snap decision to leave him in charge of the boat. So out went we into the sea, pulling the three screaming women with us, and holding them afloat until boats in our vicinity rushed to the rescue, and helped us aboard.

Awe-struck, we watched the conger in the skiff, threshing around like an enraged psychopath. Eventually he got out, line and all, and we got in. Closely we inspected the bite marks he had left on the seats, and thanked God, that we had escaped without the loss of life or limb.

'What are we going to do with this boat?' asked Ambrose.

'We're not going to row it back to Howth. We'd drop dead of exhaustion before we'd be halfway there.' said Mike.

'We'll carry it on our head's by road. It's only a few hours walk,' suggested I.

'Teddy, you're as helpful as ever,' said Ambrose.

'Why don't we haul it up on Dollymount Strand, and go back by bus,' said Eithne.

That's what we did do. It's still there for all to see. It needs a new coat of paint - what's left of it.

#####

One dull November evening Cecil, Sylvester and I were sitting in the kitchen chatting about nothing in particular, when Julia, on a day off work, arrived in from shopping in the city.

'Anything interesting happen to you in town today, Julia?' enquired her husband.

'There certainly did. And I'm not over it yet.'

'I hope to God that you weren't mugged,' said he, standing up.

'Sit down, Cecil. It was nothing like that. When I had my shopping done I went to Bernie Shinners' cafe for a cup of coffee, and a Danish pastry. I wasn't long there, when a low-sized gentleman, in his mid-sixties, with lovely white hair, and a harassed look on his face, walked in, ordered a pot of tea for two, and sat opposite me - two tables away. I continued glancing through "The Irish Chronicle" while I was wondering what I'd get you for your lunch.

'The next thing I noticed was a tall, broad, battleship, seventy if she was a day, towering over the white-haired man, abusing him in a low vicious tone, at the rate of about a hundred words a minute; while he sat there like a lamb, looking up at her, not uttering a word.

'I was watching, but pretending I wasn't, because she often looked over to see if I was.

'Eventually she left.

'He looked over at me. Gave me a shy smile. I burst out laughing.

'Then I happened to turn my eyes towards the doorway.

'To my terror she was framed in it, glowering at me. Over she marched, and came to a halt in front of me:

'Are you involved with that man?' said she in a menacing tone, and her index finger pointing in his direction.

'I nearly wet my panties with fright. 'No,' said I. 'No. I never saw him before in my life! As sure as God is my judge."

'You better stay clear of him or I'll swing for you,' said she.

'I grabbed my purse, and bag of groceries, paid my bill, and came straight home.'

'Julia! If we ever happen to be in town, and come across that ould rip point her out to me, and I'll give her a dose of her own medicine that she'll remember for a long time,' said Cecil.

'Isn't it amazing the number of husbands, and wives who spend their time fighting with each other,' said I.

'I believe we'd be more amazed if we found out the number of couples who go through phases of not talking to each other. They go around their homes passing each other like strangers, or else passing notes to each other,' said Julia.

'That brings back memories for me, of an argy-bargy the wife and I had, as a result of which we didn't speak to each other for a fortnight,' said Sylvester. 'I found it highly inconvenient, because if I needed something, such as a change of socks, I hadn't a clue where to go rooting for them, but I was determined that I wouldn't be the first to break the silence.

'During the course of our tongue-tied hostilities, one morning at breakfast I made the mistake of passing her a note. She indicated that she didn't favour that form of intercourse, by tearing the note to shreds, and then allowing the tiny pieces to flutter down around my head, while I sat at the kitchen table eating humble pie.'

'I'll bet you a penny that you don't remember what that row was about,' said Julia.

'You'd lose the bet,' answered Sylvester. 'She suggested that we'd go away on a holiday, and I said it would be cheaper to fight at home.'

'All our neighbours go off on holidays,' said she.

'All our neighbours don't spend all their time fighting,' said I.

'If you don't bring me away I'll go myself,' said she.

'I'll give you a fiver never to come back,' said I.

'That generous offer stirred her to tell me that I was good for nothing, that my father, and mother were good for nothing, that all belonging to me were good for nothing, and that she'd never lower herself to speak to me again.'

'Suit yourself,' said I.

'You were totally at fault, Sylvester. You should be ashamed of yourself for not bringing her off on a holiday,' rebuked Julia.

'You're absolutely right, but what good is it regretting it now,' answered he.

'Which of you made the first move to speak again?' asked Cecil.

'The morning after she had showered me with the confetti, to my surprise, she threw in the towel. When I went in to the kitchen for my breakfast she looked down at Rory, our Scotch terrier. He cocked his ears, and looked up at her with rapt attention.

'Rory!' said she, "I wonder what he'd like for his breakfast."'

'Tell her, Rory,' said I, 'that I'll just have a boiled egg, and two slices of dry toast.'

'We carried on like that for a couple of weeks, getting on great, with Rory as the interpreter, but gradually, we slipped back into our mud-slinging habits, and eventually parted, as you know.'

'Sylvester!' said Julia, 'if what you're after telling us is typical of the way you treated her, you must shoulder most of the blame for your relationship going wrong. You admit that you should have given her a holiday. Yet when a row developed over that, you dug in your heels, and refused to be the one to make up. She broke the ice by talking to you through the dog, which shows she was willing, despite your contrariness, to try to salvage the marriage from the rocks it was heading for.'

'I won't attempt to defend myself,' said Sylvester. 'At times I feel guilty about it, but regrets are useless. I heard from a mutual friend that she has another man now. I wish her well.'

'Tell us,' said Cecil, 'what was the straw that broke the camel's back!'

'The last day we were together in the one house I remember coming home, well-oiled, at about ten that morning - having been missing for the previous four days. She met me at the hall door, her arms akimbo, her eyes ablaze.

'Is my breakfast ready?' said I, as if I had been out in the garden pruning roses.

'I've put up with too much from you for too long. Either you guarantee me here and now that you'll give up the drink or I'm leaving this very day.'

'No one asked you to stay,' said I, as I brushed past her to go upstairs, and sleep it off.

'I woke a few hours later with a splitting headache and a dehydrated dipsomaniac's thirst. While I was throwing on my clothes to go out for the cure I was glad to hear her working below in the kitchen. I believe she wouldn't have left only I refused her the last favour she sought from me. As I was going out the door she asked me to post a letter for her.

'I told her I wasn't able.

'That night, when I returned she was gone. On the kitchen table was an unsigned note with one word: "Goodbye."'

'It's surprising she never contacted you since,' said I.

'It doesn't surprise me,' said Cecil.

#####

The late Lizzie Ruane was the rudest person I ever met at a card table. Naturally my mate thought her personality was worth painting as this proves:

WHAT A WOMAN!
By Cecil Chuckleworth

I've met many people in my day. While age has blotted most of them from my memory, some come floating back to the forefront of my mind quite often, among them Lizzie Ruane. Through us both being members of the Edenstown Bridge Club I became acquainted with her, originally a West of Ireland woman.

Everyone called her 'Old Mrs Ruane,' not because she was old, even though she was ninety if she was a day, but because there was also a young Mrs Ruane a member.

'Old Mrs Ruane' was the best hand I ever met at insulting people and getting away with it. Others might think the same thoughts as she, but they'd stifle them, or choose safe ground on which to air them. That wasn't her style as those who had been on the receiving end of her viperish tongue would readily testify.

Among her hapless victims was Ted Lyons, a middle-aged, civil servant, who had been regarded as a confirmed bachelor. Ted, who wouldn't say boo to a goose, suffered severely all his life from asthma, and seldom enjoyed two consecutive days of good health.

He caused a sensation in the club by going off, and getting married to a girl in her late teens!

On his first night back at the club, instead of congratulating him, as the rest of us felt it our duty to do, she embarrassed the sensitive among us by accosting him with:

'You're a selfish old bugger that's always threatening to wheeze your last breath, and you sneak off and marry a slip of a girl so that you can boss her around the house. I'll say a prayer that the Lord will forgive you.'

He never came near the club again.

When new members join the Edenstown club they are invariably told who the best players are. Legend has it that she hadn't her backside warmed there when she first showed her teeth. Our outstanding player by a long shot was Hugh O'Neill. His regular partner was arrogant Larry McFadden who never left anyone in doubt that he considered himself to be the top dog.

On being formally introduced to them Mrs Ruane said to Hugh: 'I hear you're the best player in the club.'

Then she turned to McFadden, and said: 'I hear you think you're the best player in the club.'

Looking at the rippling wrinkles on her face and throat, one might not realise that in her day she had been an attractive looking woman, who had boasted a bosom that drew many's the man's eye. A bosom which she apparently had believed would benefit from exposure to the air as she was never averse to flaunting its merits with daring low-cut dresses especially at the bridge table.

Once when she was playing against two men they scored a good result on the first hand. Nothing daunted she more than recovered the score on the second.

'That's tit for tat,' remarked one of the males.

'Ah! but my tit proved to be much bigger than your tat,' responded she.

'Agreed,' conceded he admiringly.

A brief encounter she had with another member of the opposite sex at a Hallowe'en party in the club was not of as flippant a nature.

Mr O'Reilly, a thick-witted businessman, tried to pull his roots rank on Mrs Ruane while the party was in full swing. He took on the wrong woman.

Going past her table his coat caught in her gin and tonic hurtling it to the floor.

He walked on.

'Mr O'Reilly!' she shouted. 'You spilled my drink.'

He came back. Looked down at her.

'Mrs Ruane! All belonging to me for generations past have come from Edenstown. You're nothing more than a common blow-in who wouldn't be tolerated in any other town in Ireland!'

(What his ancestry had to do with him spilling the old dear's drink is beyond my understanding).

She a keen student of local family history peered up at him.

'You don't have to remind me that all belonging to you come from Edenstown. Didn't 'Flasher' O'Reilly, your grandfather do six months in the local jail for indecent exposure. Hadn't your grandmother, on your mother's side, an even more colourful history - '

'Mrs Ruane! Would you mind lowering your voice, everyone's looking at us. I'll replace the drink I knocked over on you. What was it?'

'A large gin, and tonic please, with ice and lemon.'

When he returned with the drink she thanked him for it, and winked at her partner, who too was aware that the glass knocked over was virtually empty.

Not too long before I left Edenstown, she, a widow woman for thirty odd years, invited three ladies to her home for a game. By a coincidence - I presume - all three of her guests were in the deserted wives category. Their husbands had done a bunk, and were never seen nor heard tell of in the area again.

As customary in most private houses where bridge is played, the game over, the card table was put aside, and all moved their chairs in to the fire to round off the evening with a friendly chat.

Mrs Ruane, as widows often do, brought up the subject of her 'poor dead husband,' and moaned and groaned and sobbed, as she recalled the way he used to take her on his knee every evening after tea.

The women uttered suitable noises.

Then, the hostess excused herself to go to the bathroom, seemingly overcome with grief, but really to eavesdrop at the door.

The moment she was gone the three of them looked at each other, and burst into peals of laughter.

'Sitting on his knee how are yeh!' said one of them, 'the luckiest thing that ever happened to him was to die.'

With that she opened the door.

'Get out fast ye bloody bitches! At least I know where my husband is. More than any of you tramps can brag about.'

#####

Towards the end of January the four of us were in the kitchen discussing the long-term effects of hell for leather drinking when Sylvester, who hadn't drawn a sober breath for a month, declared that he was going back on the long ones.

'I'll control it that way,' added he hopefully.

'That's a fallacy about drinking long ones instead of shorts, and thus controlling it,' said Cecil. 'That works only for social drinkers. Unless you want to drink yourself to death, sooner or later you'll have to face up to the fact that, like George and myself, you are an alcoholic, and an alcoholic cannot learn how to control drink. Drink will control him.'

Sylvester, not wishing to face reality, said, 'Let's get on to a more pleasant subject, Cecil. Tell us, did you ever raise your fists in a pub?'

'Never unless provoked,' answered he, as he opened a package of chewing gum, and went on, 'I spent a few months teaching in Russelstown, in the County Cavan. My local was Fiona Jackson's Tavern, which did a booming after-hours business because that was where the cops drank. So it was never raided.

'One night I fell in with a stranger in civvies who claimed that he was a policeman home on sick leave with a bad heart. We swapped drinks while he recounted his great coups as a limb of the law.

'At about two o'clock in the morning, we two being the last on the premises, Fiona informed us that she was filling our last pints, after which she went to bed, having told us to make sure that we pulled the door after us.

'I had sucked halfway down my glass in one go when he surprised me by saying that he was going to arrest me.

'I put my tumbler on the counter, and looking at his purple-veined face, asked why.

'On the grounds that you are, and have been drinking after the legal closing time!"

'What about yourself! You're breaking the law as well as me!'

'No,' said he, 'I've been here, doing my duty, keeping you under observation."

'He then told me that if I didn't come easily I'd have to go forcibly.

'Listen,' said I, grabbing him by the lapels of his jacket, 'you told me that you've a bad heart. If you attempt to bring me in, with one thump I'll find out whether you have or not!'

'A good punch line,' laughed Julia.

'What happened then?' asked Sylvester.

'Let me go,' said he.

'I let him go, and out the door he went - without finishing his pint.'

'Was he really a policeman?' asked Julia

'Not at all. I found out from the school-attendance officer, the next day, that he was a local farmer who fancied himself at playing practical jokes,'

'Had he a bad heart?'

'That was the only part of his story that was true.'

'Thanks be to God you didn't hit him, or you could have been up on a murder charge!' said she, as she got up out of her chair to make us a pot of tea.

'You must have found yourself in ridiculous situations from time to time, where you made a fool of yourself, through your heavy drinking,' said I to Sylvester.

'Too numerous to mention but I'll mention one of them,' answered he.

'I remember during the Emergency - or as some people called it,

World War Two - being sent down to Ballybeg, a little fishing port in Kerry, to do an in-depth feature on village life.

'You may not be aware that in Ireland in those days a lot of essential items were scarce - none more so than brandy. In Ballybeg, however, as in several other small harbours on the south-west coast, brandy was nearly as plentiful as fresh water, because, despite the blockade, Spanish trawlers often came in for supplies.

'Naturally, as any reasonable journalist would do, I spent most of my time, and all of my money, stuck to a high stool at Sheehy's counter, disinfecting my throat with brandy.

'The time came when I was a day or two overdue to return to Dublin, so, on this Saturday evening, in the twilight zone of an alcoholic haze, I pushed myself from Sheehy's counter, and out the door, across the road to my baby Ford, parked under an oak tree.

'I opened my case, carefully wrapped two shirts around my precious bottle of brandy, closed the case, and sat in to the car, when next thing, lo and behold, a monkey jumped up on the bonnet!

'Am I seeing things or am I not!

'Is this a monkey or am I a monkey for thinking it's a monkey!

'I gave a bang on the windscreen. What did the cheeky creature do but lift its paw, and claw back at me!

'I blessed myself, shut my eyes, and gathered my thoughts: I'm here in Ballybeg in County Kerry. I have seen a monkey sitting on the bonnet of my car. Monkeys can't be roaming the streets of Ballybeg. I'm going mad. The brandy is setting me mad. Never again, for as long as I live, will I let the taste of alcohol pass my lips.

'I rubbed my eyes and opened them. What did I see this time!

'Two monkeys gaping in at me!

'I gave a blast on the horn, and be the hokey pokey didn't both the monkeys disappear in jig time, climbing up the old oak tree out of my sight.

'I opened my case, grabbed the bottle of brandy, uncorked it, wound down the window, and poured the contents out on the road. There were three elderly locals in overcoats and caps, with hunched shoulders, standing, with their backs against Sheehy's pub across the street, staring impassively in my direction. At least, said I to myself, they don't know that I saw two monkeys.

'Off I headed for the capital, which I reached eventually.

'The features editor, as features editors often do, didn't look at my piece for a fortnight, but when he did, he liked it so much that he told me to get a photographer, and go back down to Ballybeg to have a few photographs taken to go with it.

'My father's cousin the parish priest, obliged me once more with the petrol coupons.

'Meanwhile, my will had weakened as regards the consumption of alcohol. Yes. I had gone back on the beer after three long days drought. But then I had a legitimate reason: I never saw monkeys when I was drinking beer.

'On arriving in Ballybeg the sky was too dull for taking photographs, so we adjourned to Sheehy's.

'What'll you have?' said I to the photographer.

'A bottle of stout."

'Whenever you're ready a bottle of stout, and a pint of beer please.'

'Then this hunch-shouldered old gent got up from his seat in the corner, walked over and asked me:

"What did you think of the two monkeys that escaped from the circus?"

'Two monkeys escaped from the circus! Barman, excuse me! Forget about that pint of beer. Give me a double brandy instead!'

#####

Chuckleworth was in a peevish mood when he penned this piece:

GENEROUS ME
By Cecil Chuckleworth

None have a more vexatious effect on my humour than those people who succeed in using me. Consequently, for my own peace of mind, I try to be on my guard at all times to prevent them from taking advantage of the generous side of my nature.

Only yesterday evening I was going for the bus having bought a few items in the city. I was striding along, minding my own business, wondering to myself how my next-door neighbour fiddled the money to get a new car for his wife, when I was stopped by this outwardly respectable looking fellow who had run out of matches and wished to know if I would oblige him with a light.

'Run in to the shop that you're after passing by and you'll soon be out of that predicament,' advised I, as I proceeded on my way to be obstructed twenty paces further on by a young lady who proffered me a ten-penny coin, and asked me could I change it into five-pences for the parking meter.

I told her I felt flattered that she mistook me for a bank official, but that unfortunately I wasn't of that profession.

Next a wizened newsboy waved an 'Evening Herald,' in front of my eyes, and shouted 'Paper!' into my face.

'Any eejit would know that that's paper,' said I. 'Why don't you shout something else, and maybe somebody would listen to you.'

Before I got on my bus for home I was waylaid yet again. This time by an elderly gent with a stick, who wanted to know if I would be so kind as to direct him to Duckham's Restaurant, where his considerate nephew was waiting to treat him to dinner. He looked like a man who wouldn't be able for a good meal so I sent him packing in the opposite direction.

On the bus itself I sat down on my own to be joined by an overweight woman, whom I'd prefer to have avoided, not only because she had me pinned against the window, but also because she is noted in our neighbourhood for never paying her fare if she can get a mug of a man to stump up for her. Worse still, the whole world revolves around herself and her family. No matter what subject you bring up she'll wangle it around to one of her own kith and kin.

'A cool evening, Mrs Plunkett,' said I. (Wondering to myself how she was going to drag her relations in to that remark).

'Yes indeed,' said she, 'Walter - that's my husband - said this morning that it would turn out to be a cool evening, and he's always right about the weather.'

'Does he work in the met. office?'

'No,' said she. 'Why did you ask that?'

'Because I always see him carrying an umbrella when the sun's splitting the trees, and wearing sunglasses when it's raining.'

'You must be mistaking him for somebody else.'

'Has your husband a hump and a wonky leg?'

'No!' said she emphatically.'

'Then I must be imagining,' said I.

'You must. I wouldn't marry a man with a wonky leg.'

'You'd prefer one with a hump so.'

'I didn't say that. My Walter's a fine strapping man that any woman would be proud of.'

'Is he proud of you?'

'He used to be anyway.'

'Men are terrible,' said I sympathetically, 'the way they change when a woman falls into flesh.

'They are,' said she revealingly.

With that the bus conductor came up the aisle jingling his money, intimating that he'd like us to have our fares ready.

She, as anticipated, went through her sham routine of poking in her bag, while she waited for the sucker sitting beside her to say it was alright, that he'd pay for her.

'There!' said I, looking into her handbag, 'there's a pound note. You can pay for the two of us. I've nothing on me only a tenner. I'll make it up to you again.'

She was so taken aback that she bought my ticket.

When I arrived in the front door of my own home I found I still wasn't safe from human scavengers trying to live cheaply at my expense.

There was a knock on the back door.

I opened it to see the daughter of the neighbour with the two cars armed with an empty cup in her hand.

'My mammy wants to know will you lend her a cup of sugar till tomorrow!'

'That's my cup,' said I, grabbing it from her. 'I know it by the flower pattern. Go back and tell her that if she can afford to have two cars standing in her driveway, she can afford to buy a pound of sugar.'

Being ever self-critical I wonder would I be a happier man if I act the hypocrite, and pretend I don't care when people try to use me for their own ends.

#####

One of the greatest dangers for an alcoholic off drink for some time is that he gradually forgets about the mental hell he went through because of his addiction. As a result he becomes complacent, and is no longer wary of the monster lurking in his subconscious, waiting to grasp an opportunity to take command of his life again.

That's what happened to Cecil and myself. We became too cocky for our own good and paid the penalty.

One night, after we had had a profitable visit to the dogs - successfully backing two outsiders on information received - Chuckleworth remarked to me:

'What's the point in earning easy money if you don't get rid of it quickly before inflation reduces its buying power!'

'What do you mean?'

'Let's celebrate our win with a few jars just for this one night.'

'I'm game,' said I. 'We'll go back on the dry tomorrow.'

We didn't go back on the waggon on the morrow. Nor the next day.

Julia was distraught to see her husband on the booze again. She begged him to desist. Her pleas fell on deaf ears. Nobody can help an alcoholic until he or she decides that they want help. She resorted to prayer.

Sylvester on the other hand was delighted to have two new drinking companions.

'At last we are really brothers in misery,' said he.

Apart from wakening daily with the seedy morning sickness to which we previously had been so accustomed little noteworthy happened for a few weeks. Then, one Friday - on which I had not gone to work - the editor told us that the family renting his house had taken off to warmer climes for a winter holiday. He suggested that we'd go to see his residence, which was some miles out the country, on the other side of the city. Julia declined the invitation as she was working that evening. Cecil and I reckoning that one excuse was as good as another for getting out of the house and in to a pub, declared that we couldn't wait to see the mansion.

We spent that afternoon knocking back pints in Mulligan's. Then, as we were becoming fairly full, Cecil recommended a change of diet - a switch to shorts. Sylvester enthusiastically told us that he had one room in his house, the library, which he had put out of bounds to his tenants, by having it under lock and key as he didn't want their children to be interfering with his books. Also in it he stored a substantial quantity of spirits for rainy days. Chuckleworth said we should rush there immediately in case the weather improved.

Into the Merc we scrambled, with, as usual, Cecil driving. We hadn't gone far when he pulled up at a supermarket to buy a stone of spuds, a few pounds of bacon and sausages, a dozen eggs, and several other items.

'What did you do that for?' enquired Sylvester.

'We might hole up in your house for a day or two, to keep an eye on the liquor, for as long as it lasts.'

The editor laughed, and asked, 'What about Julia?'

'I'll invite her over.'

'She won't come.'

'I know.'

Some miles further on the chauffeur received orders to turn off the main road, and take a short cut through a tough district.

We were in the middle of the estate when we met a protest group of men, women, and children, lined across the road, waving banners, and beckoning at us to go back. The story was that many accidents had occurred on this short cut due to cars speeding through. The local residents wanted it closed to outside traffic.

Mr Chuckleworth, drunk or sober, seldom listened to reason, and refused to turn back. Instead he gently nudged his way through the mob while they booed us, thumped the car, and spat on the windows. We were almost clear of them when an attention-seeker jumped on the bonnet, and began banging on the windscreen.

'A foolish man,' muttered Chuckleworth as he continued to tread softly on the accelerator, while the squatter persisted in thumping hard on the windscreen when he wasn't shaking his fist at us.

As soon as safety allowed Cecil pressed a little harder for more juice. When we reached the open country, down went the boot, which caused our uninvited passenger to change his tactics. Instead of beating the windscreen he concentrated on holding on for dear life.

Up a deserted lane sped the Merc before it stopped.

Out stepped the gorilla-shaped driver, and asked the man whose wig had been blown away by the wind if he had any regrets about having hitchhiked without permission.

'I have sir. I have.'

'Are you sure?'

'I am. I'm very sure.'

'That being the case I'll let you go in the one piece.'

Cecil got back in. Ten minutes later we were in Sylvester's house: seven bedrooms en suite, plus a dining room, breakfast room, sitting room, mod cons kitchen, and a library, in which was kept the liquor locked, and which we not yet locked, entered.

'Why did you build a mansion of this size?' asked Chuckleworth of the kind editor who was extracting the cork from a bottle of Scotch.

'I had hoped that we'd have a large family.'

'You didn't follow through with your lusty desires!'

'She got her satisfaction from denying me mine.'

'There's two sides to every story,' said Cecil.' There must have been some reason for that. My guess is that you were a useless lover.'

'Don't put any heed in him, Sylvester,' said I. 'He's only trying to wind you up. Aren't the two children you did have, doing well for themselves in England.'

'Thank God they are.'

'Fill my goblet,' said Cecil, 'and we'll drink to their health.'

'Help yourself,' said Sylvester. 'I must go out and turn on the heating.'

When he returned we settled down to the business we went there for - serious drinking. Inevitably, as froth-blowers are prone to do, we swopped stories about drunken escapades.

'The only headmaster I ever had a trace of respect for,' said Cecil, 'was Jack Moran, a man whom I often drove to distraction by my disgraceful dereliction of duties in his school in the midlands. After being there a couple of years I decided to move to fresh pastures. The evening I was leaving the school, on bidding him goodbye, he surprised me by suggesting that we'd go out for a drink that night.

'I never knew you took a drink,' said I.

'I do,' said he.

'Later, when we were chatting in our house of refuge, he revealed that he was quite a heavy boozer, but he had some kink about drinking in his own locality, and used to walk miles out the country for his jar, so that the parents in the area wouldn't know his business.

'Where will we go?' asked I.

"We'll just tip up along the canal road to 'The Harbour Bar,'" said he.

'That's six Irish miles and neither of us has a car.'

"Won't we enjoy the walk!"

'You might but I wouldn't,' said I. 'I never walked that far in my life. I'll tell you what I'll do. There's a solicitor in my digs, Jim O'Sullivan. He told me I could have his car any time I liked. I never yet availed of the offer. Now is the time for me to take advantage of his generosity.'

"Don't tell him you're going drinking," advised Jack.

'Right,' said I. 'I'll tell him I'm going off to collect a dozen day-old chicks for a neighbour.'

'Jim handed me the keys without any fuss.

'I called for Jack as soon as I had my evening meal eaten because I always believed in going to a pub early and coming home late.

"It has been freezing for hours," said he. "The roads are like glass. I think it's too dangerous to go off in a car tonight."

'Not at all,' said I. 'We've good tyres, and a good man behind the wheel. What more do you want!'

'Against his better judgment he sat in alongside me. The journey there was uneventful apart from us nearly skidding into the canal twice. We had a great night drinking hot whiskeys until we staggered out about four hours after closing time, into a thick fog.

"Are you sure you're fit to drive?" asked he anxiously.

'Of course I am,' said I. 'I never yet failed to bring a car home safely.'

"In the name of God so," said he, "we'll chance it."

'Scared out of my wits, I drove ultra-carefully. I couldn't see a stim in front of me. The further we went the slippier it became. The further we went the drowsier we grew. Then I noticed that he wasn't answering when I talked to him. Into a drunken sleep he had fallen.

'To hell with it,' said I to myself, 'I might as well have a little snooze too.' I turned off the ignition, and soon joined him in the sleep of the just.

'The first thing I felt some hours later was an unmerciful poke in the ribs. It was broad daylight, and the fog had lifted.

"Will you look where we are!" said he.

'Right in the middle of the frozen canal we were parked.

'God be praised that we weren't drowned,' said I.

"Amen," said he, "but we're not out of the woods yet."

'We'll soon fix that,' said I.

'I started up the engine, and headed for dry land, but the sudden twist I gave the tiller apparently caused the ice to begin to let us down.

"Abandon ship," ordered he with great presence of mind.

'Out we shot without waiting to close the doors, and had barely reached the bank, when, with a crack and a snort O'Sullivan's automobile surrendered to the deep.

'When I arrived back at the digs the solicitor happened to be standing at the front door.

"Where is my car, Cecil?" asked he.

'Don't worry, Jim,' said I. 'I've the exact spot marked.'

'How did he take it when you gave him the facts?' asked Sylvester.

'He didn't bat an eyelid,' answered Cecil. 'He was one of those rare guys who could treat triumph and disaster just the same. Nevertheless I'd say he was glad that he had the car comprehensively insured.'

'That incident about the car,' said I, 'reminds me of a hard chaw, by the name of Joe Hernon, whom I knew by sight in Edenstown.'

'Hernon, a bank clerk, was a man with a family but not a family man. Straight from the bank to the pub he drove every evening. Always drank on his own. Seldom talked to anybody. At about ten o'clock each night he'd zigzag home in his old battered Anglia.

'Next door to him lived the boss of the local hospital, Surgeon O'Mara, who didn't drink himself, didn't approve of anyone else drinking, and was death on drunken drivers. The surgeon had the police pestered, complaining about the menace Hernon was on the road every night.

'The police put little heed in O'Mara for a number of reasons - being drinking men themselves they were in sympathy with Hernon; they didn't like busybody O'Mara, and wouldn't satisfy him to take action; they knew that Hernon never drove at more than eight miles an hour; and it must be remembered that in those days there was very little traffic on the roads, not like nowadays.

'One night O'Mara was going home from the hospital, when yet again Hernon's Anglia was astride the middle of the road, snaking along at a snail's pace.

'The surgeon blew for Joe to pull in to his own side. Hernon went further to the right, and tauntingly signalled with his left arm for O'Mara to overtake him on the inner side, which the surgeon refused to do.

'Next thing didn't Hernon's car stall!

'Out jumped the surgeon. Opened Joe's door. Lunged for, and obtained the ignition key. Told Joe he wasn't fit to be driving, and went for the police.

'Joe poked in his waistcoat pocket; found his spare key; started up his car; and went home to bed.

'On the surgeon's insistence, two policemen followed him in their squad car, to the scene of the stalled car and the paralytic pilot.

'There was no sign of either.

'The policemen told the surgeon that they had more urgent matters to be dealing with than chasing phantom drunkards, and went off about their business.'

'I've always found the gardai understanding, and helpful,' remarked Sylvester.

'I could say the same,' said Cecil, 'apart from the night the London police refused to give George and myself free lodgings for the night.'

We continued chatting, joking, and drinking for some hours before the editor said he could feel the hunger coming at him.

'I'll cook a meal,' volunteered Cecil. 'What would you say to bacon, eggs, sausages, and chips?'

'I'd love it,' said we both.

'Right! It won't take me long.'

He went to the kitchen.

Twenty minutes later he rejoined us for an aperitif, remarking that everything was nearly ready.

It proved to be a costly aperitif.

When he returned to the kitchen the chip pan was on fire. He did what one should never do - threw water on the burning oil. Before he knew where he was the kitchen was ablaze.

Sylvester and I ambled out when we heard his shout.

'Let there be no panic,' said the editor, as he pulled shut the kitchen door. He rang the fire brigade, ushered us back to the library, and topped up our goblets, as he expressed the view that we were in for a hot time.

It took longer than expected for them to come. When they did arrive Sylvester refilled our goblets for us to drink the health of the bustling firemen as the house burned down around our ears. One of them put an axe through the French window, and asked did we know that the place was on fire.

'Don't ask nonsensical questions. Didn't we send for you!' replied Sylvester.

'Come out you drunken idiots before you're burned alive.'

'What's the weather like out there? Should we bring an umbrella?' asked the editor, staggering towards the fireman.

'Come back, Sylvester!' said Cecil. 'There are more important things than the weather to be worrying about. Give us a hand to carry out some liquor before the roof falls in.'

Laden down with bottles of brandy, whiskey, gin, and rum, we tramped on the budding snowdrops, following Reynolds to the garden shed, wherein Cecil gingerly placed his cargo on the floor, and then heeled up a wooden table, sending potted plants flying in all directions.

'Now we have a counter,' said he.

'We forgot our goblets,' said I.

'It's far from goblets you were reared,' said Cecil, as yet another Scotch was uncorked, for us to start swigging by the neck, a bench having been drawn up to the table.

'You could read "Gone With The Wind," by the light from that fire,' remarked Sylvester, before declaring that we were being anti-social, as we had not invited the firemen to join us for a drink.

The bottle absentmindedly in his fist, he meandered out to the front of the house, approached the captain, and told him that there was no need to rush the job as the place was well insured.

'Come around to the shed at the back, and have a few jars. Bring your men with you.'

'As soon as we have the fire out we will. Not till then.'

About an hour later the guests arrived.

'What'll you have?' asked Sylvester, addressing the captain.

'A drop of brandy.'

He was handed a bottle of Cognac with apologies about the absence of glasses.

'And you, what's your poison?' enquired the editor of a rotund fireman with a pocked nose.

'I'd love a whiskey if you don't mind.'

To him was handed a bottle of his heart's desire. Three others chose brandy, and the last was a rum merchant.

During the course of our impromptu party we must have fallen asleep because the firemen were in hospital when we woke up late in the morning, with Julia standing over us in the shed, a copy of the city edition of 'The Irish Chronicle,' in her hand. There was a front page story of its editor's residence having been gutted, alongside a photograph of a fire brigade which had knocked down a stationary lamppost. All the firemen had been injured, only one seriously - a fractured leg.

'Weren't we the three wise men not to go home last night, Julia!' said her husband, fishing for a compliment.

'You'd have been twice as wise if you didn't come here at all.'

'Now Julia! No lectures. We didn't take a few drinks just to give you the opportunity to talk down to us.'

'I'm disgusted with you,' said the helpless woman, as she turned on her heels, got into the Prefect, and went home.

'Thank God I'm not married. I've no one to answer to,' said I.

'Julia's alright. Gets a little excited at times,' commented the husband.

'Imagine! Those poor fellows ending up in hospital, after the heroic job they did putting out the fire,' said the editor.

'They're no heroes to me,' said Cecil. 'They're a gang of robbers. They took every last bottle of liquor we had.'

'They did not!' said Sylvester, incredulously. 'We'll have to go elsewhere for a cure so.'

'Where will we go?' asked I.

'Where else but to a pub,' answered Chuckleworth.

'I often wondered how many pubs there are between here and Turpstown,' said Reynolds.

'We'll go there, and count them on the way,' said Cecil.

After crawling into most of them but forgetting to count them we eventually arrived in Turpstown.

'We may as well stay here for the night,' said Cecil.

'Not in the car,' said Sylvester. 'We slept in a shed last night, and I don't feel the better of it yet.'

'With the amount of liquor you've down you shouldn't be able to feel anything,' commented Cecil.

'I'm not feeling great. And I'm serious,' said Sylvester.

'We'll have one more drink so, in this here joint, and then look for sleeping accommodation,' said Chuckleworth, pulling up at 'The

Windmill Bar.'

'Have it your own way,' remarked Reynolds half-heartedly.

Leaning against the counter the editor confessed that he was thinking of committing suicide.

'What way were you thinking of doing the job?' asked Chuckleworth.

'With a gun.'

'That's very messy! Did you consider gas?'

'The smell of gas makes me sick. Maybe I'll slash my wrists with a razor blade.'

'You'd want to be careful not to use a rusty one or you could get blood poisoning. Drowning is the safest way. Why don't you drown yourself?'

'I thought about that. I even picked my bridge on the Liffey. The snag is that I'm a good swimmer. I'm afraid that when I'd jump in I'd panic, and strike out for shore.'

'We'll cure that by tying your arms and legs together, and giving you a push,' said Cecil.

'I don't think you lads have any sympathy for me.'

'Is that all the thanks we get for trying to help you,' said I.

'Lads! Lads! I'm in earnest!'

'You're only indulging in self-pity, and angling for attention. Pull yourself together and don't spoil the night on us,' said Cecil.

'Maybe you're right,' said he, straightening up his shoulders.

I enquired about accommodation, and booked us into the 'Hotel Rahugh,' towards which we drove some hours later, not without incident.

Usually our chauffeur was Cecil, but when we came out of the pub at closing time, the editor and he started arguing about who was better fit to drive. Neither would yield ground. So Sylvester brought up the subject of who owned the car. The keys were flung at him, and we got in, to head for the hotel, some five miles the other side of Turpstown.

None of us noticed that the editor, seeking more room to swing out on the road, backed under another bumper, and securely hooked together the two cars.

'That car behind us is uncomfortably close,' said I to Sylvester, from the back seat, before we had gone 50 yards.

'I'll put up speed so, to get rid of him.'

The boot was put down but the tailgater stayed with us.

'I'll slow down and let the shagger pass us out.'

We slowed down.

He slowed down.

'Stop the car and back into him,' suggested Cecil.

'Obviously you want to get me into trouble,' responded Reynolds, just before a squad car, siren screaming, passed us out, and blocked the road in front of us.

'I hope your driver's licence, and insurance are in order,' whispered I as a cop opened the driver's door, and asked the editor what he was at.

'I'm at the steering wheel, but you'll have to charge the fellow behind with dangerous driving. He has been on my tail for the last five minutes trying to run me down.'

'That's going to be difficult,' said the cop. 'There's nobody in the car you towed.'

Within the hour, Mr Reynolds having been examined by a police doctor, was informed that three charges were being preferred against him - drunken driving; dangerous driving; and taking a mechanically propelled vehicle without the consent of the owner. The court was due to be held on the following Monday.

As the police had warned us that none of us was fit to drive we then had to foot it to the 'Hotel Rahugh' where we went straight to bed.

First up the next day, Sunday, I went to the desk to have my friends called as I never liked breakfasting on my own. The receptionist had her back to me, working at the switchboard, making morning calls. I took in her figure - not plump, not slim, just seductively between. Then she turned to me.

In that brief moment when our glances first met I saw haunting beauty in her sparkling, blue eyes.

'Yes. Can I help you?'

'Will you call 43 and 45 please?'

'Certainly.'

While waiting for them to surface I chatted with her. Barbara Hayden was her name. Ridiculous though it may seem, we were together only 20 minutes, yet I felt I knew her all my life, that here was a woman who understood me, complicated, immature, emotionally insecure person that I am. Before leaving her, to go to the dining room, she asked if I was married.

'Yes. I'm married to drink!'

For our breakfast, Sylvester, claiming that champagne was the best cure for a sore head, wouldn't tolerate coffee being served. So we started that day with snipes of the bubbly beverage. Then we went on to brandy. Come eight in the evening Chuckleworth and Reynolds were airborne - game for anything.

There was a lot of activity in the hotel, which aroused my friends' curiosity, as they didn't want to miss anything. They discovered that a charity bridge tournament was about to begin.

'Will we enter for it?' asked Sylvester of Cecil.

'I didn't know you played bridge,' answered Chuckleworth.

'I used to, years ago.'

'Are you any good?'

'I was good at it. Lost interest after my regular partner emigrated. Come on! We'll go in.'

'We'll see what the prizes are like before we decide whether we'll play. At these drives there's often trash given out fit only for a Hallowe'en cracker.'

In to the thronged ballroom they went.

'Who is the boss-man here?' asked Chuckleworth of a well togged out lady.

'You mean the tournament director I presume.'

'Yes Mam, that's who I mean.'

'He is over there, taking entries. Mr Moynihan is his name. He'll look after you. You'll find him super efficient.'

'Will I!' said Chuckleworth, who then went over to that gentleman - a small skinny guy.

'Are you Moynihan?' asked Cecil.

'Yes. I'm Mr Moynihan. Do you want to enter?'

'Show me the prizes first.'

'What! An unheard of request. I've run charity drives for years, but this is the first time ever! that someone demanded to see the prizes before entering.'

'It's my money that's involved not yours.'

'You must be as mean as sin.'

'The prizes must be no good when you're ashamed to show them to me.'

'Rubbish! The gifts donated by our generous sponsors are on

display up there on the stage.'

Right enough, they were good prizes: a fine selection of Waterford Glass, half-sets of China, bottles of spirits, and various other items which one would love to win.

While Chuckleworth was inspecting them, and deciding which of them he'd like to bring home to Julia as a peace offering, Sylvester paid their entry fee.

As he accepted the money, Mr Moynihan told the editor that it was with reluctance he was allowing Chuckleworth to play, that if he wasn't drunk he was next door to it. Which diagnosis amused Mr Reynolds as he was every bit as far gone as Cecil.

Tournament directors - who act as referees in bridge - are seldom asked to give rulings at charity drives. The players, almost without exception, enter into the spirit of the evening, and regard such events as an opportunity for some harmless fun. They would be ashamed to call the tournament director.

There was no shame in Chuckleworth. From the start he kept Mr Moynihan on his toes. For every footy little infringement he was called, and each time he had to rule against his own Turpstown members in Cecil's favour, because our friend knew the Laws of Duplicate Bridge like the back of his hand.

It didn't help Mr Moynihan's temper either, that both my mates delayed the competition time and again, by their frequent trips to the bar. Nor was he pleased with Cecil poking fun at the local parish priest. His reverence made a silly mistake, which gifted a great score to Cecil, who, to show his appreciation, started serenading the holy man with, 'For he's a jolly good fellow,' in his tone deaf voice.

'No singing allowed,' said Moynihan to Chuckleworth, who shortly after that fell asleep when it was his turn to play a card.

'No sleeping allowed,' said Sylvester who got him awake eventually by trying to pull the chair from under him.

'Jacus! I'm not playing bridge. Am I!' exclaimed Cecil, who then studied his cards for an age, trying to gather his wits.

One of his opponents remonstrated with him for his slowness in playing a card, asserting that he had nothing to be thinking about, whereupon Cecil accused her of looking in to his hand or else she wouldn't know whether or not he had a problem as to which card he should play!

Distressed at being branded a cheat she summoned the tournament director - her husband!

Moynihan, white with rage told Cecil that he was expelling him from the tournament. Chuckleworth made to give him a jab on the jaw. He ducked, and ran up on the stage to announce that he was suspending the competition until the hooligan left the room.

Cecil's reaction was to go in pursuit of him, during which the unfortunate wretch must have gone into a drunken blackout, as he grabbed the prizes, and flung ammunition such as vases, bowls, biscuit tins, and lampshades in the general direction of Moynihan, to the accompaniment of screams from the ladies. The bridge-playing males of Turpstown rushed him. Sylvester went to his assistance. They were not subdued until the hotel manager brought in a net which was thrown over them.

The police arrived to take them off for an overnight stay in the station. Next morning they were up before District Justice Seamus Ogle on various charges.

Judge Ogle was endowed with a weakness not ideal for dispensing justice. He was seldom sober on the bench; and was always biased in favour of those who appeared before him through their being partial to booze.

The evidence - including Sylvester's separate drunken driving charges - having been heard, Mr Ogle summed up by slurring:

'These are two terrible men who have committed dreadful offences; but for the fact that there are extenuating circumstances I would have no hesitation in sending them to jail for six months. However, while I don't approve of any man drinking more than he can hold, it must be taken into consideration that both defendants apparently have a drink problem.

'What I invite them to do, is to enter and remain in the alcoholic unit of a hospital for a minimum period of three weeks, to be dried out, and then come back to me on this day month with a psychiatrist's report on their progress. Otherwise I will have to send them to prison.'

As neither was anxious to do a spell in jail they gave the required undertaking, and the case was adjourned.

I, having already collected the car, the three of us went home to Julia, who had been out of her mind with worry about her husband. She was relieved to learn that they were going in to hospital.

Our local doctor made the necessary arrangements, and on the following day, Tuesday, they were admitted to the alcoholic unit of a psychiatric hospital - paralytic drunk.

On Wednesday evening Julia went to see them. She had wanted me to accompany her. I saw no point in visiting patients who'd be vegetables from heavy sedation in the early process of drying out. Besides, I had a date to bring Barbara Hayden, to the Abbey Theatre to see Patrick Kavanagh's classic, 'Tarry Flynn.'

Anyway, Julia, having arrived at the hospital, was directed up the stairs, and through a door, which, without a key, could be opened only from the outside. Along the corridor nervously she walked; and into the ward. There they were; both ghostly pale. Heavily drugged. Fast asleep.

Looking at them, normally so vivacious, now so quiet, a tender wave of sympathy engulfed her. She hesitated. Then sat down on the chair between their beds, and started crying softly to herself.

A few minutes later a priest came in to the ward. Saw her obviously distressed. Approached.

'What's wrong, my child?'

She sobbed her way through the sad story of her poor husband, and his pal.

'You have nothing to worry about. They'll be grand in a few days. I'll give them sound advice. I'll put them on the road to sobriety. You can be sure of that. Does that make you feel better?'

Julia was indeed consoled to learn that there was such a nice, understanding chaplain on the premises.

As she was drying her eyes, and thanking him, another patient came in to the ward. The priest looked him up and down. Then went for him. Grabbed him by the throat. Nearly choked him as he roared in to his face:

'Take off my duckin dressing gown at once, or I'll kick your arse till it's black and blue!'

Which reminded Julia that she was in a madhouse, and that the priest was an inmate.

A few days later I bought a six-pack of coke in 'The Sober Saloon,' a pub directly across the road from the hospital, and in I went to visit my friends.

Both were out of bed, nattering with the three other patients in the ward.

'Ah, there you are, George,' said Sylvester. 'It's good to see you.'

'You took your time in coming,' was Cecil's greeting.

'What have you got there?' asked the editor.

'A half-dozen coke.'

'A what!'

'Just a few coke as a token of good fellowship.'

'For goodness sake are you gone off your rocker! What put it in your head that Cecil, and myself are coke drinkers?'

'What did you want me to bring in! This is an alcoholic unit in a psychiatric hospital, and you're not here for housemaid's knee.'

'Is that so! Well if you want to know, there's nothing wrong with me that a drink won't cure.'

'Jacus, Sylvester, I can't go out again.'

'And what's to stop you from going out again! Aren't you able to walk!'

'You're being most unreasonable.'

'Is it the money you're thinking of? If it is I'll give it to you.'

'Give it to me so, and tell me what you want.'

'Go across the road to "The Sober Saloon." Order a six-pack of coke. Tell the barman to throw a good sup out of each of them, and to refill them with Scotch, and to recap them carefully.'

Reluctantly I did as bid, and returned to my mates.

'More coke,' remarked one of the patients who had been given two of the original bottles by the editor.

'You've had enough already. Any more would only sicken you,' remarked Sylvester, as he took the six-pack, and offered to share them with Chuckleworth.

'Don't tempt me Sylvester. There may be another drunken bout in me, but there mightn't be another recovery.'

'You've become sensible all of a sudden.'

'The thought struck me that the next time I'm in a coffin I mightn't hear Lazarus barking.'

'Fair enough. I'll have all the more for myself.'

While Sylvester was polishing off his 'coke' I chatted with them until the evacuation bell clanged.

As I was walking out by the main exit the doorman stopped me.

'Are you by any chance going in the direction of Wicklow?' asked he.

'I am.'

'Would you have any objection to giving me a lift?'

'Not in the least. Come on.'

As he got in to the car I introduced myself. He told me his name was Terence Cassidy.

'A tough old job you've got there, Terence!'

'You don't know the half of it. There's never a week goes by but I catch visitors trying to smuggle drink in to that place.

'You don't mean to tell me,' said I, 'that people would do such a thing as that!'

'Indeed they would, if they got away with it; but I'd know them a mile away. I'd know them by the guilty look in their eye. Not one has ever yet passed me, and I'm there over thirty years.'

'That's a record you can be proud of!'

I dropped him outside his own door, thinking to myself how happy people like Terence are, to believe they are infallible in their judgment of others.

I too was happy as I continued on my way to the 'Hotel Rahugh' for a date with the new love in my life, Barbara. Mainly because I was enamoured of her I had decided to have another go at abstaining from the drink.

For the remainder of their stay Julia and I visited the patients every day. I refused to bring in any more 'coke' for Sylvester; not for fear of being caught. I wanted to give the poor fellow a chance to pull himself together.

I got to know Sean Cox, one of the other patients in the unit, very well, through chatting with him and from Sylvester, and Cecil filling me in on his chequered career.

Sean, a labourer, was a chronic alcoholic, who had been hospitalised many times. On his initial hospitalisation he found himself in a large public ward in a mental hospital. He was the only alcoholic. The rest of the patients suffered, God help them, from various delusions.

For some weeks prior to his admission he had dire difficulty in getting to sleep. Nor did the problem diminish on his first night in the institution. Due to the amount of drink he had aboard he was not given tranquilising medication. And it seemed that there was a conspiracy among the other patients to prevent him dozing off.

Every time he shut his eyes the guy in the bed on his right hopped out, and over to him, with the promise that: 'As soon as you fall asleep I'm going to cut your throat from ear to ear.'

Which Sean found to be an inducement to stay on the alert.

Eventually the cutthroat chap himself fell asleep, and Sean relaxed somewhat. He had almost reached the point of dropping off when the bus conductor opposite him got up, came to the end of our friend's bed, and shook it violently.

Sean, looking at him in his middle-of-the thigh nightshirt, asked:

'What do you want?'

'You didn't pay your fare!'

Trying to calm him down Cox said:

'I'll give you my name and address.'

'I don't want your friggin name and address. I'm used to you getting on here and never paying your fare. Unless you fork up now I'm throwing you off.'

'How much do you want?'

'How far are you going?'

'To the next stop.'

'That'll be nine pence.'

Cox reached under his pillow for his purse, and handed the fare to the conductor, who then whispered to him to take good care of his money as a lot of pickpockets travelled that route.

Shortly before midnight the fellow on Cox's left jumped out of his bed, and started shouting for his clothes because he had an appointment to meet Jesus at twelve o'clock. He didn't want to keep Him waiting. To Sean's relief a nurse and doctor came along, and after some argument persuaded him to wait until tomorrow to meet Jesus.

The next night Cox fell asleep early without any trouble. He wasn't pleased when the night nurse wakened him to give him his prescribed sleeping tablets.

After two days he was allowed out of bed, and used to pass the time walking up and down a long wide corridor, at one end of which was, on a mahogany table, a huge goldfish bowl, inhabited by 27 of the species.

He noticed that the cutthroat specialist - McSweeney by name - used to spend hours studying them, apparently fascinated by their colour and movement. Then one evening, with him at the opposite end of the corridor, he saw McSweeney dipping his hand into the bowl, grabbing the goldfish and popping them into his mouth. By the time Sean arrived at the table the bowl was empty. He asked McSweeney did he do it because he was hungry.

'No. I wanted to stop them grinning at me. And I don't like the way you're grinning at me now!'

Thanks to Sean's entertaining company, my two friends found that the three weeks passed quickly. Sad to say, while Cecil was resolved to stay on the dry, Sylvester hadn't the remotest intention of doing so.

Our parish priest, Father Paddy, a recovering alcoholic, had visited them regularly, and had implored Sylvester to give sobriety a fair trial. Reynolds politely pretended that he was interested in learning to live without alcohol, while at the same time stubbornly maintained that if he went about it the right way he could control his drinking, and that a bottle of whiskey a day was a good man's fault. Deep down I believe he knew he was wrong even though drinking alcoholics are noted for being geniuses at fooling themselves.

Before giving them their reports the psychiatrist tried to persuade the editor to remain on for further treatment. Reynolds thanked him for his concern but declined the invitation.

The gist of the report on Cecil was that he had made satisfactory progress while that on Sylvester indicated that he had made none.

On the Tuesday evening Julia and I collected them. Getting in to the car Reynolds moaned that he was badly in need of a cure for his hospital hangover, and enquired about how much drink there was back in our home. Julia emphatically told him that there was none. He remedied the situation by buying two bottles of Scotch in an off-licence. He drank on his own in the kitchen that night, as the reunited couple rushed to bed early, and I went off and collected my girlfriend, Barbara, whom I brought to Rodney and Margaret Dillon's house where we had a delectable meal.

After Cecil had left teaching Rodney was chosen as the new principal. The day he was appointed he complimented me on the way I was pulling my weight in the recent past, and expressed the hope that I would continue to do so. I assured him that I was fed up to the teeth of the attention I got from inspectors and would do enough to keep them off my back. Which I did until I went back on the bottle, and was once more on the high road to the gutter when Barbara Hayden came in to my life.

She it was who gave me a reason for living when I had revived the wish to drink myself to death. Too seldom have I previously experienced the peace which she engenders in my soul by spontaneously sharing with me the beauty, the goodness of the enthralling woman she is. I find it impossible to paint with words the exciting loveliness I see in her, but, to my astonishment, I have on tape a few tunes which accurately express for me her adorable personality - an intense personality, bursting with vitality, sensitivity, and gaiety.

We experience ecstatic moments together; moments when we don't speak; moments when I feel that I am a complete being, because she is by my side.

I love her for many reasons, one of which you may find strange. She is no way clothes conscious, dresses dowdily. Perhaps her lack of taste appeals to me because I myself am always scruffy.

Rodney and Margaret made us feel very much at home in their house. It must have been obvious to them that we were in love because they ribbed us about when we were going to have 'the big day,' even though we had been doing a line for only a couple of weeks!

I answered that the big day would be next Monday when Cecil and Sylvester would be reappearing in court, each armed with a headshrinker's report.

Throughout the week Cecil behaved impeccably. He even bought flowers for Julia as a token of his regret for all the worry he had caused her. He assured her that she need have no fear of him ever drinking again, which made her very happy; but we were all very unhappy about Sylvester, who returned home heavily boozed each night, and didn't come home at all on the Sunday night, opting instead for an all-night session with his cronies in the Hotel Russell.

We collected him there on the Monday morning, footless, and drove to Turpstown. Cecil and I linked him in to the courthouse, Julia, and Barbara timidly following.

He was not the only person assisted in to court under the influence that morning. District Justice Seamus Ogle also had been on an all-night session. Majestically he arrived, a police man on each side of him, a half an hour late, with his silver mop of hair tousled, his flybuttons open, a shoe in one hand, and his tie in the other.

The first case down for hearing was our friends.

'Ah yes,' said Mr Ogle, 'I remember these two men. Have you undergone the treatment I recommended?'

The reports were handed to him. He read them while helping himself to what he casually called, 'a drop of tea,' from a hip flask.

'Mr Reynolds, I observe that according to this report you have made no progress whatsoever. Why?'

'Your worship,' babbled Sylvester, 'I have done my best to stay off drink. It's a terrible struggle. I can't seem to make it. I'm drunk again now. I don't know why. If you let me off this time I'll have another go at it.'

'At the drink?' asked the justice.

'Yes,' said Sylvester, who meant the opposite.

'And you Mr Chuckleworth! It doesn't seem to have been any trouble to you at all. The psychiatrist says that you are completely reformed.'

'Who are you to talk about psychiatrist's reports! You'd need to see one yourself. You're a public disgrace there on the bench,' which was not the wisest comment to make to a judge in his own court, and Cecil duly paid the penalty.

The judge found him guilty of contempt of court, found him guilty of all the charges preferred against him, declared that he had second thoughts about his drink problem, that in fact he obviously had no drink problem, and therefore there were no mitigating circumstances, that he was simply an out and out blackguard, that society needed to be protected from him, and so he was obliged to sentence him to six months hard labour.

Ogle sympathised with Sylvester, 'a victim of society doing his best,' and let him off under the Probation Act.

Barbara and I plan to get married when Cecil comes out of jail, which will be the full six months, as while there, he doesn't intend to be of good behaviour.

ENDS

228

Further extracts from reviews

'An absolute howl. No less a man than Con Houlihan said, "George Ryan is probably the funniest man at large today in Ireland." That is good enough for me.'

- Roy Hafford, 'The Star.'

'This book has a serious note too, giving the reader a sympathetic insight into the problems of an alcoholic. It may well prove to be a major work in the not too distant future.'

- Peter Kavanagh, 'Dundalk Democrat.'

'It's success is so assured that it's only a question of time before it's translated into morse code.'

- Kevin Marron, 'Sunday World.'

'It will certainly entertain,'

- Kieran Nally, 'Irish Independent.'

'When I put it down to answer the door my wife picked it up and refused to give it back to me...Hilarious.'

- Geoff Oakley, 'Tullamore Tribune.'

'It is an extraordinary page turner,'

- Petrina Vousden, 'Leinster Leader.'

'In this book there is a quirk of humour which I never before met. A lot of people will enjoy it.'

- Bruce Williamson, 'Irish Times.'